My Sister's Husband:

Renaissance Collection

My Sister's Husband:

Renaissance Collection

Ambria Davis

www.urbanbooks.net

Urban Books, LLC
300 Farmingdale Road, NY-Route 109
Farmingdale, NY 11735

My Sister's Husband: Renaissance Collection

ISBN 13: 978-1-62286-517-8
ISBN 10: 1-62286-517-0

First Trade Paperback Printing July 2017
Printed in the United States of America

10 9 8 7 6 5 4 3 2

*This is a work of fiction. Any references or similarities
to actual events, real people, living or dead, or to real
locales are intended to give the novel a sense of reality.
Any similarity in other names, characters, places, and
incidents is entirely coincidental.*

Distributed by Kensington Publishing Corp.
Submit orders to:
Customer Service
400 Hahn Road
Westminster, MD 21157-4627
Phone: 1-800-733-3000
Fax: 1-800-659-2436

Prologue

Brinay

I sat in the church pew, mad as all outdoors. I didn't know what to think about what was about to take place. To my family, this event was going to be wonderful and joyous, but I wasn't even in the mood. Here I was, at my sister's wedding, with all of my family around me, but I was in a sour mood. I had a smile on my face, trying my hardest to play it off, but I was burning up on the inside, and only me, the Lord, and the damn groom knew why.

"What's wrong, Nay?" my grandmother asked, placing her hand on my leg, which had started shaking. I was so busy focusing on everything else that I didn't even notice it.

"Umm . . . nothing. I'm just nervous for Sky, that's all," I lied. She looked at me as if she knew I was lying, but she didn't say anything. My granny wasn't a fool. She knew me, and she knew how much I couldn't stand Sky, so I don't know why I even said that shit to her. Had I been thinking clearly, I would've known not to, but my nerves, mixed with these pregnancy hormones, had my mind all over the place instead of where it should be.

She was about to say something, but I deaded that before she could even get a word out of her mouth. I knew she was trying to come with a lecture, but right now, I ain't had time to hear it.

"Umm . . . Excuse me, Gram. I'll be right back," I said, abruptly getting up from my seat. My big belly was now showing, and it was weighing me down. I was still small, though. The only thing big on me was my stomach, and I was happy about that. I was all baby weight, which was great for me, because I wasn't trying to gain all them pounds.

The minute I reached the double doors, I suddenly felt as if something was blocking my airway, making it hard for me to breathe.

"Where are you going, Brinay?" my father asked, stopping me.

"I'm going to step outside for a quick little minute. I need a breath of fresh air," I stuttered, rubbing my neck as I tried to fill my lungs with some air.

"Okay, baby, but don't be long, because the wedding is about to start," he said, making me want to throw up. *As if I give a fuck about this bullshit-ass wedding*, I thought to myself.

"I won't," I said, trying my best to get away from him. I walked over to the door, where I had to grab hold of the knob to keep myself from falling. I was all fucked up today.

"You don't look too good, Nay," he said, running to grab me. "Is everything all right? Is there something wrong with you or the baby? You need me to take you to the hospital or something?"

"No, Daddy, I'm fine. It's just so stuffy in there with all of the different perfumes and cologne smells all mixed up in one place. It's making me dizzy. I'm sure once I get some fresh air I'll be okay."

"Are you sure?" he asked, concerned.

"I'm positive. Me and the baby are both fine," I said, reassuring him.

"Okay, but if you need to go to the hospital, just have someone come and get me," he replied. "Hey! I thought your baby daddy was supposed to be here. You know I still want to meet the man who's gotten my baby girl knocked up."

"Umm, about that . . . He called at the last minute and said that he couldn't make it. You'll meet him some other time," I said, saying the first thing that popped up in my mind. What I wanted to say was: *He's already here, and you've already met him. Hell, you've ate with him and shook his hand*, but I decided not to. I was going to leave that mess for another day and time.

"Okay, go on and get your air and hurry back, because the wedding is going to start in a minute," he said, taking a glance at his watch.

"Okay," I replied.

Walking out the door, I damn near fell down. I walked over to the steps and took a seat. This whole overbearing event was starting to get to me. Yeah, I did tell Dontie that I didn't care, but common sense would tell the nigga that I was lying. How the fuck could I be okay with something like this? Was he truly out of his mind, or he just ain't care? This whole thing was crazy and unrealistic and extremely fucked up to me.

That day when my father said that Sky wanted all of us to be there for some announcement, I knew it was something. I just didn't know that she was going to present a man, and that the man was going to be Tae. What killed me the most was when she said they had gotten married when they went on a vacation to Jamaica. When she said that, I felt like someone had sucker punched me in my gut. It took all my breath away. I was hurt, broken, and scared. The man that I loved and was now pregnant by was married to my damn sister. To be honest, I didn't think Sky had a clue, but the look on Dontie's face was one as if he'd seen a ghost. He looked like he wanted to die when I told everyone that I was going to be a mother, and when everyone started asking about my baby's father, I looked straight at him. He must have thought that I was going to call him out, because he looked as if he was going to piss on himself or pass the hell out. He tried his hardest to inconspicuously loosen the tie that was around his neck. I wasn't going to do that, though. I was better than that. I wasn't that type of chick, so I lied to everyone, told them that my baby's father was some man back home, and ever since that day, I hadn't talked to him.

That was a few months ago, and here I was nine months pregnant, about to pop at the wedding of my child's father and the woman who would be his aunt and stepmother. *Life is surely fucked up for me,* I thought.

"Are you all right?" a voice asked from behind me. When I turned around, Chance was standing there in his white tuxedo. I rolled my eyes and turned back around, not even saying anything to him. *Fuck his ass too,* I thought. I'm sure the nigga knew that Tae had another woman. I knew he didn't know that the woman was my sister, but he damn sure knew about there being another woman. Therefore, I didn't have anything to say to his ass. I had to admit, though, that he did look hella good in that all-white. Kind of made me want to play a little game of payback with Dontie. Hell, he was keeping it in the family, so why couldn't I? Just as fast as that thought entered my head, it quickly left. I didn't have time to be playing those childish games. I was better than that. He didn't take the hint that I didn't want to be bothered, because he walked over and took a seat beside me.

"Nay, I know I'm probably one of the last people on earth that you want to talk to right now, and I don't blame you one bit—" he started to say.

"Well, if you know that, then, why are you talking to me?" I asked, interrupting him.

"Because I can see that you need a friend," he had the nerve to say. "And I'm just trying to be here for you."

"A friend? You actually think that you're my *friend,* Chance?" I asked, turning to him. "A friend wouldn't have did what you've done to me, Chance."

"Ma, you have to believe me when I say that at first, I didn't know anything about Dontie having a woman, or married, for that matter. I found out way later, and when I did find the shit out, I told him to leave you alone, but he didn't."

"Chance, you should've told me. Did you even stop to think about telling me, or did you think about that bogus-ass guy code that y'all have and are living by nowadays?" I said. "I was your fucking friend. I know Tae is your family, but I thought we had some type of respectful feelings for each other, but I guess I was wrong. Just know that I would have never done that shit to you, no matter what the circumstances were."

"Ma, it killed me to know what that nigga was doing to you. You're right, I do have respect, and I love you as if you was my family, but Dontie's blood whether or not we both like it. I did what I could've, and that was tell him to leave you alone, but don't play stupid, Nay. You knew damn well that the nigga had to have a woman somewhere in the cut. I mean, you seen the nigga mostly on the weekend. I know you ain't slow. You get straight-As in school, making the dean's list and shit. So you can't tell me that you didn't have a clue," he replied.

My eyes grew misty, because I knew what he was saying was nothing more than the truth. I'd been dealing with Tae for about a year, and other than the times when we would go on a few vacations together, I only saw him on the weekends. I never meant for any of this to happen. My whole life, I'd promised myself that I was never going to be some man's other woman, like my mother was to my father. I'd seen the things she went through daily without having him there, and I didn't have a father, so I knew that I, myself, didn't want to go through any of that. I really thought that Tae was something special and that I wouldn't have to worry about being the other woman, but somehow, I ended up being in that position anyway.

Before I knew it, the dam that I held up for the past few hours came crashing down.

"You know what? You're right. I'm not dumb, nor am I stupid. I did have some type of clue about Tae having another woman, but I didn't have the proof, so I couldn't act on the shit. Yeah, I seen him mostly on the weekends, but it never bothered me because I was so consumed with school during the week. I had a feeling, though, I just didn't think that I'd end up pregnant and the other woman would end up being my sister," I said as the tears flowed freely from my eyes. I didn't even try to wipe them away.

"It's going to be okay. It's life. You just got to get it together for you and the baby, ma. It's not about you anymore," he said, grabbing my hand. "You're going to be straight, ma. You and I both know that."

"No, I'm not, and this is not life. I'm pregnant, and I didn't want to be. I wanted to finish school, find a job and my own husband to have our kids with, but now I'm in this fucked-up situation," I said, pulling my hand away from him, "Look around you, Chance. Ain't nothing about this that's going to be good. My baby daddy is getting married to my sister, well, remarried or whatever you want to call it. Then to make matters worse, I have to sit in the pews and watch the shit, like it's okay. Ain't nothing good about that, and you know what? I'm not staying here to watch this shit."

I got up from where I was seated as quickly as my belly would allow me to and began walking down the church steps.

"Where are you going?" he asked.

"I don't know, but I'm not staying here," I said, making my way to my car.

"Ma, you can't go anywhere. The wedding's about to start," he said, following behind me.

"I don't know how many times I have to tell you that I don't care about this damn wedding," I yelled, never slowing my stride.

"Chance, come on, man. The wedding is starting," Nasir yelled from the church steps.

"A'ight, I'm coming," I heard him yell from behind me.

"Nay, stop," he said, grabbing my forearm.

"Just let me go, Chance. I need to get out of here before I lose my damn mind," I told him.

"Where are you going?" he asked.

"I don't know, but I'm getting my ass far away from here," I replied. I was almost to my car when I felt something wet dripping down my legs. When I looked down, a pool of water had puddled at my feet.

"Oh shit, it looks like your water just broke!" he yelled in a panic. "Wait right here while I go get some help," he said; then he took off running back to the church. I wasn't waiting on anything or anyone. I wobbled my ass the rest of the way to my car and got in. I started the car and zoomed out of the parking lot. It was when I got on the street that the pain of what I'm guessing was contractions started hitting me like a ton of bricks.

"*Arrgh!*" I yelled as I started breathing like the woman and Kourtney had taught me in the Lamaze class. Speaking of Kourtney, I surely do wish that she was here with me right now. She would've been so helpful. She would've known just what to do in this situation. I'm so sorry that she wasn't able to make this trip with me.

Somewhere in the car, my phone started to ring. I turned to see my purse lighting up on the seat next to me. I reached over to try to grab it when another wave of contractions began to hit me. This time, I had to grab my stomach with both hands, *that's* how painful it was, then I felt something pop between my legs. Placing one hand back on the steering wheel, I reached between my legs with the other one. When I brought my hand back up, it was covered in blood. Again my phone started ringing, but my focus was nowhere near being on my ringing phone at this moment. It was on the fact that my hand was now covered in blood.

"Oh my God! Help me, Lord, please!" I yelled, shocked because I had no idea what was going on. I began crying as I immediately started to fear the worst. My phone began to ring again, but I couldn't answer it. I was too distraught. I wasn't even paying attention to the road, and since I was crying, I wasn't able to see clearly. It was then when I felt the car veer to the right. Recognizing the danger, I turned the wheel as I tried desperately to get control of the car, but by then, it was too late. The next thing I knew, another car had plowed into the side of my car, and I hit my head on the steering wheel. The car then began to spin. It hit another car and started flipping before it fishtailed and hit something so hard that my head connected with the window this time. Blood immediately began to drip from my head. I tried to move, but I couldn't, so instead, I tried to scream, but nothing came out. The last thing I remembered before everything went black was me hoping and praying that help would get to me in time to save my baby. I wasn't even worried about me or my safety. All I was concerned about was the safety of my baby as I wished that he wasn't harmed in any way.

DONTIE

I stood at the altar as the wedding had just begun. I was on pins and needles because I knew what I now had to do. It was time for me to come clean, and even though I know it was going to hurt Sky, I couldn't stand the thought of hurting Brinay any longer. The pain I saw on her face earlier, when we first made it to the church, was a look that I'd never seen before, and it killed me to know that I was the cause of all of that. I hadn't talked to her in months, and I was dying on the inside. I missed being able to see and wake up to her face in the morning, to hold her at night, and to wake up in the middle of the night and pour my heart out to her without her judging me. I missed all that, and then some. Now that she was pregnant with my seed, all I wanted was to be there for them. I knew she was lying when she first said that the baby wasn't mine. I knew better. Brinay wasn't that type of chick, so I knew that cheating was the last thing she'd do to me. I guess she was saying that to get under my skin, and, boy, did it work. Just the thought of someone else getting what I couldn't get and needed to get was mind-blowing and cause for me to fuck everything up. I wanted everything to go back to the way it was, but I knew that would never happen.

I looked over to where I saw her sitting earlier and noticed that her seat was empty now. I searched the crowd as I tried to locate her face in the sea of people. I don't know why, but all of a sudden, this feeling hit me in the pit of my stomach, and I knew that something wasn't right. I spotted my cousin, Chance, walking down the aisle, and the look on his face let me know that something was, indeed, wrong.

"What's wrong?" I asked him when he made it to where I was standing.

"It's Brinay," he whispered but stopped when everything got too quiet.

Everyone stood to their feet as the music changed and the double doors to the church stood wide open. It was now time for Sky to make her grand entrance. I wasn't concerned about that, though. What I was more concerned about was what was going on with Brinay. I tried to get Chance's attention, but he was focused on who was about to walk down the aisle with her father to her right, just as was the rest of the room. The band changed the tempo as her cousin Keyon, or Keys, as she called herself, came up to the mic and started to sing.

"For all those times you stood by me, for all the truth that you made me see . . ."

Shorty was really singing the hell out of that song. Between how good she sounded and how beautiful Sky looked walking down that aisle, everyone was wiping their eyes. I too found myself wiping a few tears away. That's how emotional everyone was.

"I'm everything I am because you loved me."

By the time Keys was finished singing the song, Sky had already made it to the front of the church. I know she was crying, because she was a hard-core crybaby. So when I lifted the veil from over her face, just like I had thought, she had tears streaming down her face. I used my thumb to gently wipe them away. I made sure to be extra careful, because I wasn't trying to mess up any of her makeup.

"You look beautiful, ma," I said smiling. "But you need to cut all that crying out before you ruin your makeup."

"Thanks, baby, you don't look so bad yourself," she said, reaching in to give me a kiss on the lips.

The pastor cleared his throat, trying to get our attention, while everyone else around us laughed.

"We'll have time for all of that later. Let's get the ceremony started, shall we?" he said, cracking a smile.

"Sorry," we both said, apologizing at the same time. Out of the corner of my eye, I spotted one of Sky's aunts walking over to her father, who was still standing behind her. She had this look on her face as if something was wrong, but she was so afraid to tell him. I looked at Sky, who then looked at me, then to her father.

I watched as Brenda stood on her tippy toes and whispered in Brian's ear. By the way that his body tensed up and his mood quickly changed, I knew something was indeed wrong. He then walked over to Sky, and I could've sworn that I saw water in his eyes. He looked her in the eyes, then whispered something in her ear. Her eyes grew as big as saucers as she grabbed for her chest. I quickly grabbed her.

"What's wrong?" I asked, searching her eyes.

She didn't say anything. She just looked back at her father, then nodded her head. He, in turn, walked—more like ran—back up the way they just came and headed out of the church.

"Is everything okay?" the pastor asked her.

She looked at me, then turned and looked at the crowd. She then turned back to him and said, "Yes. You can continue."

"Okay," he nodded.

"What's wrong?" I asked her.

"Umm, it's Brinay," she replied. "It's no big deal, so you don't have to worry about it."

"Brinay? What's going on?" I asked her, trying to find out what she wasn't telling me.

"I just told you that it isn't a big deal, Dontie," she said, leaning in toward me. "So, let it go, please."

"If it wasn't a big deal, then why did your father just up and run out of here?" I asked, looking at her. "Tell me what's going on, Sky."

"Umm . . . She just got into a bad car accident, and she had to be airlifted to the hospital," she said, sounding as if she was irritated just talking about it.

I know this bitch ain't serious right now, I thought as I took a step back, looking at her sideways.

"Did you just say that your sister was in a bad car accident?" I asked to be sure that I heard her right.

"Yes," she said, rolling her eyes.

"And you over here acting like that's *not* a big deal?" I asked, confused. I don't know what it is, but I'd never seen them act like normal sisters do. It's like they hated each other, and one could never stand to be around the other. The only reason they would be in the same room sometimes was because of their father.

"I can't believe you're standing there acting as if your sister wasn't just airlifted to a hospital. She's pregnant, Sky! Damn."

"Oh shit, that's what I came in here for," Chance whispered from behind me. "I found Nay sitting on the steps of the church earlier. She wasn't feeling too good, so she decided to go home, but when she got up, water came leaking down her legs."

"She was in labor, and you ain't tell me, nigga?" I said, shoving him in the chest.

"Man, I forgot, with all of this shit that's going on. I don't know what to tell you and what not to tell you," he said, cutting his eyes at Sky, who was still standing there as if nothing was wrong.

"Yeah yeah yeah," I said, waving him off. "So are you going to the hospital to check on her and the baby?" I asked, turning back to Sky.

"No, I'm not. I'm going to continue on with my wedding," she responded. I was so taken aback by her comment that I really had to take a step back and look at her from a different angle. This was *not* the woman that I met almost two years ago . . . or was it? I mean, here she just said that her sister had gotten into a bad accident, and she was more worried about a fucking wedding than the safety of her sister and her nephew. I didn't see her feel one type of emotion or shed one tear about the shit.

"God, please be with me," I silently prayed to myself. This bitch had to be out of her fucking mind or just plain ole stupid. Ain't that much hate in the world that you can just not give a fuck about ya own blood. Whichever the case was, I really needed to get away before I ended up hurting her ass.

"Come on, Chance," I said, turning to my best man.

"Where are we going? You're about to get married again or whatever the hell ya call it," he asked, confused. I didn't even answer him. I didn't have time to. Shit had just hit me all of a sudden. My baby mama was in labor and had just gotten into an accident, and I was in a church about to marry her sister when I needed to be by her and my son's side. I knew the situation was fucked up, but ain't no way I was going to let my son come into the world without me being around. I'd be less of a man to even allow something like that to go down.

"Dontie," Sky called out to me, but I never answered. I kept on walking. I saw the people in the pews beginning to whisper among themselves, but I wasn't concerned or worried about any of that. What I was more worried about was the safety of my son and his mother. I knew that Sky was going to want my head on a silver platter after this, but I didn't care. My main concern right now was finding out which hospital Brinay was at and getting there as fast as I can. I'd have to worry about Sky and the rest of them nosy muthafuckers later. Right now, my son and his mother needed me by their side, and that's where I was heading. Fuck this wedding. That shit could happen another time, *if* it makes it. If Brinay or my son didn't make it out if that hospital alive, I'd never be able to live with myself.

Once I exited the church, I went straight to the limo that Sky and I had reserved for us to leave the church in. Chance ended up coming after all. We loaded into the limo without saying a word. Once inside, I instructed the driver to take me to hospital where I believed she might be. I tilted my head back and said a prayer asking God to spare both Brinay and my son's life. I know she and I weren't on the best of terms, but none of that mattered to me. Nothing in my life right now matters to me but the two of them.

"It's going to be all right, fam," Chance said, finally speaking up.

"I hope so, man, I really hope so," I replied. As I sat there waiting to arrive at the hospital, I made a promise to myself that I will always be there for my son and his mother. No matter what anyone had to say.

Chapter One

Brinay

I sat there on the toilet as I waited impatiently to read the results of the pregnancy test that I had just taken. I'd be lying if I said that I wasn't nervous and scared, because I was. It felt like I was about to catch a doggone heart attack any minute now. I was silently hoping and praying that the test would come back negative, because in all actuality, a baby was really *not* in my plans, at least, not right at this moment.

You see, I'd been sick for the past few days. At first, I tried to write it off as food poison. I even tried thinking that it was the flu, but up until two days ago, when I'd experienced the worst pain of them all, I knew otherwise. I prayed to God that I wasn't pregnant, and I tried ignoring all of the signs, but I couldn't anymore. Besides, my best friend was always in my ear about it, telling me that I was indeed pregnant. I knew I kept telling her that I wasn't, but she just insisted that I take a test anyway. She even went out and bought the damn thing.

"It's been like five minutes already. Did you go and check the thing yet?" my best friend Kourtney asked me. I'd been on the phone with her the whole time, and I was beginning to regret it. She swore that I didn't know how to tell time. To be honest, I was scared as hell to get it and read it.

"No, I didn't read it yet," I said, rolling my eyes in my head.

"What? What do you mean? Do you need me to come over there and read it for you?" she asked, sounding as serious as a heart attack.

"Kourt, chill, man. I'm just nervous about reading it. That's all," I said, calling her by her nickname.

"Girl, don't make me come over there. You know it won't probably take me all of ten minutes to make it there," she said, now sounding like she was my mother and not my friend.

"Kourtney! You don't even have to go through all of that. I'm about to go and read it right now," I said, getting up from the seat.

I swear the five, maybe six steps it took to get from the toilet to the sink felt more like fifteen to twenty steps instead. With every step that I got closer, my heart began to beat a bit faster, so fast that I could actually hear the beating in my ears. I didn't know what that stick was about to say, but I was surely about to find out, even though I didn't want to. Taking a deep breath, I closed my eyes, picked up the stick, and swallowed the lump that had formed in my throat. Bringing the stick up to eye level, my heart fell to my ass when I saw it. I damn near fainted when I saw two pink lines inside of the little square window, telling me that I was, in fact, pregnant.

"Oh my God, this can't be true," I whispered softly, still trying to deny it, even though I now had the proof in my hand.

"Well, what does it say?" Kourtney asked, sounding anxious. I didn't say anything right away. I couldn't. I was still trying to wrap my mind around the fact that I was pregnant.

"Nay, are you going to tell me what the thing says or not?" she asked, sounding a bit irritated.

"Umm . . . yeah," I said, just above a whisper.

"Well, hurry up and tell me then, before I go crazy over here."

Letting out a breath of air, I closed my eyes and said, "I'm pregnant." I said it so slow that she barely even heard what I had said.

"Huh?" she asked. "I couldn't hear you. Say that again for me."

"I said that I'm pregnant, Kourtney," I blurted out. I ain't seen no point in trying to hide it. Hell, it was going to come out one way or another.

"I knew it, I *knew*," she replied, and as if it had hit her for the first time, and she started screaming, "Oh my God, Nay, you're going to be a mommy. Congratulations!"

I sat there listening to her as she screamed with excitement. She was acting like she had won the lottery or something, while I, on the other hand, was acting the total opposite.

"You're going to be a mother. What are you going to do? Why aren't you excited?" she asked once she realized I wasn't all happy-go-lucky like she was. The truth of the matter was, I didn't know what I was going to do. I wasn't ready, nor did I want this.

"Honestly, Kourt, I can't have a baby right now. I'm still in school, and I have a year and a half left to finish. If I was to have this baby right now, all of that would change, and I've come too far to not finish school on time," I said to her. "Besides, all that extra shit that comes with a child is too much. I'm barely able to support my own self, let alone add a baby to the mix."

"Well, what are you going to do, then?"

"Right now, I really don't have a clue about what I'm going to do about the baby just yet. I'll think about it. Just let me get through this weekend at my father's house first," I replied dryly. "You know his ass had to practically beg me to come. Talking about my sister had some big announcement, and she wanted me to be there. I don't know why she wanted me to be there. We aren't even close like that."

"Oh, that's this weekend?" she asked. "I thought that was the weekend after next."

"No, unfortunately for me, that's this weekend, and I got a good mind to call and cancel on their asses," I said seriously. I really didn't feel like being bothered with or being around those wannabe white people in black folks' bodies. Now that I knew I was pregnant, I just wanted to be alone so that I could think about my situation and what I'm going to do about it. It's times like these that I wish my mother was alive to help me, but she died two years ago from cancer. Which is why I'm grateful to have Kourtney in my life. I still had my oldest brother Brandon, but he was in prison doing a bid, so that didn't and couldn't help me too much.

"I think you should go. Right now is the perfect time for you to be around your family. It can help you make whatever decision you decide to make regarding the baby," she replied. If only she knew how wrong she was. My dad's family ain't all that peachy. In fact, they ain't even sweet—they're sour as hell. I didn't need to be around those people. They were basically a family from hell. Being anywhere around them would probably make me want to get an abortion without a second thought.

I never really liked to be around my dad or his family, especially my sister and her no-good-ass mother. They hated me, and I, in turn, despised both of them. They acted as if they were too good and I was beneath them. Thank God I'm only going to be around them for three days, because I don't know if I could handle being around their asses no longer than that. The only one that I really got along with was Momo Netty, my dad's mother, and we're not always on good terms, either.

"I'll go, but not because I need to be around them. I actually need a vacation, and with the news that I've just received, this is the perfect time for one."

"Well, when are you going to tell Tae about the baby?" she asked, posing the million-dollar question.

"I haven't seen Tae in two whole weeks, so I have no idea when I'll tell him about the baby," I sadly said to her. *That's if I decide to tell him,* I thought to myself.

"Well, you could always call or text and tell him," she said, offering up a solution. Rolling my eyes in my head, I took a seat on the bed.

"I've been calling and texting Tae for days now, and he has yet to respond to anything. I'm not trying to have no man out here thinking that I'm going to chase behind him, because you know for sure that right there just ain't me. I don't even get down like that."

"Okay," she said, then the line got quiet. I'm guessing that she was over there lost in her thoughts, just as I was over here lost in mine. "Well, whatever you decide to do, just know that I'll be here for you no matter what happens, Nay," she said, making my eyes watery.

"I know, and that's why I couldn't have asked God for a better best friend. You're always there whenever for whatever I need you to be, and I absolutely love and appreciate you for that," I said, meaning each and every word. A good loyal friend was hard to come by these days. That's why I thanked God daily for blessing me with one.

"Aww . . . I love you too, Nay," she replied. I can already hear her voice cracking up.

"Oh Lord, let me go finish packing my things before you have us both on the phone crying and stuff," I said, trying to lighten the mood, because I knew my friend, and she would most definitely start crying any minute now. I told her behind that she's too doggone sensitive for me.

"I can't help it, Nay. You know I'm all softhearted, girl," she said, laughing a bit.

"I know," I said, going in on the laugh. "You need to tighten that up and get hard, my girl."

"I'm fine. Do you need me to come over and help you pack your things?" she asked, changing the subject.

"Now, how did I know you was going to ask me that?" I said, laughing at her once again.

"Because we always help each other pack when the other one is going on a trip."

"Oh yeah. I forgot," I quickly replied. "Well, I'm almost done, but thank you anyway."

"You're welcome. Just call me if you need me."

"Okay, I will. See you tomorrow."

"You too," she replied, and I hung up.

After getting off of the phone with Kourtney, I decided to try to call Tae's phone again, but like the first few times, it went straight to voice mail. I wanted to leave a message, but I opted to send a text message instead. I texted him a message telling him that I had something important to say and for him to call me immediately; then I began to pack the few things that I had left. A few minutes went by, and my phone buzzed, alerting me that I had an incoming message. I immediately stopped what I was doing and practically ran over to the phone, thinking that it was Tae. I was disappointed when I noticed that it wasn't him and that it was my father. He texted my phone wanting to know if I was still coming to the house this weekend. I started to tell his ass no, and tell him and his dysfunctional-ass family to go to hell, but I didn't. He's been texting me more than usual. I hope he wasn't trying to form some kind of father/daughter bond, because it was way too late for that. I don't know what this announcement was that my sister had to make, but I'm guessing that it was important for his ass to be stalking my phone, wondering if I was still coming. I told him that I was coming and that I'd see him tomorrow. Placing my phone back down, I went back to what I was doing.

It took me almost two hours to finish packing my things, and by that time, it was dark, and I was tired and hungry. I didn't feel like leaving my apartment, so I just made myself a sandwich, got one of those little fruit cups, and a bottle of water. I may not like or want to admit it, but I didn't want to hurt or bring harm to the baby if I decided to keep it.

When I was done eating, I took a quick bath and was ready to climb in bed. Before I got in the bed, I checked my phone and saw that Tae still hadn't responded to me, so I decided to send him one final text, and I do mean *final*.

See, I wasn't green for a minute. I had suspected that Tae had a girlfriend, but I didn't have any proof. That was . . . until he started going MIA all the time and trying to end the call in a hurry whenever we were on the phone. Even though he said he didn't, I knew better. This right here just proves to me that I was right, and now that I knew for sure, I wasn't too happy about keeping a nigga's illegitimate child. I'd basically have to do this parenting thing by myself—while he's out there probably making a family of his own. I wasn't ready for that, and I didn't sign up for the shit.

When I was done typing up everything that I needed and wanted to say to him, I sent the message and placed him on my block list. I then powered my phone off and hopped in bed. I was too tired and fed up with Dontie's shit to even give a care anymore. Being a statistic wasn't something that I had planned on doing, but things happen, and if I decided to keep this baby, I wouldn't have a problem with raising him or her on my own. I was going to give my baby the best life that I could give it. I didn't need a man here to help me, because at the end of the day, it was still *my* child, with a daddy or not. I wasn't going to worry myself or stress behind Dontie. I'm not the type of chick who'd run behind a man, and Tae will soon find that out.

Chapter Two

Brinay

When I woke up the next evening, my stomach and back were killing me. The pain was so excruciating that I was barely able to get out of bed. "Lord, please don't do this to me today," I said out loud. I pulled back the cover, slowly got out of bed, and made my way to the bathroom. I grabbed my toothbrush and prepared to brush my teeth . . . when a wave of nausea hit me. As fast as my aching body would allow me to, I made my way over to the toilet—just in time to throw up everything that I had eaten last night.

"Oh my God!" I screamed as I clutched my stomach. My stomach was hurting me so bad. I felt like something or someone was trying to dig out everything inside of it. I was bent over the toilet for five long minutes before my stomach had finally decided to calm down. Flushing the toilet, I walked back over to the faucet and rinsed out my mouth. Next, I grabbed a towel from the towel rack, wet it, and passed it over my face before I grabbed my toothbrush and brushed my teeth. When I was done, I removed my clothes and hopped in the shower.

Once in the shower, I turned the water on, made sure it wasn't too hot and stood underneath the faucet. I was hoping the warm water would somehow ease the pain that I was feeling. After a few minutes of just standing there, I grabbed my washcloth, my Dove body wash and began to wash every inch of my body that I could reach. When I was done, I rinsed off and repeated the process a few times; then I just stood underneath the water again. I didn't get out of the shower until the water began to get cold. Again, my stomach started to hurt, but not like it was hurting me before. I think I was just hungry this time, so I turned the water off and got out. Grabbing the big towel from the shower rod, I wrapped it around my body and headed to the bedroom.

Once I was inside of my room, I went to the dresser where I kept my panties and bras. I removed a black and pink lace bra and pantie set and laid it on the bed. I then walked to the closet, where I removed a purple and yellow sundress, with my yellow sandals, put them on my bed next to my bra and pantie set, then went to look at myself in the full-length mirror. I let the towel fall to my feet as I started to look over my body in the mirror. The first place my hands went to was my stomach. I stood there imagining the different ways my body might look like. I mean, I've seen plenty of pregnant women, and they had a little bump to their stomach, but not my stomach. It was damn near flat, and I couldn't imagine another life growing inside there. As if he/she knew what I was doing or thinking about him/her, I felt movement in my stomach.

"Hey, little baby, I'm Brinay, and I'm your mother," I said, rubbing my stomach. I was talking to it as if the baby knew what I was saying. "I'm scared, but I promise not to let anyone hurt you, baby." When I said that, the baby started moving nonstop. "Whoa, calm down, little one. Mommy's in enough pain already."

I was brought out of my momentary "mommy moment" when my phone began to ring. Walking over to the dresser where my phone was, I picked it up and noticed that it was Kourtney calling.

"Hey, boo," I said, answering the phone.

"Hey, baby mama!" she said, sounding like her normal jolly self. "How are you today?"

"I'm doing better today than I was yesterday," I replied. "What about you?"

"Well, that's good, and I'm doing fine," she said. "So today's Thursday. What are you doing since you don't have school today?"

"I don't know yet. Not too long ago I woke up and got out of the shower. I can't believe that I slept into the evening," I said, sounding sluggish. I was still tired.

"That's why you didn't answer me earlier. Well, let's go out and get something to eat then," she suggested.

"Umm . . . okay. What time would you like to go?" I asked her.

"Now. I'm actually on my way over to your apartment already," she said. I knew her ass was up to something since she was calling me.

"Okay. I should be ready when you get here."

"Okay, I'll see you in a minute."

"See you in a minute, girl," I said, then hung up.

I placed my phone on the charger, grabbed the bottle of cocoa butter lotion, and began to lather my body with it. When I was done, I grabbed my bra and panties and put them on. Then my dress. When I finished dressing, I slipped on my shoes and went to the bathroom so that I could do my hair. My hair had grown quite a bit these past few weeks, and now I knew why. Grabbing the brush from out of the cabinet, I brushed my hair into a ponytail. The minute I was done with my hair, someone started knocking on the door. I applied a little bit of lip gloss on my lips and grabbed my purse and keys; then I went to answer the door.

"Damn, I thought you was going to have me out here waiting on your behind forever," Kourtney said once I opened the door.

"Chile, please. Stop exaggerating. You was not out here that long," I told her. "Are you ready to go?"

"Yes, come on, because I'm starving, and now that we know that you're eating for two, I know you have to be hungry too."

"Ha-ha! So funny. Let's go before you make me change my mind on you," I said. I turned to make sure that I had locked the door, then shut it behind me.

"You're glowing. You look so cute, even when you're trying to be mean," she said, giving me a once-over.

"Thank you, ma," I replied as we made our way outside. When we got outside, we met up with this chick named Jordan. She goes to the same college as us. We even have a few classes together.

"Hey, y'all," she said, walking over to us. "Where y'all headed?"

"Hey, Jordan, how's it going? We're about to go get something to eat. You want to come?" I asked her. Out of the corner of my eye, I spotted Kourtney giving me the "look."

"Nah, I'm good. I got a ton of homework to do, and I haven't started on it yet," she replied. I know she was probably lying, because she would always do her homework before she stepped foot outside. She probably spotted the way that Kourtney had looked at her and decided not to.

"Well, okay, then. See you later, girl," I said, trying to hurry up and get her away from us before Kourtney blows up.

"Okay, I'll see y'all later," she replied. "Oh, and by the way, you look beautiful today, and you're glowing."

"Thank you," I said, cheesing hard.

"You're welcome," she replied, then walked off.

"What was that?" I asked, turning toward Kourtney.

"What are you talking about?" she asked, trying to play like she was innocent.

"Know what? Never mind. I don't even have time for this today," I said since she wanted to play like she was stupid. "We're taking your car or mine?"

"We can take my car," she replied.

"Okay," I said as I began to walk toward her car. I waited for her to unlock the doors; then we both got in. At first, she didn't say anything. She just started the car and pulled off.

"Umm . . . So, where do you want to go?" she asked once we were on the road.

"It don't matter as long as I get to put something in my stomach, because I'm starving," I said, rubbing my belly. "Where do you want to go?"

She didn't say anything. She just looked at me, smiled, and turned back to the road.

"Why are you looking at me like that?" I asked her.

"Nothing. You're just so cute when you're pregnant, that's all," she replied.

Oh Lord, here she go with this pregnancy shit again.

"Let's go to IHOP. You know they make the best pancakes," Kourtney finally decided.

"Surely do, and I could surely use some right now, with some strawberries on top," I said, licking my lips. Just thinking about it made my stomach growl.

"Aww . . . That's the baby talking there, because I remember that you couldn't stand strawberries. Now your ass over there craving them," she replied.

"No, I'm just so hungry that I'd eat anything right now."

"Uh-huh," she said as she pulled into IHOP's parking lot. She killed the engine, and we got out. I tried to play it off, but I was actually starting to like this pregnancy stuff, but I wasn't going to admit that to her, though.

When we walked into the restaurant, the place was kind of packed, but lucky for us, we found a table not too far from the entrance. Once we were seated, the waitress came straight over to us.

"Good evening, ladies, I'm Journi, and I'll be your waitress this evening," she said, handing us two menus. "Can I start off by getting you all something to drink?"

"Yes, I'll have a Sprite," Kourtney said.

"And I'll have a lemonade," I replied as I looked over my menu.

"Okay. I'll give you all a minute to look over your menus while I go and get the drinks," she replied.

"Okay," I said as she walked off.

"What are you getting?" Kourtney asked, looking at me.

"I don't know. All of this got my mouth watering. I wish I could have the whole damn menu," I said, laughing a bit.

"Well, order whatever it is that you want, because I'm paying," she said, shocking me a bit, but not too much. I knew she was doing this only to make sure that I was eating and taking care of the baby.

"I know why you're paying, but you don't have to. I'll pay for myself," I told her.

"Nay, you're my best friend, so stop tripping," she said, placing her menu on the table.

"Okay, I hear you," I replied, waving her off.

"Besides, I want to make sure that you're feeding my god baby," she added.

"See, I knew it," I said laughing. "You're going to worry yourself to death over this pregnancy thing, and you're not even the one who's pregnant."

"No, I won't. I only want to make sure that you all eat," she said, just as the waitress came back with our drinks.

"Are you ladies ready to order?" she asked, placing the drinks on the table.

"As a matter of fact, we are," I replied. "Can I get two pancakes topped with strawberries, an omelet, two pieces of bacon, and some French toast also topped with strawberries?"

"Okay," she replied as she wrote everything down in her little pad. "And for you?" she asked, turning to Kourtney.

"Just give me some grits, eggs, and two pancakes."

"Okay," she said as she began to read our orders back to us.

"Will that be all?" she asked to make sure.

"Yes, that will be all," I said. "Oh, and can you make sure that the syrup is hot?"

"Okay. Your food will be a few minutes. In the meantime, enjoy y'all's evening." She then left to go place our orders.

"So, are you ready to go to Miami tomorrow?" Kourtney asked.

"I'm as ready as I'll ever be," I replied as I took a sip from my drink.

"Have you talked to Dontie yet?"

"To be honest, Kourtney, I'm not about to worry my nerves about Dontie anymore. He's just who I thought he was, and I'm just mad at myself for falling for that bullshit." I was now feeling some type of way.

"Well, are you going to at least tell him about the baby?" she asked, beginning to annoy me. I don't know why she was so concerned with me telling Tae about my baby.

"No, and I don't plan on telling him. I'm done with Tae. I don't need a man who already has a woman. If I have to raise my baby by myself, then I will. I don't want or need Tae to help me with my baby," I said as I felt the tears welling up in my eyes. I tried to wipe away the tear that fell from my eye before she saw it, but I was too slow. She got up from where she was sitting and came to sit next to me.

"Don't worry about it. It'll be okay. I'll be here with you every step of the way. You won't be alone."

"I know." I then lay my head on her shoulder and cried. I don't know why all of a sudden I became so emotional, because this was not me. I was always the hard one out of the two. Now, I'm over here looking like Kourtney's emotional ass. It has to be this pregnancy shit. I'd just learned about it, and now I was already ready for it to be over and done with.

Chapter Three

Dontie

I stood outside on the balcony, smoking cigarette after cigarette. My nerves were shot, and I don't know what to do. I'd been up all morning trying to reach Brinay, but her phone keeps going to voice mail. I needed to get in touch with her like yesterday. When I woke up this morning, I saw that I had two new messages from her. One that said that she had something really important to tell me and that she wanted me to call her, but I guess when I didn't answer her, she decided to send me this long-ass message saying how she knew I had a woman and she wanted nothing more to do with me. I wasn't trying to hear that shit there, which is why I'd been calling and texting her phone all morning, but she didn't answer, and the shit was starting to aggravate the hell out of me. I know she probably felt some type of way because I wasn't answering her calls and texts anymore. Hell, I couldn't. Every move that I made, Sky's always making them with me. I can barely even take a shit by myself, and if she sees me leaving the room with my phone, she becomes all suspicious and shit.

See, I knew before I even got here that this trip was going to be a bad fucking idea. I don't know why I fucked around and agreed to come here in the first place. I don't like to be out of town, because I have a few businesses to run. Besides, I haven't seen Brinay in weeks, and I'm really starting to miss seeing her pretty face and hearing her beautiful voice. We'd been in Jamaica for about two weeks now, and I was more than ready to head back home to the States. I wasn't the type to leave and go on a vacation like this, but Sky had practically begged me to come, so I couldn't tell her no. Besides, if I wouldn't have come, I would have never heard the end of this, and I most definitely wasn't about hearing her bitching and moaning about why I didn't come for the next few weeks. So I gave in, and now I wished like hell that I hadn't.

As I stood there, I couldn't help but to think about Brinay, wondering what she was doing and what it was that was so important that she needed to tell me. I picked up my phone and tried to call her again, but her phone kept on going straight to voice mail. I wanted to leave her a message, but I wasn't that type of dude. Still, I couldn't help but to wonder what was going on with her. *It's bad enough that I've been thinking about her this whole trip. I'll have to be more careful, because I don't want Sky to catch on.*

"Baby, are you going to come in and pack the rest of your things? You know the flight is schedule to leave in two hours, and I'm not trying to miss it," Sky said, interrupting my thoughts. I rolled my eyes in my head, before turning to her. I can't lie, she was standing there looking just as beautiful as she was the day I first met her. Standing at five foot three and weighing about 135 pounds with a well-toned body as if she worked out twice a day, she had shoulder-length brown hair and brown eyes that matched her beautiful, light brown skin. She walked over to me, wrapped her arms around my neck, stood on her tippy toes, and placed a kiss on my lips.

"You know I love you, right?" she said, kissing me again.

"I love you too, baby girl," I responded.

"You've made me one of the happiest women on the planet," she beamed as she stared at her wedding ring. I knew I was fucking up and I should never have proposed, let alone married her with a ring that was supposed to be for Brinay, but she'd been mad since she caught me on the phone with this li'l chick named Cindy from around the way, so, it was more like some spur-of-the-moment-type shit, and I was trying to get on her good side. I wasn't nowhere near ready to get married, but she just insisted that we get married on the Jamaican beach. I tried everything not to. I even thought about her parents who I had yet to meet, but she still wanted us to get married.

"You know what would make me happy right now?" I said, licking my lips and trying to change the subject. I wasn't trying to think about the mistake that I had made, and sex was the only thing that would help me not to think about it. I grabbed her around her waist and placed her on the balcony railing.

"Dontie, put me down before you drop me," she said, trying to climb off the railing.

"Chill out. I'm not going to drop you," I said, parting her legs.

"Babe, you know we can't do that right now. We still have to pack the rest of our things before our flight leaves, and I don't know about you, but I'm not trying to miss this plane at all," she said, trying to push me back.

"I promise to make it quick," I said, moving her from the railing to the table.

"Okay, but if we miss our flight, I'm blaming it on you," she said, opening her bathrobe. My dick instantly grew a few inches as I noticed that she didn't have anything on beneath it. I stuck a finger inside of her to see if she was ready for me. A smiled formed on my face when I pulled my finger out and noticed that it was soaking wet.

"I see that *somebody's* happy to see me," I said, freeing my dick from my pants. Grabbing it, I then placed it at her opening. Gently, I began to rub it back and forth between her lips.

"Dontie!" she said, whining. Her eyes looked as if she was going to pass out any minute now. "Stop playing," she said, and with one powerful thrust, I entered her.

"Oh, Dontie, fuck!" I didn't move right away. I just stood there, enjoying the way her walls felt clutching my dick like a glove.

"This is supposed to be a quickie, remember?" she said, reminding me. Snapping out of it, I began to pump in and out of her.

"Oh my God!" she moaned. She wrapped her legs around my waist and began to ride me from the bottom. I picked her up and gave it to her like that. She reached in and began to suck on my neck.

"*Sssh*," I hissed. She knew just what she was doing. That was my spot, and that shit always turned me on. I quickly pulled out of her and began walking us inside of the suite. Once inside, I walked over to the bed and laid her down. I bent down and began rubbing the head of my dick at her opening again. Since she wanted to play, I decided to play that game with her. I then gave her a few inches before pulling all the way out of her, doing it all over again, and when she least expected it, I plugged all the way in her, hitting the bottom of her pussy.

"Oh my Jesus, Tae," she moaned out. I was momentary confused by that, because the only one who called me that, besides my mother, was Brinay.

"Turn over," I said, pulling out of her. She turned over and got on all fours, arched her back, and spread her ass cheeks with her hands. Sliding my dick back inside of her, I then went to work. Roughly and hungrily, I began to fuck the shit out of her.

"Slow down, Tae," she said, calling me by that name again, which only made me think of Brinay again. I then went into a zone as I picked up speed and began power driving her ass. The only thing on my mind right now was Brinay.

"Babe, slow down," she cried out, but her pleas fell on deaf ears. I was already in a zone, thinking about Brinay and the last time we had sex. Right now, nothing but a nut was going to stop me. As I pumped in and out of her, I could feel my nut building up.

"Dontie, stop it!" she yelled from under me. She tried to move, but the grip that I had on her waist prevented her from doing so. My nut was right there, I could feel it.

"Tae!" she yelled just as an image of Brinay popped inside of my head, sending me over the edge.

"*Aaargh,*" I said as I released. When I was done, I rolled over on my back, trying to catch my breath.

"What the hell was that about?" she asked, jumping up from the bed.

"Why are you tripping, Sky?" I asked, sitting up on my elbows.

"What the fuck you mean, why am I tripping?" she yelled. I knew I had done fucked up, and I knew for sure that she was mad, because she was one who rarely cursed. I wanted to bust out laughing, because cursing wasn't her style. She was a suburban chick who liked to act ghetto but failed at it. I knew she wanted to be hard, which is why I loved watching her try hard to do so.

"Sky, I don't have time for your shit. So, chill, please, because I'm not trying to hear that shit today." I fell back on the bed, trying to catch my breath. On the inside, I was dying laughing, but still, I knew I had fucked up by fucking her like that, but I couldn't help it. I missed my baby Brinay.

"Well, it's too damn bad because you're about to hear it then," she said.

No, I'm not, I thought as I got up from the bed and made my way to the bathroom. She stepped in my way before I could make it in there.

"Yo, Sky, I'ma need you to chill the hell out."

"Dontie, why every time you fuck up, *I'm* the one who needs to chill?" she asked, poking my chest with her index finger.

"Really, Sky? How did *I* fuck up? What are you talking about?" I asked her. I could already feel myself about to blow up on her ass. I silently counted to ten in my head. I had to keep myself from blowing my top, because Sky was really about to get it. She nagged and fussed too much for me. That's why I always like to be around Brinay. She didn't fuss. She let a nigga be, and she didn't nag me.

"You know what, Dontie? Forget about it," she said, moving to the side.

I stood there for a minute just looking at her. I don't know what her angle is, but I was not about to feed into her bullshit. I wanted to say something, but instead, I didn't. I proceeded to the bathroom to take a shower.

Once I was in the shower, I stood there letting the warm water run over my face. I'd been so stressed lately, and this trip wasn't making the shit no better. I stood there thinking about my life and how I was living it. Sky had no idea about my other dealings, and I was trying my hardest to keep that shit away from her, but that was proving to be a task in itself. I'd been with Sky for a minute, but I could slowly feel myself letting go. Then I had Brinay, and shorty was everything to me. She'd always be there to listen to my problems and help out if she could. It didn't matter what I did, she didn't care. Her only thing was that I be careful and come back in one piece. She was all right. She wasn't trying to be my mother most of the time, which is how I found myself, slowly but surely, falling in love with her.

I was deep in my thoughts when I felt Sky get into the shower behind me. At first, she didn't say anything. She just moved over to me, wrapped her arms around me, and lay her head against my back. For a minute we just stood there, lost in our thoughts as the water beat against our skin.

"I'm sorry, baby," she said. I heard her, barely. So I turned around and held her in my arms.

"That's okay, ma, and I'm sorry too," I said as I rubbed her back.

"I love you, Dontie," she said, looking into my eyes. "Promise me that you will never leave me, Tae."

There she go with this Tae shit again. I don't know where she got that name from, but she needs to quit calling me that. She probably remembers my mother saying that, but she needs to stop, for real. She always gets like this when we get into a fight or disagreement . . . like I could promise her that I would never leave her. Hell, people change every day, and the way things are going with her, I couldn't guarantee that we'd be together forever, especially knowing that I was falling in love with another woman.

Do I really want to be with this girl forever? I thought to myself.

I hesitated a bit before I spoke. "I love you too, and I will never leave you," I said, leaving out the word *promise*.

"Now, come on. I'm sure we don't have much time left, and I'm not trying to miss that plane."

I grabbed the washcloth, lathered it up with some body wash, and began to wash her. When I was done, she took the cloth out of my hands, put some body wash on it, and washed my body. We took two more turns washing each other's body before we hopped out of the shower,

Ambria Davis

got dressed, packed the rest of our things, and headed straight for the airport. I was hoping like hell that we didn't miss our flight, because I was going to be pissed the fuck off.

Chapter Four

Sky

We made it to the airport just in time to catch our flights. I was glad that we didn't have to schedule another flight, because I would've been supermad. I had too many things to do back at home, and that would've messed everything up, and I wouldn't have been a happy camper at all.

I sat there on the computer, going over the file that my boss had sent over to me. I wanted to ask him why he didn't get my assistant to do it, but I knew better. As soon as I got back, I was going to be looking for a new assistant, because the one I got was no good.

"Put that computer away, Sky. You'll have enough time to do that on Monday," Dontie said, scaring the shit out of me. I thought his ass was sleeping, but I guess I thought wrong.

"I know, but my boss e-mailed me this file, and he said that he needed it back as soon as possible," I said, never moving my eyes from the computer screen. He sighed and sat back in his seat. He hated it when I was supposed to be on vacation but still worked. That's one of his problems with me, but he had to get over it, because that was how my job worked. I made sure to save the file that I was working on before I closed the computer and turned to him. I don't know what's been going on with him, but lately, something has been bothering him. He thought that I didn't notice it, but I did.

As he sat there with his eyes closed, I couldn't help but to wonder what it was that was bothering him so much.

"You just going to stare at me, or are you going to say whatever it is that's on your mind?" he asked. He didn't open his eyes, so I don't know how he knew I was staring at him.

"What's wrong with you, Dontie? What's going on?" I asked, concerned.

"Ain't nothing wrong with me, and there's nothing going on," he said dryly. I grabbed his face and turned it my way, forcing him to open his eyes.

"Babe, I don't want to fight with you anymore. I want us to go back to the way things used to be, you know, before all the fussing and fighting started." I looked into his eyes.

"Ma, I'm telling you, ain't wrong with us. Yeah, we may fuss and fight sometimes, but what couple doesn't?" he replied.

"Yeah, I know that, but lately, things between us just ain't right, and I want us to fix it."

"What's changed besides the fact that our jobs keep us extrabusy these days?" he asked.

"Yeah, but it's something else, Tae. I know it is," I whined.

"Look, ma, everything is gravy with us. Stop trying to find something wrong when there's nothing wrong. Don't worry yourself, because it's nothing," he said, placing a kiss on my lips. "Don't trip."

"Okay," I said, dropping the issue. If he said that there wasn't anything wrong, then there wasn't. I wasn't trying to go looking for something wrong when he said there wasn't anything. I folded my arms across my chest and sat there thinking. I couldn't help but to think that there was something that he wasn't telling me. I only prayed that I wasn't about to lose my man.

"Oh, I need you to clear whatever it is that you have planned for the weekend," I said, remembering that my father planned something for the family this weekend.

"Why?" he asked, now sitting up.

"Because my parents are doing something at the house for our family, and I want you to come with me," I responded.

"Why you want me to meet your parents now?" he asked, shocking the hell out of me. I had no idea why he didn't want to meet my parents.

"Dontie, we've been messing around for over two years. I think it's finally time for you to meet my family. Babe, I really want you to be there. Can you reschedule whatever it is that you have to do?"

"Nah, I can't. I told you that I'm going to be back Saturday."

"Okay, cool. I'll just go to the mall that morning and get us something to put on, so you won't have to."

"That's cool, but don't pick out nothing girly," he said, serious.

"Babe, I got this," I replied, smiling.

"Umm-hmmm," was all he said.

As I sat there, I couldn't help but to remember the first day that I met Dontie . . . *I was walking in the mall, trying to find a pair of shoes for the next day. As I passed by store after store, I spotted the prettiest pair of Jimmy Choos that I just had to have. Never mind that they were kind of sluttish, I still had to have them. I was standing in the mirror, admiring the way they looked on my feet. Once I was positive that these were the ones that I wanted, I took them off, placed them in the box, and headed to pay for them at the register. I was almost to the counter when I heard a voice coming from behind me.*

"Excuse me, ma, but I was just passing by when I happened to spot you from the window. I know you don't know me, but I was wondering if I could get your name and maybe your number," he said from behind me.

Rolling my eyes, I tried not to sound so irritated. "I'm sorry, but right now is not the time. Besides, ya pickup game is weak, and I don't pick up men from out of the mall." I didn't bother to turn around.

"Well, I'm sorry that I wasted your time. Enjoy the rest of your day," he replied. I don't know why I did it, but something inside of me was telling me to turn around. When I did, I stood staring at the most handsome man that I'd ever seen. I don't know what his name is, but his mother should've named him Adonis.

"Umm . . . Wh-wh-what did you say your name was again?" I asked, stuttering. I'm pretty sure God had a hand in making this man, who stood at approximately six foot two with a chocolate complexion, hazel eyes, full lips, and his hair in a low-cut fade. I could've sworn my heart skipped a beat or two, just looking at him.

"I didn't, but my name is Dontie," he said, reaching his hand out to shake mine.

"My name is Sky," I replied, shaking his hand. "I'm sorry about what I said to you earlier. I'm tired, and I really don't pick up men in the mall."

"It's cool, I'm not tripping, ma. You good," he said; then he smiled, showing off a perfect set of teeth.

"Still, I want to apologize to you," I insisted.

"I told you that you're good, ma. You don't have to apologize about anything," he said. "But what you could do to make it all better is give me your phone number and agree to go out on a date with me."

I stood there giving him the once-over, and I can't lie . . . Dude was fine. But I'd seen his kind already. He looked to be a few years younger than me, and he was a thug. I could tell just by looking at him. I didn't normally date them, nor did I hold any type of conversation with them, but I couldn't help but to forget about all of that. This man was an exception to the rule, and I didn't mind breaking it. Something about him screamed trouble, but still, something told me to give him a try, so I went ahead and gave him my number just to see how things were going to go. He tried to pay for my shoes, but I wasn't that type of girl. I was independent, so I paid for my own things. Besides, I didn't want him to spend his last few dollars trying to stunt for me. He ended up calling me the next day, trying to get to know me. He wanted to take me out on a date, but work had me swamped, and I couldn't go. He just took my conversation for now and promised that he was going to wait.

We ended up going on a date that weekend, and every-thing was perfect. I found out that he owned two car washes, a few used car dealerships, and some magazine thingy, so I knew for sure that he had some good money. Immediately, everything I thought about him changed. Needless to say, that was over two years ago, and Dontie and I are still going strong. We have our ups and downs, but no relationship is perfect.

The jerking of the plane brought me out of my thoughts. I looked over at Dontie to find him sound asleep. I wish I could lay my ass down, but I had some work to do. Grabbing the computer, I went back to what I was doing. I wanted to make sure that I finished with this project before we landed so that my focus can be on this week-end. This weekend was so important to me, and I wanted to make sure that I wasn't consumed with work and stuff. This was the first time that my parents and Dontie were going to meet, and I only hoped that everything went the way that I planned it in my head. I wanted my man and my parents to get along great, because I planned on spending the rest of my life with this man.

Chapter Five

Brinay

By the time the waiter came back to the table with our food, I was ready to go. I was in no mood to be around anyone, and I'd completely lost my appetite. All I wanted to do was go home, get in my bed, and watch television. I didn't feel like being bothered with anyone at the moment, not even with Kourtney. I just wanted to be alone, by myself, so I could be lost in my own thoughts.

"So, where do you want to go?" she asked once we were back into the car.

"To be honest, all I really want to do is go home and sleep until tomorrow, when I have to leave," I replied, strapping my seat belt.

"Come on. Nay, I know you're feeling a certain type of way, but don't do that," she said, pulling out of the parking lot.

"Do what?" I asked her. I had no idea what she was talking about.

"Shut people out," she replied. "Every time something goes wrong with you, you try to shut people out. That's no good, and it's not happening today. Tomorrow, you're leaving me for a few days, and I want to spend some time with you."

"I'm not shutting you out, Kourtney. I just want to go home, get in my bed, and go to sleep. How is that shutting you out?" I told her. I don't know what was up with her, but I was not in the mood for no bullshit.

"Okay," was all she said as she made her way back to my apartment. I knew she was mad, because for the rest of the ride home, she didn't say anything. She only drove, which wasn't usual at all.

"Kourt," I said, trying to get her attention, but I was stopped by an excruciating pain in my lower abdomen. "*Arrgh*," I cried out, holding my stomach.

"What's wrong, Nay?" she asked me.

"My stomach hurts, that's all," I said to her.

"Well, do you want to go to the hospital or something?" she asked as she began to panic a bit.

"No, I'm fine," I said, trying to calm her down, even though *I* was the one in pain. I tried to sit up straight, but I couldn't.

"No, you're not fine, and I'm going to take you to the hospital right now," she said, sounding as if she was about to go crazy.

"No. I told you that I'm fine. All I really need to do is go home, take some medicine, and lie down for a bit," I tried to protest. "I'm going to be just fine."

"Are you sure?"

"Yes," I replied, still holding my stomach.

"Really, are you *sure,* Brinay?" she asked for reassurance.

"I'm positive. All I want to do is go home, go to bed, and get some sleep," I said to her.

"Okay, but I'm not leaving you until I know that you're all right," she replied.

"Okay, that's fine," I responded. I knew that if I would've tried to say no, she wouldn't have let me. She was very caring, and she didn't like when someone she really cared about was hurt and stuff.

When we pulled up to my apartment building, she found a spot in the front of the building, parked the car, and hurriedly ran to my side of the car. I already had the door open trying to get out, but it was hard to do, so she ended up helping me.

"Nay, are you 100 percent positive that you don't want me to take you to the hospital?" she asked as we made our way to my apartment. It was a good thing that I lived on the first floor, because I'm not sure if I could have made it any farther.

"I'm sure," I replied. *I hope she stops asking me that,* I thought to myself. I don't want to go to no damn hospital, and I don't know why she didn't see that yet.

"Okay," she replied. "Hold on while I open the door," she said as she leaned my body against the wall by the door. She pulled out the set of keys that I had given her and unlocked the door. "Come on," she replied, turning to help me. She helped me all the way into the bedroom, where I lay down on the bed.

"I'll be right back. I'm going to go and get your food and stuff from the car," she said once she made sure that I was okay. "Don't move."

I wanted to ask her how was I going to move, but I didn't. Instead, I lay back on the bed and waited for her to return. Not even five minutes later, she was walking back inside the room.

"Damn, what did you do? Run?" I asked her.

"Well, yes," she said, laughing. "I wanted to make sure that I got back to you in case you may have needed me or something, so I ran to the car."

"I'm okay, Kourt. It was probably my emotions and the fact that I haven't eaten anything yet," I replied, sitting up as best as I could.

"I know, which is why I have your food in the micro-wave, and you're going to tell me where the Tylenols are," she said, getting up from where she had taken a seat.

"They're in the cabinet above the microwave, and catch me a bottle of water while you're at it," I replied.

"Anything for you, baby mama," she said, cracking a smile.

"All right, baby daddy," I replied, winking at her. She damn near fell to the floor laughing. She was so silly sometimes.

"You too foolish. I'll be right back with your things. Then I'll help you take a bath and get ready for bed." She left the room to go and get the things from the kitchen.

"Here," Kourtney said, reentering the room. I sat up as she handed me the container that I had gotten from IHOP that was filled with the food that I couldn't eat earlier and the pills with the water. She then walked toward the other side of the bed with her own container and sat down.

"Where's the remote?" she asked.

"It's over there on the dresser," I replied as I began to stuff my face. I hadn't realized that I was that hungry until I was actually stuffing food into my mouth.

"I told you that you was hungry, lady. Over here trying to starve my god baby and stuff. Don't make me have to whoop ya behind next time."

I didn't say anything. All I did was look at her, roll my eyes, and continue to eat my food. I wasn't worrying about her one bit. I was more interested in this food than what she had to say anyway.

"I think I'm going to call my dad and cancel my trip," I said after I stuffed the last bit of food into my mouth. "I don't feel up to it anymore."

"Are you sure?" she asked, removing her focus from the TV to me.

"Yes. Like, even though I'm feeling better now, I don't think I'm in no shape to be driving on the road all them hours by myself, and I'm more than sure that I'd be feeling worse when I get there and see all those people who I can't stand hanging around," I said as I got out of bed and prepared to head to the kitchen . . . then a thought came to mind.

"Unless you want to come with me."

"Are you asking me to come with you?" she asked, getting off the bed and following behind me.

"Yes, I am," I replied, trashing the container. I then walked over to the refrigerator, grabbed another bottle of water, removed the top, and proceeded to down the water. "Damn, that was good."

"Well, in that case, I'd love to. I haven't been to Miami in a minute, and I'm in dire need of a vacation," she said as she placed the remainder of her food in the micro-wave as I handed her a bottle of water.

"Oh! I need to go home and pack."

"Yes, you do, because we're leaving in the morning," I said, taking a seat on a chair by the table.

"Well, get up off your behind and come on," she said, walking over to me and pulling me out of the chair.

"Can't you handle it yourself?" I asked sitting, back down on the chair. "I'm still feeling a little bad, and I want to lie down a bit."

"Yes, I can, and you can do that at my house," she said as she headed to my bedroom. She returned moments later with my shoes, purse, and keys.

"Okay, but I'm telling you right now that I'm not lifting a finger. So don't ask me," I said as I slipped my shoes on to my feet, grabbed my things out of her hand, and headed for the door with her following behind me.

"That's cool, Nay. I wasn't going to ask, and I didn't plan on letting you help me anyway," she said, following behind me. I'd just reached the door when my phone started to ring. Pulling it from my purse, I saw that it was a number that I didn't recognize, so I didn't answer it. I simply ignored the call and dropped it back in my purse.

"Who was that?" Kourtney asked.

"It was an unsaved number, and you know I don't answer calls from numbers that are not saved in my phone," I said, opening the door and almost falling down as I bumped into a hard chest. I looked up and saw one of the last two people I'd expect to see right now.

"What are you doing here, Chance? Is something wrong?" I asked, staring Dontie's cousin in the face.

"That's what I came to find out," he replied, looking at me with concern. "Dontie sent me over here to check on you, saying that he's been trying to call you, but he's getting your voice mail every time."

"Well, I'm fine, as you can see," I said, pushing past him. "Tell Dontie to kiss my ass and go to hell, because like I said to him before this, I'm through with his ass, so he don't need to be worried about me and what's going on over here."

I left his ass standing right where he was. I liked him, but the mere thought of Dontie's ass worrying about me made my skin crawl. He wasn't worrying about me before when I kept calling and texting his ass for two weeks straight, and he ain't replied to any of my attempts to contact him, so I don't know why he sent his cousin over here to check on me, because I wasn't flattered one bit. I didn't need him to worry about me anymore, because I was through with him.

"Ma, please. You know I fucks with you the long way, and I love you like my actual family. So I wasn't just doing this for him. I came to check on you for myself also. I don't care what's going on with you and Dontie. Just know that I'll be here for you whenever you need me. I just needed to make sure that you was fine, because when he called, he sounded worried," he said, stopping me.

"Look, Chance, I appreciate that, I do, and I'll always look at you as my family too, but I'm not fucking with Dontie's ass no more. So you don't have to come check on me when he asks you to," I told him. I really did like Chance like a brother, but I wasn't messing with Dontie no more, and I needed him to know that.

"Well, I did my part. Just call me if you need me, ma," he said, then left.

"Oh no. Don't let Dontie bring your mood to that level again," Kourtney said, walking over to me and grabbing my arm. "Come on, let's go to my house so I can pack, so we won't be late tomorrow when it's time for us to leave."

"Yeah, you're right. Let's go, because if I don't make it, I know my father will be very disappointed," I said as we walked out of the building. I really couldn't wait for all of this to be over and done with so I could just get my life back in order and get ready for motherhood. This stuff was already stressful, but I couldn't let anything else mess with my emotions, and I knew firsthand something was going to happen once I got to Miami. I only hoped that it didn't proved to be too much on me and the baby.

Chapter Six

Dontie

I was more than happy when our plane arrived at Miami International. I didn't know how much I'd actually missed being home until I walked out of the airport and into the amazing Miami air. Like always, the sun was shining, the breeze was blowing, and it wasn't too hot, which was perfect. I was glad to experience the beautiful weather.

"Come on, Dontie, the car is waiting on us over there," Sky said, interrupting my thoughts.

"Next time we go on a trip, please try not to bring your whole damn closet," I told her. She already had an ass load of things, not to mention the things she bought while we were down there. It was just too much, and I was barely able to hold everything.

"Yeah, whatever. Just come on so we can get home, because I'm tired and sticky. All I want to do is take a bath and lie down for a minute," she said, placing her shades on her face and walking toward the car. She didn't offer to help with not one of the bags that I had in my hands. I don't know why she always felt as if she was too much for the next person, because really and truly, she wasn't.

"Yeah, bitch, the minute I get home, I'm ghost," I said under my breath as I followed behind her. Once we made it to the car, like always, she got in without trying to help me, and I was left to help the driver with the bags. Once everything was inside of the trunk, I hopped in the car. I was about to give her ass a piece of my mind when my phone began to ring. Looking at the phone, I noticed that it was my cousin Chance calling me. Since I knew what he was calling me about and I was in the car with Sky, I let the call roll to voice mail. *I'll call him back when I make it to the house*, I thought as I slipped my phone into my pocket.

I lay my head back and thought about Brinay. *I've been torn up over the fact that she called herself ending things with me. I know I've been MIA for a while, but I didn't think she'd be in her feelings and try to break things off. On top of all that, she hasn't been answering the phone, which is why I sent Chance over there to check on her. I wasn't sure if she was okay or if something had happened to her. I needed to know, but I couldn't answer the phone and risk the chance of Sky finding out about her. I mean, I wanted Sky, but she wasn't Brinay. Had I met Brinay first, Sky wouldn't be in the picture. The only reason I'm still with her is because I don't want to hurt her.*

"Dontie," Sky said, calling out to me. I was so deep in my thoughts that I had barely heard her. If it wasn't for the fact that she started waving her fingers back and forth in front of my face, I don't think I would've.

"What's up, ma?" I replied as she snapped me back to reality. I looked out of the window and noticed that we were almost to our house. Since we didn't live too far from the airport, it took us no time at all to make it home.

"I was telling you that I have to run to the office and get a few things once we get home," she said.

"Sky, we just got back from our vacation. Whatever it is that needs to be done at the office can wait until Monday morning, when you're due to go back to work," I told her.

She was beginning to get on my last fucking nerve with all this working shit. I mean, she just took a two-week vacation from work, so why in the hell was she trying to go back so fast?

"I know, baby, but I need to get all of this done before tomorrow. I promise that after I'm done with this, I won't be doing anything else until Monday," she said just as the car pulled up to the house. She didn't even wait for the car to come to a complete stop before she got out and practically ran inside the house. Lately, I don't know what's been up with her, but all she does is work, work, and work. I'm starting to believe that something else is going on at that office where she works. I just don't know what it is yet, but I'm going to find out.

After getting all the bags from out of the car, I left them sitting in the middle of the living-room floor. I then made my way upstairs to our bedroom. Since I could hear the water running in the bathroom, I knew that she was already in the shower. I walked over to the dresser, removed a pair of boxers and a wife beater, and headed to take a shower in the bathroom down the hall. Hopefully, when I get out of the shower, she'd already be gone, because I wanted to chew in her ass so bad but decided against it. Besides, I had to go and see what was up with Brinay, so fuck whatever it was that she was about to do.

I didn't take that long in the shower. I was basically in and out in a heartbeat. When I was done, I dried off, threw my clothes on, and went to the bedroom. Like I had hoped, she was already gone once I entered the room, so it took me no time to throw some clothes on and head out the door. Before I left, I made sure to lock the door. I hopped in my smoked-gray Mercedes-Benz S-Class and headed straight for the highway. I didn't have much time, and even though I wanted to go make my rounds around the block, I didn't since I promised Sky that I was going to be back in time for her little "event" at her parents' house. Instead, I decided to phone my dude, Jessie.

"'Sup with ya, boss man," he said, answering the phone.

"Ain't shit. How's everything going on around the way?" I asked him.

"Everything's fine. There wasn't one problem while you was gone," he replied. "You back in the States yet?"

"Well, that's good, and yeah, I just got back not too long ago," I said just as my phone began to beep. Pulling the phone from my ear, I noticed that it was Chance calling me back.

"Cool, so that means we're going to see you on the block today?" he asked.

"Nah, I got some other business to take care of. I won't make rounds until Sunday," I said to him. "But tell everyone that I'm back, and if you need me, you can call me."

"All right, man. I'll let them know."

"Well, I got to take this call. Just call me if someone needs me," I said and hung up the phone. I immediately dialed Chance's number back.

"What's up, li'l nigga," I said once he picked up the phone.

"Ain't shit, man. What's up with you? How's everything? You still on vacation?"

"Nah, I just got back home. You did what I asked you to do for me?" I asked, referring to Brinay.

"Umm . . . Yeah, I went," he said.

"Well, what happened? Is she okay? Is something wrong? Did she say why she wasn't answering the phone?" I asked, spitting out one question after the next. I needed to know why she wasn't answering my calls and texts.

"To be honest, man, she said she was okay and to tell you that she wasn't fucking with you no more," he replied. "She also told me to tell you to leave her the fuck alone."

I didn't say anything. I couldn't. I just sat there taking in everything that he had just said to me. I don't know what was going on or what I did to her to make her feel that way, but I needed to fix whatever it was. I wasn't trying to lose her, and I damn sure wasn't about to let her find another nigga to deal with. Yeah, I know I sound cheeky and whatnot, but I don't give a fuck. I wanted Brinay in my life, and I wasn't about to let her go that easily.

"All right, man," I said after a minute.

"What are you going to do?" he asked. "I know you, and you like her, so I know you're not about to let her go that easy."

"Man, I don't know. I'm on my way coming up there right now. I just hope that she lets me in so we can sit down and talk about whatever problem it is that we have, because I'm not trying to lose her, nor will I let her go," I said as serious as a heart attack. "All right, man. Holla at me when you touch down. I have to go."

"See you when you get here," he replied.

"All right, man. I'll see you in a few hours," I said, hanging up the phone.

I didn't know how to feel about what Chance just told me. I mean, I knew she sent me a text message and all, but I thought that she was just going through something. Now that she said it to him and I'm hearing it from someone else, I know that it wasn't just a phase that she was going through. She's really through with me, and I don't know why, but I planned on finding out as soon as I made it there. I knew one thing for sure . . . I wasn't coming back to Florida without squashing whatever beef we had between us and getting my boo back.

My mind was so clouded with thoughts of Brinay that the seven-and-a-half hours it took me to get to South

Carolina felt way less than that. I had powered my phone off and rode the whole way in silence. I wanted to be able to focus, and my mind needed to be clear when I arrived there. I didn't need any distractions, and I know that if I would've kept my phone on, then Sky would've ended up calling and wondering where I was. Like I said before, I don't know what's going on with her, but something most definitely ain't right. Right now, I don't have the time to find out, though. I needed to get my shit right here in SC first; then I'd worry about what's going on down in Miami.

When I pulled up to Brinay's apartment building, I spotted her car in her designated parking spot, so I know that meant she was there. I hurried to find a spot, got out of the car, and practically ran my ass all the way inside to her door. When I made it to the door, I began banging like I was the fucking police. I wasn't about to leave until she answered the door. I ain't give a fuck that she had neighbors, I needed to see her, and I wasn't going to stop until I did. Before I knew it, about twenty minutes had passed, and I was still there knocking on the door, waiting for someone to answer it.

"Excuse me, sir?" I heard a voice say from behind me. When I turned around, I was face-to-face with Ms. Cannon, the lady from down the hall. "Oh, Dontie, it's you."

"Hey, Ms. Cannon. Yes, it's me. Have you seen Nay today?" I asked her. I knew her from the several times before when I'd been over to see Brinay. I'd helped her with her groceries and things around her apartment. She was also one of those nosy neighbors that everyone had, so I know that she'd tell me what was up and why Brinay wasn't answering the door.

"Son, Nay left this morning," she replied.

"Huh?" I asked, not sure if I heard her right. I know she didn't just say that Brinay left this morning.

"She and her friend Kourtney left this morning. I think they were going on a trip," she repeated herself.

"Well, did they say where they were going?" I asked, hopeful. I needed to see her that bad.

"No, I'm afraid not," she said, looking sympathetic. Now I knew why she wasn't answering the door. She wasn't there.

"Okay, thank you," I replied, feeling like a fool. "I have to go. I'll see you later." With that being said, I took one last look at her door and left. When I got back in the car, I pulled my phone out and dialed her number, but like all the other times before, it went straight to voice mail.

"Fuck," I yelled, banging my hand against the steering wheel. I sat there not knowing what to do. I'd come all the way from Miami to see her, only for her not to be here. I looked at the clock and noticed that it was getting late. I started up the car and headed over to my auntie's house. Hopefully, Chance would be there when I get there, because he was the only one who'd be able to get the answers that I needed.

Chapter Seven

Brinay

We've been on the road since nine o'clock this morning, and I was all too happy when we made it to Miami. It was almost five o'clock that evening, but I was just happy not to be cooped up in a car no more. We ended up renting a room at a hotel out in Miami, because I wasn't trying to be staying at my father's house. Shoot, I barely wanted to be here for Sky's little "announcement," let alone be staying under one roof with those people. I knew for a fact that something was bound to happen, especially since my father's wife, Veronica, couldn't stand my guts, and the feeling was mutual. I wasn't in no rush to see her or my father's face. I still don't know why in the hell they wanted me to be there, because as far as Sky and I were concerned, we weren't sisters at all. I mean, we had the same blood flowing through our veins, but that was about it.

You see, my sister was one of those uppity, sadity-ass chicks. Yeah, she was basically born with a silver spoon in her mouth, but that still didn't give her any right to think that she was better than me, or the next person, for that matter. That's why I never got along with her . . . well, for that reason and every time that I'd go over there, she and her mother would use me and abuse me. They'd do things like call me all kinds of names, pull my hair, make me take cold baths, and make me eat their scraps. Hell, half of the time, I'd go without eating. That went on for about a year, until I finally got the nerve to tell my father, but that didn't go too well, because he accused me of lying and whooped me. He also threatened me and told me that if I told my mother, I'd be sorry. Needless to say, I didn't tell, because I was too scared to.

Things changed one weekend when I went home after visiting my father's house. I had a couple of bruises on my back, and I was extremely hungry. My mother asked me what had happened, but I didn't tell her for fear that my father was going to do something to me. It wasn't until I went to school and one of my teachers saw the bruises and threatened to call CPS that I finally decided to tell the truth. My mother wasn't happy with me at all, and I'm more than sure that day my father wished that he never made me, because my mother went in on all of them. She whooped Veronica's ass so bad that she had to go to a hospital.

My mother ended up beating *me* after that. She said that I should've told her sooner. Even though I told her that my father had threatened me, she said that I should've still said something to her. Needless to say, that was the day that I disowned my father. It wasn't until after my mother died that I decided to let him back into my life. I was grown now, and no one could bring any harm to me without me harming them back, so like I said, I wasn't too thrilled about seeing them. The only person who I planned to see today was my grandma, and that was going to be after I took myself a little catnap.

When we pulled up to the Ramada Inn Hotel, it was already a quarter to five. There were more people at the hotel than I expected, so it was hard for us to find a parking space. We ended up having to park at the back of the hotel. I can't lie, that was a far little walk from there to the front of the hotel, but I wasn't complaining. We hopped out of the car, grabbed our bags, and headed for the hotel lobby.

Luckily, it took us no longer than ten minutes to check in and receive our keys. We then headed to our room, where I ran straight to the bathroom. I made it there just in time to puke up the Big Mac meal that I'd gotten from McDonald's a few hours ago.

"I really think you should go to the hospital or at least see a doctor," Kourt said, entering the bathroom.

"I don't need no doctor, Kourtney. I'm fine," I said as I rinsed my mouth out.

"You're not fine, Nay. You've been in pain since yesterday, and it doesn't look like it's getting any better," she said, beginning to aggravate the hell out of me.

"I told you that I was fine. I need to lie down, that's it," I said, walking out of the room. I began to strip out of my clothes, leaving on just my bra and panties. Pulling back the cover, I then hopped in the bed. "Can you turn the air on?"

"Yes, sure," she said as she went to turn the thermostat down. Instantly, the air came on and began to cool the room down. "Better?" she asked.

"Yes, thank you," I replied yawning. I could already feel myself falling asleep.

"Well, I'm about to go sightseeing while you take a nap. I'll see you later. Call me if you need me," she said, grabbing her purse and heading for the door.

"Okay," I replied, and with that, she left.

Just as I began to fall asleep, my phone started to ring. Frustrated and tired, I turned over, letting the call roll over to voice mail. A few minutes later, it started ringing again, but just like the first time, I ignored it, with hopes that whoever it was would get the hint and stop calling. Unfortunately, they didn't get the hint, because they called again. Angrily, I got up from the bed and went to retrieve my purse from off the desk that was sitting across from the bed. I fished my phone out and placed my purse back on the table. Since it had stopped ringing, I didn't even bother to see who it was calling. I placed it on the nightstand that stood next to the bed and hopped back in. No sooner had I'd placed my head on the pillow, my phone started ringing *again*.

"Shit," I said, reaching for the phone.

"Hello!" I yelled, answering the phone with an attitude. I didn't bother to check to see who it was, because whoever it was, they were about to get the business. "This better be a matter of life and death since ya calling me like this."

"So this is what I got to do to get you to answer the phone?" I heard a voice say, making me pause. I knew that voice all too well. *But how the hell is he calling me, when I know I blocked his number*, I thought to myself. I pulled the phone from my ear, and that's when I saw that he was calling me from Chance's phone. "Where are you?"

"What do you want, Dontie?" I asked, aggravated. I did not feel like talking to him right now, and I was in no mood to let him upset me. "I'm not in the mood for nothing right now, so you're going to have to make this quick."

"So that's how you coming? That's what we on now?" he asked, not answering my question.

I sighed, because I wasn't trying to go there with Dontie. He always had a way of getting to me, and my ass was always stupid enough to let him. Had I known that it was him calling my phone, I wouldn't have answered it, because I knew what this man could do to me.

"Tell me where you at," he asked again.

"I don't know what you're talking about, boo," I said this time, ignoring his question and playing stupid.

"Brinay, for real, ma, don't play stupid with me right now. I've been calling you for days, and your phone goes straight to voice mail," he responded. I knew he was mad, but I really didn't give a damn.

"It don't take a rocket scientist to figure out what's going on," he continued. I wished his ass was in front of me right now so that I could slap the shit out of him.

"Yeah yeah yeah, and I've been calling your ass for weeks, and you wasn't answering my phone calls—nor was you answering my text messages. So please explain to me why the fuck you bugging about me not answering you?" I said, getting heated. I don't know why he was on my case when he'd been ignoring me for weeks. I know damn well he saw the message that I had sent to him, so again, I was sitting over here wondering why he was calling me.

"Ma, look! I was out of the country handling some business. I just got back today. That's why I couldn't answer the phone," he had the nerve to say. I rolled my eyes in my head, because I knew damn well he wasn't out of town on business. He must have forgotten that I knew what he did for a living.

"I want to see you, baby. Tell me where you at," he pleaded.

"You must really think that I'm stupid, Tae," I told him, "You don't need to be worrying about where I'm at. You wasn't worrying about me when you kept ignoring me."

"No, I don't think that you're stupid, but I'm telling you the truth. Nay, stop all that playing and tell me where you at."

"Look, Dontie, I'm not about to go back and forth with you. You can't reach me, so that should tell you something. Stop calling my phone, because I'm not trying to be bothered with your ass no more. Go back to whatever bitch you took on a vacation with you, because I know for a fact that you wasn't out there handling no 'business'!" I yelled.

"Ma, just tell me where you're at so I can come and see you."

"Dontie, what part of *I'm not trying to be bothered with you* don't you understand? I'm good on you. I know you got a woman, and I'm not trying to go down that road. I ain't trying to be no nigga's side bitch, bottom bitch, or other bitch. So you can go back to your woman and leave me alone, because we're done, and I mean that," I said and hung up.

I then powered my phone off, because I knew that he was going to call me back, and I wasn't in the mood for that. All I wanted to do is take a nap, but I couldn't even do that, so instead of taking a nap like I had planned, I got up and went to take a bath. Maybe that would relieve some of the tension and stress from my body.

I got my body wash, my iPod, my speaker, and my vanilla-scented candles and headed for the bathroom. When I got in there, I placed everything on the sink and went to start my bath, making sure that the water was at a nice temperature. I then spread the candles around and lit them. Next, I grabbed my iPod, chose my slow mix playlist, and hooked it to the speaker. I then removed my bra and panties and slid down in the tub. I swear, the minute I sat down in the tub, I felt some tension leaving.

As I sat there, listening to Pandora, I couldn't help but to think about Dontie and the conversation that we had earlier. I knew for sure that he had a woman. Hell, he didn't even deny it when I said it. Well, I know that I hung up on him, but still, he could've interrupted me and said that it wasn't true, but he didn't. I shook my head and chuckled. I'm in love with someone else's man, and I'm having his baby. *Ain't that some shit,* I thought.

I don't know why I was so surprised. I'd only seen him on weekends since we started dating. I never thought much of it, because I was busy with school and whatnot, and he had to work, but the signs were there, and they've been there. I just turned a blind eye to them. Don't get me wrong, though, I'm far from being one of those bird, bum project chicks. I never needed a man for anything. Seeing Kourtney with her little boyfriends made me want one, so when Tae came along, it was perfect timing. For the most part, I think I was just lonely. My mother was dead, my brother was in jail, and my father was in a whole 'nother state, not that I'd mess with him like that. I only had Kourtney, and at times, she'd be with her man, and I'd be left alone on weekends with nothing to do.

That's why I didn't think anything of Tae only being around mostly on the weekends . . . until about a couple of months ago, when I caught him on the phone. He was whispering, which was something that he never did when he was around me. He never did that no matter what, even when he was conducting his illegal business. I'd be right there, and he would go on and act like it was noth-ing, so when I rolled up on him and he was whispering, I *knew* it had to be some chick that he was talking to.

I wanted to chew him out, but I didn't. I left it at that, because I knew that time would tell. Whatever it was that was going on, I'd soon find out. I just didn't think that I'd end up pregnant and about to have this man's baby. Before I knew it, my eyelids were getting heavy, and I fell asleep right in the tub.

An hour later, I was awakened by someone knocking on the bathroom door. I jumped up, splashing water all over the floor. I was so disorientated that I'd forgotten about where I was.

"You okay in there?" I heard Kourtney ask. I took a look around and remembered where I was.

"Yes, I'll be out in a minute," I said, sitting up. I pulled the plug and started to let the water drain out. I stood up, cut on the shower, grabbed a washcloth, and began to scrub myself. When I was done, I stood under the running water and rinsed my body off. I then lathered the washcloth with more body wash and repeated the process. When I was done, I turned the water off and got out. I grabbed a towel from the counter and began to dry off. When I was done, I threw on a shirt and some shorts, blew the candles out, grabbed my iPod and speaker, and headed into the bedroom. When I walked in the room, Kourtney was sitting on the bed waiting on me.

"How are you feeling?" she asked, taking off her shoes.

"I feel great. How was the sightseeing?" I asked, placing the iPod and speaker on the nightstand.

"It was great. I love the weather out here. We should hit up a beach before we leave this weekend," she said, heading over to where her suitcase was. She grabbed it and placed it on the bed, opening it.

"We could do that," I replied, taking a seat on the bed. "What time is it?"

"It's almost eight o'clock," she replied as she gathered her clothes. I guess she was about to go take a shower. "You still want to go and see your grandmother?"

"Nah, it's kind of late. I'll just wait to see her tomorrow," I said, reaching for the remote and turning the TV on.

"Okay."

"Guess who called me today," I said as I flipped through the channels, trying to find something to put on. I settled on reruns of *Martin,* which used to be my favorite show when I was a kid.

"Who?" she asked, looking at me.

"Dontie."

"What? I thought you put him on the block list. How was he able to call you?" she asked, taking a seat on the bed.

"I did. He called me off of Chance's phone. I guess he's in South Carolina," I replied.

"Well, what did he want?"

"He came at me on some bullshit, asking me why I wasn't answering the phone for him and wanting to know where I was, talking 'bout he was coming see me."

"What did you tell him?"

"I told his ass that I wasn't trying to be bothered with him, and for him to stop calling me because we was done," I said, shrugging my shoulders.

"Girl, you lying," she said.

"No, I'm not. I meant what I said. I'm done with Tae. He wasn't answering the phone for me them weeks when I was calling him, so I gave him his walking papers," I said to her.

"Well, what are you going to do about the baby? Are you going to tell him?" she asked.

"Nah, I don't plan on tellin' his ass shit. I'm good on Tae. I'm going to raise my child by myself without him," I said, serious as a heart attack. I'd made up my mind. When he said that bullshit about him being out of the country on business, I knew for a fact that that wasn't the case, and I wasn't about to play myself or my child for a man who already had a woman. Me and my child will be good, and I know that. Nigga had the nerve to say something about him being out of the country, talking 'bout that's why he wasn't answering the phone. I ain't stupid. I know his ass was out of the country with some chick, and I'm not about to even play them games with him.

"Well, that's on you, but I still think that you should have at least told him about the baby," she had the nerve to say.

"You ain't just heard what I said? I'm good, and my baby will be good. We don't need Tae's ass, and I'm going to show him that," I said, side eyeing her.

"Okay then," she said, getting up from the bed and walking into the bathroom.

A few minutes later, I heard the water running. I got up from the bed and went to look out of the window. As I stood there, I couldn't help but to think about my mother and what she'd want me to do. Nine times out of ten, she'd say the same thing Kourtney was saying. She'd want me to tell Dontie about the baby. She wouldn't be worrying about if he had a woman or not.

"Ma, I miss you so much. I wish you was here with me now. Continue to watch over me and my baby. I love you," I said, looking into the sky. I then looked out at all of the people walking and riding around the city. Miami was my hometown before I moved to South Carolina, and to be honest, I was missing home. Many nights I found myself thinking about moving back, but then I thought about my mother dying and thought, why come back? There was nothing good here for me. Yes, I had boo-coo memories of my mother here, but she wasn't here anymore. Just as much as I was missing here, I wanted to stay far away from here, not to mention that my father and his family were here, and Lord knows how much I *didn't* want to be around them. The only thing that I actually wanted to be here for was my brother. He had a little over a year left, and I wanted to be here when he got out. Because of him, I was thinking really hard about coming back. I never told anyone, but I still had the house that my mother used to stay in, so it wouldn't be like I didn't have a place to stay if I did decide to come back. Hopefully, I'd decide before I had my baby.

"What's wrong?" Kourtney asked, scaring the shit out of me.

"Nothing, but you just scared the shit out of me," I said, grabbing my chest and trying to steady my racing heart. I didn't even hear when she cut the water off.

"I'm sorry," she replied.

"That's cool. I was just thinking," I said, walking back over to the bed.

"About?" she asked, placing her things back in the suitcase. Once she was done, she placed the suitcase on the side of the bed and climbed in.

"My mother and how much I miss her," I said sadly.

"It's going to be all right. I know you miss her, but she's up in heaven right now looking down on you," she replied, getting up and walking over to me.

"I know, but I miss her so much, and now that I'm having a baby, all I do is think about her and how she's going to miss out on seeing her first grandchild," I said breaking down. I don't know where that shit came from, but all of a sudden I became so emotional.

"It's going to be OK, Nay," Kourtney said, rubbing me and trying to soothe me.

"I know, but I miss her so much. I wish she was here with me right now," I said, crying into her chest.

"She *is* right here with you. You already know what you have to do, Nay."

"I know," I said as I attempted to dry my eyes. She was right. I knew what I had to do. I was just being stubborn and ignoring it.

"You straight?" she asked once I had pulled back.

"Yes," I replied as I began to calm down. "Thanks."

"You don't have to thank me all the time, Nay. You're my best friend. It's my job to be here for you, and I will," she said.

"I know, but I'm so damn emotional nowadays," I replied, laughing.

"That's them hormones doing that to ya," she said, joining in with a few chuckles of her own.

"Got to be, because I was never this vulnerable. That's your job. I think you're rubbing off on me. Move back," I said, playfully pushing her.

"Oh, that's cold," she replied. "But for real, you good?"

"Yes, I'm fine. Now let's go to bed, 'cause only the Lord knows how much I'm going to need all of my energy to deal with these people tomorrow," I said, making my way back over to the bed. I pulled back the cover and got in.

"I'll say a prayer just for you," she joked before she got in the other bed.

"I'm going to need it, girl," I said. "Good night. See you in the morning."

"Good night, baby mama. I'll see you in the morning too," she replied, turning off the lamp since it was closer to her.

I silently lay there, thinking to myself. I'd been through too much, and I knew I had to tell Dontie about the baby whether or not I wanted to. I just hoped he was cool with us being coparents, because I was not trying to go there with him no more. I'd call him tomorrow when I got up. Hopefully, he wouldn't be too mad not to answer me. *Lord be with me,* I thought, saying a silent prayer to myself, 'cause he already knew the situation I was in and how it was going to turn out. I then turned over and found a comfortable position before drifting off to sleep.

Chapter Eight

Sky

I couldn't for the life of me understand why Randell would send me a document to work on, knowing that I was on vacation with my man. I know he was probably feeling some type of way, but I didn't care. I told him that I couldn't see him anymore before Dontie, and, of course, I even left to go on a trip with him, and now that Dontie done asked me to be his wife and we're actually married, I wanted—no, I *needed*—him to stay as far away from me as possible. I know he was my boss and all, but I wasn't trying to lose my man over no old guy who's already married.

I lied and told Dontie that I had to go to the office, but truth be told, I didn't. Well, I did stop in at the office, but that was only for a little while. I was now on my way to meet Randell at the Ramada Inn Hotel. I don't know why he wants me to come there when clearly I told his old ass that we were over. I've been having an affair with this man since forever and a day, including the whole time that I've been dating Dontie, and I was ready for all of that to be over. I was too young, beautiful, and fly to be some old man's *other* woman. It was time for him to be fully involved with his wife or find him another young chick to mess with. Either way, I was taking myself out of the equation. Yes, the man was the CEO of the company, and, yes, he had benefits that were hell a worth it, but I couldn't continue the affair, nor could I keep up with this game of charades anymore. That wasn't me, and I wasn't trying to let him label and degrade me like that. Our relationship, that's *if* you can call it a relationship, has run its course. I was meant to be somebody's wife, and that somebody is Dontie.

When I pulled up to the hotel, I parked my car all the way in the back of the hotel. I was more than sure that I wouldn't bump into anyone that I knew, but it was better to be safe than to be sorry. I pulled down my visor and proceeded to check my makeup, adding a little more lip gloss to my already glossy lips. When I was convinced that everything was all right, I grabbed the keys out of the ignition and got out. I then pulled out my phone and dialed his number, all the while making my way to the front of the hotel.

"What room are you in?" I asked once he answered the phone.

"I'm in room 230. It's on the second floor. I left a key for you at the front desk, so it shouldn't be hard for you to get up here," he replied.

"Okay," I said and hung up just as I made it to the front door. Walking into the hotel, I threw my shades on my face as I made my way to the checkout desk.

"Hi, my name is Sky. Randell left a key at the front desk for me. It's room 230," I said to the little girl standing there.

"Ummm, yes, can you hold on for a minute, please?" she said as she searched for something. A few minutes later she found it. "Yes, here you go, ma'am. I'm sorry about the delay."

"That's okay. Thank you," I said, placing my shades back on my face. She's lucky that I wasn't in a rush to see this old-ass man, because I had a good mind to curse her little slow ass out for playing with me. With the key card in my hand, I made my way to the elevators. Just as I made it there, one was opening. I hurried on, pressed the second floor, and waited for the doors to close. A few seconds later, I was riding the elevator to the second floor as my heart began to race.

"Lord Jesus, please help me," I said out loud. I don't know why I was so nervous when I'd been fucking with Randell for some time. I don't know if it was because I was about to finally say good-bye to him for good or something else, but I had this weird feeling in the pit of my stomach that made me want to turn around right at that minute. Just as that thought came to my mind, the elevator door opened, and I spotted Randell waiting for me by the room door.

I was disgusted just by the sight of his old ass. I don't know why his old ass doesn't stalk his wife the way he be stalking me. I was not even into his ass like that. Truth be told, I never was. I only wanted and *needed* him to get in a higher position at my job, and now that I've gotten that, I don't see any use for his ass no more. True, he does lavish me with some nice-ass gifts—the man went as far as to buy me a car, but that shit was material things, and like I said, he was married. I had a man now, a husband, who happened to have my heart. What we had is over and done with, and I needed him to get with the program before this ends badly for both of us—mainly him, though.

"What's up, beautiful?" he said, handing me a single rose. I looked at him disgusted with not only him, but myself. He actually thought that the shit he was pulling was cool, but it was far from it. I didn't even bother to speak or take the rose. I pushed past him and went straight into the room. When I got inside the room, there were candles lit all over the place, which only disgusted me some more. He was really going out of his way, but that doesn't surprise me, because this was just how

Randell was, and Randell was always going to be Randell. I actually would've thought this was nice had it been with my husband and not him, but it wasn't, and I didn't. This man really thought he was going to get some ass, but he had another thought coming. I noticed that there was a chair over by the window, so I walked over and happily sat down, placing my purse at my feet.

"What's going on with you? Why you acting crazy?" he asked, closing the door behind him. Again, I didn't bother to answer his ass. I crossed my legs and placed my hands in my lap. "What did I do to deserve the silent treatment, Skylar?"

"Randell, you can cut all that out. You know just what you're doing," I said, not even buying into his game.

"Honestly, I don't know. Maybe you should tell me what it was that I did wrong," he said, grabbing the other chair in the room. He picked it up and set it next to the one that I was in.

"I told you that we can't do this anymore, so I don't know why you insisted on me even coming over here," I said, rolling my eyes. "You already know that."

"Skylar, baby, you know what I told you when you first said that," he said, rubbing his hand up and down my left thigh. "I'm not letting you go, so you might as well get that thought out of your pretty little head."

"I don't care what you said. What I said I meant, so I think you should stop calling me and find you another employee to screw," I said, shaking my leg so that his hand would fall. I then uncrossed my legs and crossed them back, putting the other leg over the one he was just rubbing on. "In fact, why don't you call your wife? You *do* remember her, *don't* you?"

"I don't want any other employee, nor do I want to call my wife. I want you, and you're going to give me what I want, Skylar, so I don't know why you insist on playing these childish games," he said, raising his voice a bit. I knew what he was doing. He wanted to get a rise out of me, but I ain't have time for him and this shit.

"Look, I don't have time to be playing with you. I'm more than sure that your wife is looking for you, as my husband should be looking for me, so it's time for me to go and for you to stop calling me," I said, grabbing my purse and standing up.

"Don't worry about my wife, but did you just say your *husband?*" he asked, putting his hand out to stop me.

"Yes, I did. My husband," I said, holding up my hand that held my wedding ring. I made sure to wiggle my finger for emphasis.

"To that thug you call a boyfriend?" he asked in disbelief.

"His name is Dontie, and he's not a thug," I replied, defending my husband.

"Oh, he's a thug, all right. You're just too blind to see it. Or maybe you just don't *want* to see it. Whatever the case is, the man is a straight thug," he said with a light chuckle.

"Look, if that's all, I have to get going before my husband starts to worry or get suspicious. I can't be out all hours of the night, and it is almost past midnight. We did just get back from vacation. You *do* know that, right?"

"Yes, I know that, but I'm not worrying about what you were doing. All I'm concerned about right now is you doing me."

I turned to see if this man was joking, but the look on his face told me otherwise.

"Look, I tried to be nice with your ass, but it's quite obvious that you like when I bring that bitch up out of me, so let me tell you one thing."

"Oh, *do* tell," he said as his eyes began to light up. I was starting to believe that this old nigga got off on this shit or something like that.

"I said that we was over, and I meant that shit. You're a married man, and I'm a married woman now. What happened between us before can never happen again. That shit is in the fucking past, and it needs to stay there. You don't own me. I own myself, and when I say that something is over, you better believe that it is," I said, turning my back and heading to the door. My hand was on the knob, and I was getting ready to open the door when he finally decided to speak.

"You're wrong, you know. I *do* own you, whether or not you like it," he said from behind me. When he said that, I turned back around, marched over to him, and slapped the shit out of him.

"You *don't* own not a muthafucking thing over here. I don't know where you got that idea from, but you can get that shit out of your muthafucking head right-fucking-now. You don't own me. I'm not the type of chick who'll let a nigga run her. That ain't me," I said flipping out on him. The nigga didn't say anything. All he did was smile. He liked when I got ghetto with his ass. The nerve of this old-ass nigga to fucking think he could own me is crazy!

"Oh, but see, that's where you're wrong. Remember your job and the position that you're now in. *I* did that. That luxury car that you're now driving around, *I* bought that. That house that you live in, *I* paid for that, and just how I gave you all of that, I can take that away from you," he replied, shocking me a bit. I looked at this nigga to see if he was serious—and he was. I knew this day was going to come. I just didn't think he was actually going to hold that shit over my head.

"Nigga, please, all of that don't mean a damn thing to me. You must got me confused with the next bitch. My father *bleeds* money, and anything I want and ask for, I can have with one phone call, so you threatening to take all of that away don't scare me one bit. Fuck with me and I will make your life a living hell. Just try me," I said, calling his bluff. I wasn't going to call my father for a thing. I just needed him to think that I was going to.

"Ha ha ha ha ha!" He sat there laughing. I don't know why he was laughing, because I didn't see a damn thing funny that I said.

"You and I both know that you're clearly not 'bout that life, not like you think you are," he said, adding air quotes.

"Try me and see," I said, matching his tone. He got up from his seat and walked over to the table where he had champagne sitting in a bucket of ice. He removed the bottle, grabbed the two champagne flutes, and poured the amber liquid into each. He then placed the bottle back in the bucket and walked over to where I was.

"Little girl, your threats don't scare me, and I'm more than sure that your bark is way louder than your bite. Now, I would advise you to take this and have yourself a nice seat on that bed," he said, handing me a glass of champagne. I looked at the glass and hesitated before taking it and making my way to the bed. I watched as he took off his jacket, loosened his tie, and made his way into the bathroom.

When he was gone, I placed my purse and the glass on the nightstand and proceeded to take off my shoes. I then went into my purse and pulled out a medicine bottle. I dropped two tablets into my hand before putting the bottle back into my purse. When I was done, I threw the two pills in my mouth, grabbed the glass, and downed the champagne. I then placed the glass on the table as I waited for the pills to take effect.

Once I started to feel the pills, I began to get undressed. When I was down to nothing but my birthday suit, I lay on the bed, spread my legs wide, and began playing with myself. I knew that I needed to get myself ready for this quick episode, and I for damn sure couldn't count on

Randell to get me aroused. The only thing he was good for was giving head, and even that itself wasn't A-1.

My mind immediately went to the last time Dontie and I had sex, before we boarded the flight to come home. I stuck a finger in my wet honeypot and moved my hand in a circular motion, as I thought about how good it was. I started playing with my breast with my other hand, rolling my nipple between my thumb and index finger. Since my breasts were big, I brought one up to my mouth and began sucking on my already sensitive nipples. That was another thing that drove me crazy when having sex. I loved for someone to suck on my breasts.

"Ooooooh," I moaned once my finger had made it to my spot. I planted my foot on the bed and lifted my ass a bit, allowing my finger to go deeper. I then inserted another finger, driving my own self insane. If there was one thing that I knew how to do, it was to please myself. I spent many nights without a man before Dontie came along.

Removing my hand from my breast, I brought it down between my legs and began circling my clitoris. I could already feel my nut building up as I began pressing hard. I pulled my finger out, turned over, and got on my knees. I was just about to place my fingers back where they'd come from, when Randell moved my hand to the side, messing my nut all up.

I opened my eyes and was about to chew him out, but I figured once his lips were on my on my clit, I'd think different.

"Allow me to do that for you," he said, licking his lips.

Opening my legs, he took one look at my wet pussy and dove in. He started off licking it first. I don't know if he was trying to tease me or not, but I thrust my hips to his lips, letting my shit coat his lips, chin, and everything else that was in the way. He must have gotten the hint, because next thing I knew, he was sucking the hell out of my pussy. He was doing it so good that I had to push up a little. It wasn't until he felt my legs shaking that he started sucking and slurping all the juices out of me. I don't know if he hadn't eaten or what, but this nigga was eating my shit like it was his last meal.

"Oh shit, Randellllllll. Oh shit, I'm about to come. Don't stop! Right there. Right theeeere!" I yelled, grabbing at the sheets on the bed. "I'm about to come!"

"Ummm . . . Come for me, baby," he moaned, looking at me. My juices were all over his lips. He then locked me down, where he proceeded to put a serious whooping on my shit. I don't know why, but for some strange reason, dude was showing out, and I loved it. A minute later, I was coming, and like a good boy, he made sure to suck everything up. I know what was going to happen next, and that's what I was regretting in my head, so I closed my eyes as I prepared for him to enter me. A few minutes went by, and I was still waiting . . . until I opened my eyes and noticed that he was standing over by the window nursing a drink.

"What the hell is wrong with this man?" I asked myself.

"You can get up now and head home to your husband," he said, never turning around. He must have read my mind, because I surely was wondering what the fuck was going on. I didn't give him a chance to change his mind, nor did I feel bad for not giving him any, and even though I was horny and in need, I pushed that to the back of my mind. I hurriedly threw on my sweat suit and tennis shoes, grabbed my bag and cell phone, and was out the door in two and a half minutes. It was only when I was out of the room and standing in the hallway that I noticed that my clothes weren't fixed properly.

Shit. That's just my damn luck, I thought. I looked down the hallway to see if someone was coming. Throwing on my pants first, I wasn't aware that they were on backward. I prepared to take them off when the door across the room came open. I looked up to see who it was, but before I could get a good look at whoever it was, the chick closed the door.

If I'm not mistaken, that chick looked just like my little sister.

"But why would she be here?" I asked myself. I must be tripping because I know I didn't invite her, and if I did, she wouldn't have come anyway. I must be still feeling high from the pills that I'd taken or whatever, I guess. Hunching my shoulders, I made sure that my clothes were on and fixed properly this time before I picked my purse up from the floor. I then remembered that Daddy sent me a text saying that he had invited Brinay. At first, I was mad, but then I was like okay or whatever. I hadn't seen her in years, so it was probably best for her to come. I didn't move right away, though. I was hoping that the chick would open the door again so I can see for sure if it was my sister. A few minutes went by without her coming back out of the room, so I proceeded to the elevator. I looked at my watch and noticed that it was almost two o'clock in the morning. It was a good thing that Dontie wasn't home, because I surely would've been in a world of trouble. I know I smelled like nut, and if he was home, I probably would've gotten my ass whooped, so the first thing I was going to do when I did make it home was hit the shower and get in bed. It had been a long day. I just hope that tomorrow is better than this.

BRINAY

I was in the room watching *Martin* when I got up out of the bed. I don't know why I couldn't sleep, but I felt restless, so I decided to go and take a walk on the beach. I removed my bedclothes and found a shirt and pants in my night bag. I then went to my suitcase and grabbed my tennis shoes. Grabbing the room key that was sitting on the table by the door, I opened the door, and then stood shocked as I watched some chick get dressed in the hallway across from my room. At first, I was going to offer for her to come and use the bathroom, but when I got a good look at who the woman was, I immediately closed the door.

"Oh my God, did she see me?" I asked no one in particular. I stood there, shocked as I leaned against the door, trying to calm my speeding heart. I don't know why seeing my sister always made me nervous, but I was feeling a little scared, as if she were my mother who I hadn't seen in a minute and was waiting on her to judge me or something.

"What's wrong?" Kourtney asked, now scaring the shit out me. "You look like someone is after you or you've seen a ghost."

Hell, I did basically, I thought to myself.

"Oh, nothing's wrong. I couldn't sleep, so I was about to go outside and take a walk on the beach. Go back to sleep," I told her, trying to steady my already rapid heartbeat.

"You want me to come with you?" she asked, trying to get up out of the bed. I know that she was tired, because she was rubbing her eyes.

"No, ma'am," I said, putting my hands up to stop her. "I'm good. You can go back to bed."

"Okay," she replied, lying back down in the bed.

I opened the door and left before she would change her mind, because she was known for doing that. I slowly turned around, thinking that I was going to bump into Sky, but when I did, she wasn't there. I looked over by the elevator just in time to see it closing.

"Damn," I said, defeated. I don't know why, but I wanted to see her. I *needed* to see her. I wanted her to see me and see the woman that I've become. I ran over to the stairs, knowing that the elevator wouldn't be back in time. Since the hotel didn't have that many floors, it took no time for me to make it to the lobby. When I got there, she was nowhere in sight. I walked outside, trying to see if I could spot her, but I couldn't. "What the hell was she doing here, and why the hell was she out in the hallway fixing her clothes?" I repeatedly asked myself. Knowing I didn't have the answer to my own questions, I decided to leave it alone. For now, anyway.

"Oh well. I guess I'll see her tomorrow then," I said. I wasn't even in the mood to go for a walk anymore. I went back inside the hotel and headed straight to my room. When I got inside the room, I stripped out of my clothes and put my nightclothes back on. I hopped back in bed and prayed that sleep would take over soon, because I needed all of my energy for tomorrow.

Chapter Nine

Dontie

I don't know what was up with Brinay, but I was going to find out. I'd just have to wait until after tomorrow, after this dinner that's supposed to be so important to Sky and her parents. I wanted to call and cancel and find out right this minute what was up with Nay, but I knew Sky, and if she's running around like a chicken with her head cut off, then it's truly important to her. Plus, she said that I was finally about to get to meet her sister that never comes around. I hope her sister didn't look just like her or resemble her, because I was going to have to date them both. Nah, I'm just playing. I wouldn't do no bullshit like that. I decided to just go, and after that, I'd be making my way back to South Carolina. I didn't know where Brinay was, but I do know that she had to come home one of these days. She wouldn't be wherever she was forever.

"What's up, man?" Chance asked, looking at me with those intense eyes.

"Bruh, to be honest, I don't know what's up," I said, placing my head in my hands.

"Well, what are you going to do?"

"I don't know. I was thinking that I'd just go back to Miami tonight because I have some event to tend to; then I'd just come back up here Sunday afternoon. She wouldn't tell me where she was, but she has to come home someday."

"Man, shit is fucked up," he replied.

"Tell me about it. I don't know what's gotten into her, but I need her to get it together and quick. I'm not letting her go, man, I don't care what I have to do," I said, getting up.

"I feel ya, man. Brinay is really a good girl. She's going to school, and I don't see her around here with a bunch of dudes, like some of these fees be," he said as we walked to the door.

"That's why I'm not trying to lose her, man. I already know shorty is good. I just got to get my shit together before it's too late," I said as I made my way to my car.

"Look, Dontie," he said, stopping me, "I know you like Brinay, but I also know what type of dude you is."

"Look, if you talking about me selling drugs, she already knows about that," I interrupted him.

"Nah, I'm not talking about that, although you need to keep that shit away from her also," he replied. "I'm talking about you and the many women that you have. When we were in school, you always had a flock of bitches sweating you, and only the Lord knows how many of them you actually fucked. You didn't leave that playboy's mentality in high school, though. You brought it into your adult life. Brinay is a good chick, if you know you can't and won't do right by her, then let her be. She already been through enough. You don't need to add to her plate."

I opened my mouth to say something, but nothing came out. I knew what he was saying was true, but I couldn't have my little cousin checking me. "Why you so concerned about what I do to Brinay? What, you like her? Or are you fucking her when I'm not around here? What is it?" I asked, beginning to get upset.

"Fam, you got me fucked up. I would never do some shiesty shit like that. I only called you about that shit with Brinay because I care about her, and not like a lover.

Truth be told, I knew her before you, and if I wanted to fuck with her, I could've, way before you ever came around here, so don't even go there with me."

"So what? This some jealous type shit? You mad because I came in your town and got the bitch you wanted?"

"Nah, nigga, pussy don't make nor break me. There's a whole sea load of pussy out here. I wouldn't dare beef with a nigga, especially my fam, behind one," he said, looking at me with disappointment. "I ain't ever the type of nigga to get jealous because a nigga in my family got something good. Excuse me for caring or giving a fuck, but I'll see you later," he said, and with that said, he left me out there in the night to think about what just went down.

I wanted to walk back in the house and apologize, because first of all, he's family, and second of all, I know he was only being concerned about Brinay. I knew how close they've gotten, and I could understand where he's coming from. I really didn't want to go off on him like that. I was just frustrated and clueless, and right now, I don't know what else to do. I was in my feelings, so it was real easy for me to go from zero to 100 real quick, without thinking. *I'll apologize to him when I get back,* I thought as I hopped in the car. I threw on a CD that had a mix of songs by R. Kelly, Trey Songz, and Jahiem. I then started the car and headed to the highway, making my way back to Miami, only wishing that tomorrow would hurry up and come so that I can get this day over with and get my girl back.

During my ride, the song "Last Time" came blasting through the speaker. I reached over and turned up the volume as I began to sing off-key with him.

"I'm living two different lives
One girl in the day, you in the night
And even though this ain't right
I just can't get enough . . ."

I know this wasn't my current situation, but I'd be damned if it wasn't something similar to it. I was living two different lives, with two different women who lived in two totally different states, and ain't none of them know about it. Hell, my family barely knows about it. My mother is the only one who knows about both Brinay and Skylar, and she's been getting in my ass daily. I can hear her now.

"Dontie, that's not right, son. You can't be in a relationship with two women at the same time," she'd say. Every time I went over to her house or she'd come to visit me, she's be speaking 'bout the same thing. I knew she was right, but I had two of the baddest bitches to ever walk this planet. I wasn't trying to give that up. It wasn't like they stayed in the same state. Sky stays in Florida, and Brinay stays in South Carolina, so I was good. Ain't like they were going to just bump into each one day at the mall, so I wasn't worried about them ever meeting up with each other. I just wanted me and Brinay to get back on good terms so everything could go back to how it was.

Midway through the ride, my phone dinged. I looked at it to see that I had a message from Brinay. I was too bucked that my mind was momentary blocked by seeing her name. I was so happy that she'd texted me . . . that was, until I started reading the message. It was then that I realized that it wasn't what I thought it was. I wanted to be mad or pissed, but I couldn't do anything but respect her. She was that bitch. The way she wasn't needy and didn't need a man for anything really did something to me. She had this mentality and attitude of one of the bravest and thuggish bitches, and I just had to have her. I don't care what she said. I was going to show up at her house and bring her flowers and gifts at her school until she took me back or else took a restraining order out on me, and even that wouldn't stop me. It don't matter what she did or what I had to do. I was going to get her back one way or another.

I know it was selfish of me, but this was the woman that I wanted to have my children. It was crazy, because I didn't know how that was going to happen or even *if* it was going to happen. All I knew was that's what I wanted, but if I had to choose out of the two, I really don't know who I'd choose. I quickly replied back to her. I knew she wasn't going to text back, so I threw the phone on the passenger seat and enjoyed what time I had left to make it back to Miami. I couldn't wait for this weekend to be over with so that we can be able to meet and talk about this like two grown adults. Hopefully, she'd accept what I had to say and not run away.

Chapter Ten

Brinay

The next day came by faster than I thought it would, and to be honest, I was nowhere near ready for any of it. My stomach was killing me once again, and I didn't have time for that. I already had too much to do, and the pain wasn't doing anything but slowing me down.

"Nay," Kourtney said, coming out of the bathroom with a towel wrapped around her.

"Yeah, what's up?" I asked her. I was still lying in the bed. I didn't want to tell her that my stomach was hurting me again, because she was going to try to force me to go to the hospital, and I really wasn't trying to go there.

"Why are you not up yet?" she asked. "Is something wrong with you again?"

"Nah, I'm still tired. That's all," I said, lying.

"Well, come on and get up. You know we have a lot of things to do today, and you still being in the bed will only slow things down," she said, walking over to the bed.

"Just give me five more minutes, Kourt," I begged, pulling the covers over my head.

"No, ma'am, you said that fifteen minutes ago. It's time to get up," she said, yanking the covers off of me.

"You know you could've waited, right?" I said, turning over, giving her an evil glare. I sighed, then got out of the bed.

"If I would've waited, you would've been lying in bed all damn day, and you know it," she replied. She was right, because that's how I was. When I was tired, I was tired, and I didn't like doing anything.

"Girl, don't do me like that. I just had a long night, and I'm really not ready for today at all," I said, getting up out of the bed and taking a much-needed stretch. "I'm about to go hop in the shower right quick. When I get out, we can go to the mall or whatever."

"Okay," she said as she began to get dressed.

I collected everything that I needed, then headed into the bathroom. I was going to make it quick, because I wasn't trying to be on the road all day. I wanted to take a nap so that I could be well rested for later on.

"So, where are we going first?" Kourtney asked as we waited for the elevator to come.

"I don't know. I got to go to the salon to get my hair done, and I got to run in the mall to find something quick and easy to put on," I replied just as the elevator came. We waited for the few people that were already on there to get off; then we got on.

"I may just go to the mall first and get my hair done after. I'm not trying to have my hair looking a mess," I said, pushing the button for the first floor.

"True that. It makes sense for us to go shopping first, then to get our hair done after. It's a good thing we already have our nails and toes done. All I need is a quick color change; then I'm good to go," she said, looking at her hands and feet.

"Me too," I replied just as the elevator came to a stop on the first floor.

We got off and proceeded to walk to the front door. Once we made it outside, I had to throw my shades on. It felt good, but the sun was shining too bright for my eyes. We began walking toward the back of the hotel where our car was parked.

"I hope we can find a spot closer to the front of the hotel when we get back," I said just as we made it to the car.

"Who you telling? That was a nice little walk there," Kourtney chimed. I pulled the keys out of my purse, unlocked the door, and we got in. I started the car, but I didn't move right away.

"So what mall are we going to?" I asked, turning to her.

"I don't know. This is your town. I don't know much of nothing, so whichever mall you choose is going to be fine with me," she replied, placing her seat beat on. I did the same.

"Okay," I said, putting the car in reverse and backing out of the parking spot. I pulled off and headed straight to the best mall in Miami, the Dolphin Mall. Everybody knew that if they were to ever visit Miami, then they'd have to shop at the Dolphin Mall. It was one of the best places to shop, and the clothes and prices were great. Also, it wasn't that far from where we were, so that was a plus too.

"So, Nay, have you spoken to Dontie today?" Kourtney asked out of the blue.

"Nah, I haven't, and I'm not looking forward to it. The only time that I'm going to call him is tomorrow so that we can talk about the baby. That's it," I told her.

"So you *did* tell him about the baby?"

"No, I haven't. I'm going to tell him all of that tomorrow when he comes. What he does or doesn't do is up to him. I'm not begging and pleading to no one about anything," I said. I was really tired of the bullshit, and I wanted all of it to just be over with. "I'm tired of looking out for other people and their feelings when it comes to shit. I'm about to start letting the chips fall where they may, no matter what or who it hurts, because no one's concerned with me or mine, so that's how I'm going to start treating everyone."

"I feel ya," she replied. We didn't say anything the rest of the ride to the mall. The only sound that could be heard was the music on the radio. Other than that, we were both quiet.

Ten minutes later, we were pulling up to the mall. Considering that it was an early Saturday morning, the mall was stupid packed. The whole damn parking lot was filled up. If it wasn't for someone coming out and leaving, I don't think we would've found a close spot to park.

"I really hope all these people are not in this mall right now," Kourtney huffed once we parked.

"I hope so too," I said. I turned off the car, and we got out.

"I'm trying to make this as quick as possible. I'm only looking for something comfortable and simple. I'm not looking for nothing expensive to go pretend around people who I don't even care about," I said as we made our way toward the mall entrance.

"Ain't shit about this going to be right anyways, so why would I spend my money when I know damn well that something wrong is going to go down?"

Walking into the mall, I was somewhat hurt. I thought for sure that we were going to be in and out since it was early in the morning, but I was wrong. The minute we stepped foot in the mall, I wanted to step foot right back out of there. I damn sure wasn't looking forward to trying to fight my way through this crowd of people.

"Damn," I said under my breath. I was regretting that I didn't go to the mall back in South Carolina. That would've been much easier and less stressful.

"Where do you want to begin?" Kourtney asked as we looked around at all of the people walking about.

"I guess we can start looking in Forever 21. You know a girl can never go wrong in there," I said, giving her one of them girlish laughs.

"Right," she said, doing the same.

"Come on," I said as I began walking in the direction of the store. I hadn't been in here in so long, and I must admit that the state of Florida was doing great. This mall was so big and so beautiful that I couldn't help but to stop and admire it.

I swear the little walk it took for us to get to Forever 21 had me all kinds of tired. I wanted to sit down on the bench because my back was hurting me.

"Come on, fat mama. I already see ya slowing down," Kourtney said, grabbing my arm and walking through the door.

"I don't know how you know it. I was just thinking that I needed a seat."

"You got pregnant women problems," she said, blushing. She always did that when we were talking about something in reference to the baby or my pregnancy. "I think we should find you one of them maternity stores up in here."

"I'm not about to go there with you, girl," I said, rolling my eyes at her.

"Aww, boo, don't take it personal. I was only playing with you and nanny's baby," she said, rubbing my stomach.

"Oh, I didn't," I replied. "Nah, let's try to find something so we can get up out of this mall."

"Okay," she said.

"If you see something nice, call me."

"I gotcha," she said. She went her way, and I went mine.

I had only been in there a few minutes, and I could already tell that I wasn't going to find anything in there.

Half of the things weren't my type. I was choosy when it came to my attire, so I knew it was going to be hard.

"Nay," I heard Kourtney calling my name, but I didn't see her.

"I'm over by the belts," I said to her. A few seconds later I spotted her.

"You didn't find anything you like, huh?" she asked.

"Nah," I said, turning my nose up.

"I figured that, because I didn't see anything in here that you like or would wear," she replied. "But look," she said, holding up a knee-length gray skirt, with a teal-colored shirt that had a long V that stopped almost to her navel.

"Oh, I like that," I said, giving her a high five.

"You didn't find any shoes and jewelry in here?" I asked her.

"Nope," she said, shaking her head. "I didn't see anything that would go with this."

"Okay, well, come on. Let's go try this on and see how it fits you," I said, heading to the dressing room.

"Umm . . . We need a dressing room," I said to one of the girls standing by the counter.

"Okay," she said coming from behind the counter, key in hand. "How many?"

"Two," Kourtney replied, holding up the two items that she had just found.

"Okay, you can go in dressing room number two," she said, opening it.

"Thanks," Kourtney said.

"No problem, you're welcome," the girl replied, walking back to where she'd just come from.

"Brinay? Brinay Williams?" someone said from behind me. I turned to find some light-skinned chick standing there. I just stood there staring at her, because I didn't have a clue who she was.

"Umm, I don't want to seem rude, but I'm clueless. Can you tell me who you are?" I asked, not trying to seem like I was stuck-up or something.

"It's me, Latoya. Latoya Washington," she replied.

"Latoya Washington," I said, repeating the name and trying to see if it would ring a bell somewhere in my head.

"Yeah, we went to high school together. We took Mr. Carter's chemistry and physics class together," she said, trying to jog my memory.

"Oh, Toya," I said, finally remembering who she was. "What happened to that little sweet girl that I remember, because as you can see, she's surely not there anymore."

She laughed, "Nah, I'm not that little girl anymore. I'm all grown up now," she said with a smile, giving me a hug. "How have you been? I haven't seen you in a minute."

"I've been doing great, and yourself? I don't live in Florida anymore, so that's probably why you don't see me as much," I said hugging her back.

"All is well. I'm still living, so I won't complain," she responded. "So what brings you down here?"

"Just coming to visit my family for the weekend, that's all."

"Oh, that's good. How has your brother been? I ain't seen him in a while."

"Brandon's been good. He's almost done with his bid, so you'll be seeing him in a minute."

"Nay," Kourtney said, stepping out of the dressing room as I turned to look at her. "What you think? Oh, hey."

"Hello," Toya said, waving.

"Kourtney, this is Latoya. Toya, this is my best friend Kourtney," I said, introducing the two of them.

"Nice to meet you," Kourtney said, reaching her hand out for Latoya to shake.

"Likewise," Toya responded, returning the gesture.

"Now, about that outfit, it looks great. You look great. I think you should buy it," I said, nodding my head in approval. The skirt and shirt fitted and looked fantastic on her.

"Okay. Let me take this off and go and see if they have another one like these in my size. You know I don't buy anything I try on," she said, heading back into the dressing room.

"Don't I know it," I said, laughing at her, because I was the same way. I wasn't trying to buy anything that I had already tried on. That was a no-no.

"We have to hang out before you leave to go back home," Toya said.

"Let me get your number," I suggested, turning back to her and handing her my phone. She took the phone and programmed her number in it, then handed it back to me.

"I'll call you when I have some free time because we most definitely have to get together before I leave to go back home."

"Okay. I'll be waiting," she said.

"All right," I replied, and with that, she left.

"Come on, I'm ready," Kourtney said, walking out of the dressing room.

"Okay. I've already wasted enough time in here as it is," I replied, walking out of the dressing-room area. She went to the area where she first found the things and exchanged them for some unworn ones. We then headed to the counter so that she could pay for them.

"I hope I can find some shoes to go with this," she said, handing her things to the woman at the front counter.

"I'm sure you'll find something. You already have an outfit. Finding shoes shouldn't be that hard to do," I said to her. "Unlike me, my ass have to find every damn thing. Hopefully, it won't take me forever and a day."

"That'll be forty-six dollars and seventy-eight cents," the lady said, giving Kourtney her total.

"Here you go." She handed her a bill, then waited for her change and her bag.

"Fifty-three dollars and twenty-two cents is your change. Have a great day and thank you for shopping at Forever 21," the lady said, handing her the bag, receipt, and her change.

"Thanks, and you too," Kourtney replied. "Okay, I'm ready," she then said, turning to me.

"All right, come on, because if I don't find anything I like in here, I'm just going to wear something that I brought with me," I said as we headed for the door. I was damn near out the door when I spotted one of the chicks that worked there, hanging new items on a rack in the corner of the store.

"Hold up right quick," I said, spotting this yellow top that I just had to have. If anyone knew me, they knew for sure that yellow was definitely my favorite color.

"Umm, excuse me, but can I have a look at that shirt right there," I said, pointing to the shirt that caught my attention.

"Sure," she said, handing me the garment. I looked at it for a minute and knew that I *had* to have it.

"Do they have this in a medium?" I asked her. I'd normally wear a size small, but since the shirt wasn't stretch material and I was pregnant, I wasn't trying to suffocate my child.

"Yes, here you go, ma'am," she said, handing me the shirt that I needed.

"Thanks," I said as I continued to look at the items that she had on her cart. I also grabbed a peach-colored blazer, which stopped at my elbow, to go over the shirt since it had spaghetti straps.

"And she finds something that she likes in here after all," Kourtney said sarcastically.

"Actually, I did," I said, beaming. I was so happy that I didn't have to play all morning in these people's stores.

"Now all you need is some pants, and you'll be almost there, like me."

"Girl, I spotted some jean capris in here on the sales rack," I said, making my way over to where I had seen the pants when I first walked in. I had to pass by a few other things before I finally found a pair in my size. "Bingo! Here I go!"

"All right. Now beat ya feet. We still have to go look for some shoes and stop by the nail salon to get a color change on our nails and toes, plus we have to do our hair," she said, motioning for me to hurry up and go and get checked out.

"Girl, you play too much, but I think I'll probably just do my own hair, because I'm not trying to be up in the salon all day, and I want to take a nap before it's time to roll," I said, placing my things on the counter.

"Yeah, I was thinking the same thing," she said, cosigning with me. "Hopefully, they have a nail salon in here where we could just get our color changed and find our shoes in here as well. That way, we'll be able to grab something to eat in the food court, then head back to the hotel so we can both take a nap."

"Your total is going to be thirty-seven dollars and sixty-five cents."

"Here you go," I said, handing her two twenty-dollar bills. She handed me my bag, my receipt, and change, and we were on our way. Everything was fast and easy and was going so well. I was actually starting to smile. I just hoped that nothing got in our way.

We didn't finish shopping until well after twelve in the afternoon. To say that I was tired and beat was an understatement. I was well past hungry, and my feet were killing me. All I wanted to do was to eat, go back to the hotel room, and dive straight in the bed.

"Yooo, I'm starving over here," I said, rubbing my stomach while desperately trying to hold all of my bags in the other hand. "Plus, my arms hurt."

"I told you not to buy all of that stuff. Most of that was things you didn't need anyway," Kourt said laughing. "You want to stop by the food court and grab something to eat?"

"I don't care, as long as we get something, because if I wait one more minute, I'm sure I'll be on my way to starvation."

"All right, come on. Let's get a table so we can put all of these bags down first," she said, leading the way to the food court area. There were so many people there that we barely could find a damn table. I was getting more and more pissed off by the minute.

"Look, there's a spot over there," Kourtney said, pointing to a table where a lady and two kids had just gotten up from. "I'll hurry and go get it before someone else tries to take it," she said, walking off. She was walking so fast that I thought she had fire in her pants or had to pee or something. I was walking so slow that she had left me behind in her first few steps.

"Damn! Let me find out you speed walk in your free time," I said once I had reached the table, all out of breath. I placed my bags on the floor and took a seat. Then I removed my shoes and rubbed my feet.

"I see you got jokes, huh? I wasn't trying to let no one take our spot," she laughed. "Your ass was walking all slow. I thought it was going to take you a whole day to get here, and put them stanky-ass feet away."

"Ha-ha. Now I see *you* got jokes," I said sarcastically. "I told you that my damn feet was hurting . . . shit. You should be massaging them anyways, since you took forever to find some shoes that you liked."

"Yeah, right! I ain't touching them things. You crazy," she said, turning up her nose.

"I thought I was your baby mama," I asked, faking like I was hurt. "You're going to do me like that?"

"You are, boo, and I'd do a whole lot for you, but touching your stank-ass feet ain't one of them, ya feel me?" I said talking like she be talking when she's mad.

"Girl, bye," I said, waving her off. "You need a little more work; then you probably can hang with it."

"Ha-ha. Whatever. What you want to eat, baby mama?" she said, changing the subject.

"I don't care, just get me something to eat before I die of starvation," I said, clutching my growling stomach. It was so empty, and I was so hungry that it started to hurt. My baby started kicking, so I knew for sure that it was time to eat.

"No, ma'am, I'm not about to stand in line and get something for you to eat, only for me to come back and you say that you don't want that," she said, placing her hand on her hips. "You know you picky as hell, Nay."

"Honestly, right now, I'd really eat anything, so can you hurry up and go ahead and get me something to eat, please," I practically begged her.

"Okay, okay, don't bite my head off," she said, throwing her hands up. "I'll be right back."

I shook my head at myself, knowing that I was wrong for talking to her that way. Hell, she was getting on my damn nerves, though. I told her that I was really hungry, and she wanted to play games. She should know better than to deprive a pregnant woman of food. They'll get hostile; well, that's what I heard.

While she was gone, I decided to take a look around. There were really a lot of people at the mall today. I looked over to my left and spotted some lady and her baby sitting by a table near me. She was bent over to feed ice cream to the baby, who was sitting in the stroller. I thought it was cute. It had me kind of wondering how things would be when I had my baby. I actually couldn't wait to find out. I only hoped that I'd be as good of a mother as that lady. *Hell, I don't know the first thing about being a mother,* I thought.

I was about to look for Kourtney when my phone started to ring. Since it was in my purse, and my purse was on the floor, I removed my foot from my lap and grabbed my purse. Taking the phone out of my purse, I noticed that it was Dontie calling me. *I should have never taken his ass off of the block list,* I thought, sending his call to voice mail. I didn't have time for him right now. All he was going to do was make me mad, and I didn't need any of that right now.

"Here you go," Kourtney said, placing a salad and water in front of me.

"Thanks, and I'm sorry for blowing up on you. I was just that hungry," I said, sincerely apologizing to her.

"Oh, girl, I'm not worried about you one bit," she said, waving me off. "If I had a dollar for each time that you've blown up, I'd be hood rich," she replied.

"Still, I want you to know that I'm sorry. I don't want to mess up our friendship over nothing." I grabbed her hand.

"Really, Nay, I'm okay. I know that it's the baby and the hormones that have to be blowing up like that, so I'm not worried, nor are my feelings hurt. I do accept your apology, though, baby mama," she said giving, my hand a gentle squeeze.

"I said that I was going to be here, no matter what, so you better go ahead and get used to me, because your little temper tantrums will not run me anywhere," Kourtney continued.

"That's why I love you. You're so understanding, even when you shouldn't be," I said sincerely. "I'd kiss you if I didn't think people would think that we were gay."

"Oh no. You can keep those lips over there, ma'am. I don't know what or who they've been on," she said, playfully frowning.

"Girl, whatever. Don't even try to play me like that. You know I don't do them kind of things with my mouth," I said, just as my phone started to ring.

"Yeah, tell me anything," she replied, rolling her eyes.

"No, you didn't," I said picking up my phone. When I noticed that it was Dontie's ass calling me, I put it back down on the table without even answering it. "My God, why won't he leave me alone!"

"Who?" she asked, but I didn't answer her. I was momentarily blinded, better yet, shocked, by the sight of Dontie walking through the food court.

"Where the fuck did he come from, and how the hell did he know I was here?" I said, not meaning to curse. It just slipped out of my mouth.

"Who?" she asked, turning and trying to see who I was looking at.

"Dontie," I replied.

"Girl, you lying!"

"I wish that I was. Come on, let's go before he sees me," I said frantically as I began to pack up my things.

"Why? We haven't finished eating yet," she replied.

"Because I don't *want* to see him, at least not now," I said, getting up from my seat. I picked up my bags and purse and waited for her. "Hurry up, Kourtney!"

"I'm coming, girl, hold on," she responded. I thought I was going to pass the hell out. Dontie was so close to my table, and he didn't even see me. I watched as he picked up the phone, dialed a number, and put it to his ear. *Please don't let him be calling me,* I thought as I tried to locate my phone.

"Okay, I'm ready," she said as K. Michelle's and R. Kelly's "Baby, You and I" song came blasting through my phone. Even though the mall was packed, my phone had still rung loud. I hurried to try to silence the thing, but my nerves were so bad that it became a challenge to do so. I looked down to turn it off, and when I looked back up, he had turned and was now looking at me. For a minute, we just stood there staring at each other, not saying a word, staring at each other as if we were the only two people in the mall at that moment. I wanted to hate him or even curse him out, but I couldn't. Looking at him reminded me of how and why I fell in love with him in the first place.

Dontie stood at about five foot eight, weighed about 200 pounds solid, and he had a chocolate complexion. He kept a fade that was fresh every single time that I saw him, with a pair of brown eyes and the prettiest smile that I've ever seen on a man. This man was handsome as fuck, which made it easy for me to love him and hard for me to stay mad at him. He moved his mouth to speak, but no words came out. I guess he was just as speechless as I was.

"Come on, Kourt," I said, abruptly walking off in the opposite direction from him.

"Nay, chill out. You getting yourself worked up for nothing," she said, trying to catch up with me. It was now my turn to be walking like someone had lit a fire under my ass. I didn't answer her, I was too busy trying to get as far away from Dontie as I could get.

"Brinay!" I heard him yell my name, but I kept it pushing.

"What, Kourtney?" I asked, now yelling, but never slowing my stride.

"Can you please slow down?" she asked, sounding out of breath.

"I'll slow down when I make it to the parking lot and away from Dontie," I said as I continued to walk. I was almost to the exit . . . when all of my bags dropped out of my hands. My hands shook badly as I tried to pick them up. "Shit," I said, because all of my things that I'd just bought in Victoria's Secret were now on the floor.

"Let me help you, ma," a voice said, causing me to freeze in place. I knew that voice and who it belonged to all too well. I played on the floor, trying my hardest not to get up and have to look him in the eye. "You can turn around, ma. I won't hurt, bite, or do anything to you."

Slowly, I turned around. I childishly wished that when I turned, I'd spin myself so fast that I'd ended up some place else, but when I spotted him still standing there with his phone in his hand, I knew that I couldn't. *So much for the Wizard of Oz,* I thought to myself.

"Thank you, sir," I said, grabbing my bags from out of his hands. I didn't even look up. I didn't want to see his face. "Come on, Kourtney."

"Whoa! Brinay, chill out and talk to me," he said, grabbing my arm.

"Dontie, let go of my arm, please. I have nothing to say to you right now." I tried to pull my arm from out of his grasp, but he didn't let it go.

"Oh, so that's what we on now? You 'round here playing these little kiddies'-ass games. What, you feeling some type of way or something?" he asked. I still hadn't turned around to face him.

"For real, bruh, just let go of my arm," I said calmly.

"Nah, ma. I'm not letting you go until you turn around and talk to me."

"I just told you that I have nothing to say to you right now," I said in a low tone, "so can you please just let me go so I can get up out of here. I have places to go and people to see."

"Ma, I ain't letting you go until we talk, so you can just cut all that other shit out," he said, hitting a nerve. He fucked with my nerves so bad, that before I knew what I was doing, I turned around and slapped the taste out of his mouth.

"What the fuck is wrong with you?" he asked, holding his face. I looked at him, then to the hand that I used to slap him with, then back at him before I took off, dropping everything except my purse and phone.

"Brinay," Kourtney said, running behind me. I didn't stop, though. I was trying to get the hell out of there.

Chapter Eleven

Dontie

When I woke up this morning, I was feeling some type of way. I was still mad about what happened between Chance and I, and on top of that, I still wasn't able to talk to Brinay like I wanted to. Not to mention that Sky was over here talking my damn head off about meeting her family. I ain't want be bothered with that shit none whatsoever, so I was kind of zoned out instead of listening to anything that she was over there saying.

"Baby?" she called out to me. "Dontie."

"Huh, huh?" I asked, snapping out of my thoughts, "What's up, ma?"

"Where were you?" she asked, looking at me from across the table.

"What are you talking about? I was right here," I replied.

"I've been talking to you, but you've been distant. It's like you're here physically, but your mind is somewhere else. What's up with that?" she asked, moving her plate from in front of her.

"Nah, I was just thinking about a few things, that's all," I said to her.

"Uh-huh! Well, we need to hurry up and head to the mall. You know it's Saturday, and there'll be a lot of people there trying to find whatever deals that they can find," she said, getting up from the table.

"I thought we already had everything that we need. What are we going to the mall for?" I asked, still seated. I wasn't in the mood to go anywhere.

"I got a few things I need to get for tonight."

"Nah, ma, I'm good. You can go to the mall. I'll just see you when you get back," I said, getting up from the table. "I'm going take a nap."

"Dontie, don't start with your shit. I need you to come with me to the mall, so you might as well come on," she said with her hands on her hips.

"Ma, I already told you that I'm not coming, so you might as well just go ahead and be on ya way."

"Look, I don't know what happened to you overnight, but you've been acting all shitty since you woke up this morning. You need to get yourself together, po'tna," she had the nerve to say.

"Ain't shit happened to me. I just don't feel like going to the mall. Damn!" I yelled. "You always be bugging a nigga. Go on with that shit, cuz I'm not for it today, Sky."

"Really? I'm not trying to go there with you either. All I ask is for you to go to the mall with me, and you come with shit," she responded. "I'm your *wife* now. You should *want* to be around me more."

Yeah, and I'm beginning to regret making your ass that, I thought to myself. I was getting tired of her shit, and we haven't been married for all of two-and-a-half weeks. It was bad enough that I ain't really bought the ring for her ass to begin with. Now she was making me begin to really regret the choice of marrying her.

"Sky, for real, ma, I'm not in the mood to even go anywhere. Why you can't just go without me?" I asked, trying to approach her in a different way.

"Because I can't, *that's* why," she said, rolling her eyes.

"Lord, why me?" I asked.

"Why you *what,* huh? So what, you want to call it quits or something, Dontie?" she asked, walking toward me.

"I didn't say that, Sky," I replied calmly.

"You didn't have to. Your attitude and the way you're acting says it all," she said, putting her hands in my face. I had to count to ten in my head to keep myself from choking her ass.

"Sky, I'm no woman beater, and I've never put my hands on a woman before in my life, so I'm going to kindly ask that you *never*, in your life, put your hands on me again," I said, remaining calm.

"Or *what? What're* you going to do?" she said, pushing my head back with her index finger. "You better get your shit together."

I don't know why she was acting hard all of a sudden, but I was not feeling it, so to keep myself from knocking her fucking head from off of her shoulders, I didn't say anything.

"If you ain't ready in the next minute, I'm leaving your ass right there, and you'll have no other choice but to go to the mall by your damn self," I threw in before I exited the kitchen. I went straight to the room and threw on a fresh white tee, some khaki cargo shorts, and a pair of fresh white Adidas. I didn't put on any jewelry. I just threw on my Rolex, grabbed my keys, and headed back out the door.

When I made it back to the living room, she was standing there waiting for me by the door with her purse on her shoulder. I didn't say anything to her. I opened the door and went straight to my car, leaving the door open behind me. I made it to the car in five seconds flat and got in. She was speed walking to catch up. I was starting up the car when she opened the door and climbed in.

"You really need to cut that shit out," she said, grabbing her seat belt and putting it on. I didn't respond to her, nor did I even bother to put on my seat belt. I knew how much that drove her crazy, and I wanted to piss her off like she did to me. I just put the car in gear and drove off.

Ambria Davis

"So you're not going to put your seat belt on, Dontie?" she asked. Again, I ignored her. I grabbed my Lil Wayne's "Sorry for the Wait" two mixtape, placed it in the radio, and tuned the volume up. I knew she was heated because she folded her arms across her chest and started mumbling to herself. I didn't wanted to hear, nor did I care about, whatever it was that she was saying. I just bobbed my head along to the music the whole ride to the mall.

That was how I ended up at Dolphin's Mall early in the morning. I was still mad at Sky, and she was obviously mad at me, because when we walked in the mall, we both went our separate ways. I wasn't really tripping off nothing, so when she walked in her own direction, I was fine with that. Like I said, I really didn't have anything to get from the mall, and I didn't know what she was coming to get, so I decided to window-shop until she was finished. I bypassed a few stores when my stomach decided to start talking to me. Since Sky had messed up my breakfast, I hadn't eaten anything yet, so I made my way toward the food court to grab me some grub.

On my way to the food court, I decided to call Brinay. I wanted so badly to be in her presence, to be able to hold her, to feel her, to kiss her, but I knew she needed time. Right now, I'd just have to settle on hearing her voice, even though she might curse me out or have an attitude. I didn't care or mind at all, though. Placing the phone to my ear, it rang a few times; then it cut straight to voice mail. I wanted to be mad, but I couldn't. I was just surprised that she took me off of the blocked list, so I was one step closer to getting back on her good side, I guess. *I'll give her a few minutes before I'll call her back,* I thought just as my phone started to ring. I noticed that it was Chance calling. I didn't know what he wanted since we weren't on the best of terms, but he *was* family, and I wasn't going to put him off just because we had one little argument.

"What's up, man?" I asked, answering the phone.

"Ain't shit, man, I just touched down. Where you at?" he replied.

"Where? You in Miami?" I asked, shocked.

"Yeah, man, remember you wanted me to come to that little thingy with your girl and her family tonight?"

"Oh yeah, I forgot that I asked you to come with me, man. I'm at the mall right now, though. What you about to get into?" I said. I had totally forgotten that I had asked him to come with me, but I was surprised that he actually came.

"You thought I was going to let you get thrown to the wolves by yaself, nigga? I'm about to head to the telly and catch a nap, man. That ride was long, and I was tired as fuck. I almost ran off the road a few times," he joked. See, that's what I loved about that little nigga. No matter what went down between us, he was never one to hold a grudge. He would always be the first one to speak and squash the shit. Occasionally, I had to ask myself if we were really related, because we were complete opposites sometimes.

"All right, man. I'll see you when you come by the house later on. Go and get yourself some rest, bruh. Hit me up when you wake up."

"All right, fam. I'll see you later, bruh," he said, and we hung up.

I'd made my way across the food court, trying to find a table. The place was insanely packed, and there was not one open table in sight.

"I don't know why everyone is in the mall today, and that's why I didn't want to come," I said to myself. I'm sure if Sky was right in front of me, I'd have to curse her ass out for bitching about not finding a seat when I told her ass not to come here in the first place. If there was one thing that she knew how to do for sure, it was bitching.

Giving up the idea of finding a table where I'd be able to sit down, I grabbed my phone and dialed Brinay's number again. It started ringing . . . but then the craziest thing happened, making my whole body go still. I heard the sound of a ringtone that I was all too familiar with. Any other time, I wouldn't think about it, but since I was calling Brinay's phone and the exact lyrics that she had set for my ring tone were now playing, I thought about it.

"It can't be her," I said, turning to where the sound was now coming from. When I turned around, I was staring straight at the woman who had my heart. She wasn't looking at me at first, but when she looked up, she looked just as surprised as I was. I moved my mouth to say something to her, but nothing came out. I didn't know what to say to her now that she was here. Then her face changed, and she looked as if she was disgusted and mad about seeing me. Before I could say something, she took off walking in the opposite direction of me.

I wanted to call out to her, but I didn't want to make a scene, so instead, I calmly but swiftly walked behind her. I wanted to wait until we got outside into the parking lot to confront her, because I knew Sky was in the mall somewhere shopping, and I didn't want to risk the possibility of them seeing each other. We were almost to the exit when all of a sudden, her bags dropped out of her hands. I guess she was that nervous or scared to see me that she dropped everything.

I watched her as she scrambled to pick everything up from off the floor. Her hands were trembling so bad that she couldn't do it, so I decided to help her. Once I'd picked up everything, I handed her the bags. She didn't even look at me. She simply said thank you, grabbed her bags, and tried to walk off, but I stopped her. I wasn't about to let her get away from me that easily. I wanted— no—I *needed* to talk to her, and I was going to do just that regardless of whether she wanted to.

We stood there saying a few words before she and her friend headed to the exit, with me right behind her. I know I was playing it close, but right now, I wasn't thinking straight. I needed Brinay like the air that I breathe, and even though I was now married to Sky, nothing was going to change that, which is why I was following her, trying to make things right with her. I waited until we made it to their car and out of earshot before I spoke.

"Come here, Nay," I said, grabbing her into a hug. She resisted a bit before she gave in. Lord knows how bad I couldn't wait to do this right here. I'd been dying for weeks to do this, and now that I was able to, I didn't want to let her go.

"Let go of me, Tae," she said, trying to push me off of her, but instead, I held her tighter.

"Stop! You're squeezing me too tight," she yelled, trying to push me again. This time, I let her go. "What are you doing here, and what do you want?" she asked.

"The question is, what are *you* doing here?" I asked her.

"I'm minding my own business. Now, what do you want, Tae? I have things to do, and you're obviously holding me up," she said, catching an attitude.

"Can you give us a minute, ma?" I asked her friend, who was waiting off to the side of her.

"You okay?" her friend asked her.

"Yeah, I'm good. Go ahead and get in the car. I'll be there in a minute," she told her. She looked at me, then rolled her eyes before walking around to the car and getting in.

"Nay, you got ya space. Start talking because a minute is all you're going to get, baby," she said with her hand on her hips.

I went to grab her hand, but she stopped me. "If I was you, I wouldn't touch me."

"Okay," I said, moving my hand back and placing both of them in my pockets. I didn't say anything. For a moment, I stood there, staring at her, admiring her beauty. For some strange reason, she had this beautiful glow on her face that I've never seen before, and I instantly got a bit jealous. I don't know if it was because of some man, but I started mugging her.

"Look, if you ain't gon' say shit, then I'm out," she said, moving toward the car.

"Ma, chill," I said, grabbing her arm. "I miss you, baby."

"Nah, you don't miss me, Tae," she replied, jacking her arms from my grasp.

"I *do* miss you. Why have you been ignoring me?" I asked.

"Dontie, I'm going to be quite honest with you. I don't know who you think you are, but I'm *not* that chick. I'm not about to let no man come in my life thinking he can play me. See, I know your kind, and I tried to overlook it, but you've made it quite damn obvious a few times. See, at first, I wasn't worrying about it, or maybe I tried to deny it, but I know you got some chick, besides me, who you mess with. Now, I'm not mad, nor am I tripping about the shit at all. I just needed you to know that I know," she started to say, but I had to cut her off.

"Man, it's not even like that," I said, lying through my damn teeth. "I was out of the country on business, and I told you that already. I don't know why you can't believe me when I say that."

"Tae, please, I know when you're lying, and you're doing it right now. If you was out of the country on *business,* like you said, then why didn't you call me?" she asked, pausing for me to answer. When I didn't say anything as fast as she wanted me to, she continued. "That's what I thought. You got me bent, twisted, and mistaken for the next bitch. I will *not* let you play me. I'm a bitch who don't need a man for anything. Hell, I don't even put up with the nigga who gave birth to me, and we share the same fucking blood. So, you can miss me with all of that shit you're spitting out of your mouth right now, li'l daddy. Like I said before, I'm done with you, so you can stop calling me and start calling your next bitch as much as you be calling and stalking me," she said, loud enough for the people who were in earshot to hear.

"Can you please lower your voice? You're starting to draw attention to us," I said calmly.

"Can you kiss my ass where the sun don't shine and get the fuck up out of my face?"

I was surprised to hear her talking like that to me, but then again, I wasn't surprised. I knew sooner or later that she was going to begin getting tired of me not being there all of the time and basically not answering her phone calls, but I didn't know that it was going to start sooner rather than later. I looked her in the eyes to try to explain it to her, but I didn't. What I saw was nothing but sadness and hurt, and I was deeply hurt to know that I was the cause of all of that, and there was nothing that I could do to fix it.

"Brinay, I'm really sor—"

"You're what, Dontie? You're *sorry?* Is *that* what you was going to say?" she asked with glassy eyes. "Oh, you're sorry, all right. A sorry excuse for a man. I can't believe after all of these years, I let a man like you come in and hurt me. Oh, don't worry about it anymore, because we're going to be fine without you," she said, letting the tears that were threatening to fall run freely.

"Baby, don't cry. What can I do to make it up to you?" I asked, trying to step closer to her.

"Don't come near me, Tae. What you can and will do is leave me the hell alone, because I'm over you. There's no need for you to call or text me anymore."

"Baby, you don't mean that," I said just as my phone began to ring. I looked at it and noticed that it was Sky calling me.

"What that? Ya bitch calling you, huh?" she asked with her hands on her hips. I didn't answer her, because I knew that if I lied to her, I would only be hurting her more.

"Know what, Tae? Fuck you!" and with that, she hopped in the car and rolled out.

I stood there feeling helpless and lost as I watched her car disappear from the mall's parking lot. On one hand, I wanted to go after her, and on another hand, I knew that I couldn't. My mind was telling me that it was time for me to let her go, but my heart was saying something much different. I didn't know how everything was going to play out, but I was going to let her cool off for a minute; then I was going to try to win my girl back, because I don't know if I could live without her in my life.

"You ain't hear me calling your phone, Tae?" a voice asked from behind me. I turned to find Sky standing there with one hand full of bags, and the other hand on her hip.

"Nah, I ain't hear ya," I said, walking off toward the car.

"Don't give me that attitude, Dontie, because I've just about had it with you this morning," she said as she stomped behind me.

"Skylar, ya better quit while you're ahead," I said just as we arrived at the car. We were walking so fast, I'm sure the people who saw us thought that we were crazy or something.

"I don't have to do anything I don't want to," she said, putting her bags in the trunk. "You're the one with the jacked up attitude, not me."

"Sky, if you don't get your stupid, ignorant, irrelevant, dumb ass in this car, you're going to make me do something that I will *not* regret."

"Look, like I said earlier, I don't know what or who done pissed you off, but I'ma need you to get it together before you make *me* do something *I'm* going to regret!"

I didn't pay that ho no mind, because I knew if we kept going back and forth, I was going to hurt her ass, and I wasn't going to think twice about it. I simply got in the car and waited for her. When she did get situated, I started the car and drove off. I was driving so fast that I flew through two traffic lights.

"Could you kill us any faster? Damn!" she yelled.

"I wish I could kill your ass instead," I mumbled under my breath.

"Tae, on the real, you need to slow down before we be wrapped around a damn pole somewhere," she said. I knew that we were almost home, and I didn't want to hear her mouth anymore, so I slowed down. "Thank you."

The next five minutes it took to get to the house was spent in complete silence. She was trapped in her thoughts over there, and I was over here lost in mine. There's been a lot of tension between us lately, and I was starting to think that we were never supposed to get married in the first place. There ain't no way we've been together for over two-and-something years without any problems, and now that we've signed papers on each other, now, all these problems come. Something was up. I already knew what my problem was, I just had to find out what hers was.

Pulling into the driveway, I parked in front of the door so that she could get out.

"You're not coming in the house?" she asked once she noticed that I hadn't cut the engine off and didn't move from my seat.

"Nah, I'm bouta go out for a minute," I replied, never looking at her. I kept my eyes focused on my phone in my hand.

"You *do* know that it's after two, and the dinner at my father's house starts at seven this evening, right?"

"Yeah, I know. I'm just going out for a few. I'll be back in time," I said. From the corner of my eyes, I watched her mouth open, then close back immediately. I really hoped that she was not about to start bitching again.

"Okay," she said, shocking me. I just knew for a fact that she was going to start yapping her mouth off, but she didn't. She simply got out of the car, then walked to the back of the trunk to get her things. Once she had everything, she closed the trunk and made her way inside.

Once I saw that the door was open and she had started walking inside of the house, I pulled off. I needed to ease my mind and smoke a blunt bad. I was all fucked up, and the only one who'd be able to help me out wasn't talking to me. I promise that I was going to find out wherever she was staying before she left and make things right again. Brinay was going to forgive me, and I was going to make sure that she did, even if I had to get on my knees and beg her. I was going to get my girl back, and that was that.

Chapter Twelve

Brinay

When I left the mall, I didn't know where I was headed. All I knew was that I had to get the hell away from that place fast. I was so nervous, mad, and pissed off that I hadn't noticed that I was speeding until Kourtney said something.

"Can you please slow down, Nay, before we end up in an accident!" she screamed, holding on tightly to her seat belt as if it wasn't gripping her tight enough.

"I'm sorry. I don't know where my mind was," I said, taking my foot off the pedal and reducing my speed. I can't believe that I let Dontie and his drama, or whatever you want to call it, get me worked up again.

"It's cool," she replied; then she changed her tone. "Are you okay, Nay?"

"Yes, I'm fine now," I replied, not believing myself. I was still shaking, and my eyes were still watery. I don't know why I just insisted on letting this man move me to places emotionally that I've never been to before. It's like he's breaking down all of the walls and barriers that I've placed up, and I can't control my own feelings anymore.

"No, you're not. I can still see that you're shaking, and the tears in your eyes that are threatening to fall are visible. You don't have to play or pretend with me. I'm your friend. You can always talk to me, Brinay. I promised I would never judge you on anything . . . no matter how horrific or terrible it is," she said, easing my nervousness a bit. "I told you that no matter what happens, I will always, and I do mean *always,* be there for you."

"I just don't know what to do," I said, shaking my head. "On one hand, I want this man to stay as far away from me as possible, but on the other hand, all I want is to love him, hold him, and feel him. Hell, I'd do anything just to be near him. I love him, and I know you can see that. I think I love him even more, now that we're going to have a baby together. Yeah, I know that's stupid of me to say that, but I can't help it, Kourtney."

"You're not stupid, Nay. It's called life. Everybody goes through that. You can't help who you love, and I'm not going to try to judge you on the situation that you're in, because like I said, everyone goes through that, some more than others. I do want you to think about this some more and understand what you do before you do it. I don't want you to be unhappy, but I also don't want you to settle for less than you're worth. So if you want, Dontie, then go ahead and see how things go."

"But the fact that I think—no—I *know* that he has another girl somewhere out there isn't really sitting well with me. I don't do that. I'm not *other woman* material. I don't play second to nobody. My mother did that, and that's how I got here. I'm not trying to go down that same path in life. You don't know the things I've been through with being my father's bastard/outside child. Like my sister and her mother treated me so bad and called me all kinds of names. They looked down on me, causing everybody else in the family to look down on me. I'm not about to let my child go through or be subject to the same thing I've been through. That ain't going to happen. I'd die or do hard time before I let anyone do anything like that to one of mine," I said, letting a lonely tear roll down my face as I sat there and confessed my fears to my best friend.

The pain of knowing that my child could possibly go through the same thing that I've gone through in life was unbearable, and it made me not want to have a child at all. Knowing that someone, someone who's supposed to show love to and for you, could cause you so much hurt and pain is crazy. I made a vow to never let that happen, and I won't, not as long as I'm alive and kicking.

"That won't happen, not while you're alive, or while I am," she finally said after a moment of silence. "We're going to be here, and I'm pretty sure that Dontie won't allow anyone to harm his child either."

"No, he's not," I said. "I've decided not to tell him about the baby, Kourt."

"Why not?" she asked in disbelief.

"Because I've decided not to," I simply replied.

"Are you sure that's what you want to do?"

"I'm positive. I don't have time for Dontie to be back and forth in my child's life like he's doing me. So to prevent him from hurting my baby, I've decided not to tell him at all."

"Okay," was all she said. I could see it in her eyes that she wanted to say something else, but she didn't. "Where are we going?" she asked, changing the subject.

"I want to make a stop before we head back to the hotel," I said, pulling into a grocery store. "You don't even have to come. I'll be in and out in a minute," I said, getting out. I didn't even cut the car off, because I was only going to be in there for a minute, two tops.

I hurried into the grocery store, trying to find what I was looking for. When I spotted the sign that said floral department, I speed walked in that direction. I carefully skimmed through the section, looking for what I'd come in here for. Once I had what I needed, I headed to the checkout counter. On my way to the front of the store, I bumped into this fine dude.

"Umm, excuse me, I'm sorry," I said apologizing because it was totally my fault.

"No, ma, I'm truly sorry. I'm sure that it was my fault," he replied.

"No, it was mine. I was so busy trying to get out of here that I wasn't paying attention to where I was going," I said sadly.

"And where are you going in such a hurry, ma'am?" he asked, obviously flirting.

"Look, I know what you're trying to do, but you can cut it out," I said, stopping him before he could fully start.

"Oh yeah, and what is that?"

"You're trying to flirt with me, but I can guarantee you that you don't want me," I said, being honest.

"And why is that?" he asked, rubbing his chin.

"Because you don't."

"Why don't you tell me why, and I'll choose if I want you or not," he said with a small smile on his face.

"Okay," I said, giving in. "You're not going to want me because I'm pregnant, and since I've just met you, of course, we know that the baby ain't yours," I said. I stood there for a few seconds before I walked off. I knew that would do it just as soon as I said the word *pregnant*. Ain't no man want to take care of a child, especially one that ain't his.

"Wait wait wait, hold on, ma," he said, running to catch up with me. I looked back at him and kept on walking. I ain't had time for this nigga. I had just made it to the register and placed my flowers on the counter when he caught up to me. "Why you giving me a hard time, ma?"

"Look, I already told you that you ain't goin' to want me, so why is ya bothering me?" I asked, turning back to him.

"You didn't give me a chance to answer you," he said. Had I not been mad with Dontie, I probably would've given the man a chance.

"I didn't have to. Your silence said it all for you," I replied.

"It wasn't that I was silent. I was just trying to see if you was playing with me or not. It doesn't bother me that you're pregnant. Hell, I'm not one of those niggas out in the streets. I can hold my own, and even though I know your baby ain't mine, if we were to develop something, I want you to know that I'll be there for both of y'all," he said.

I looked at him like he was losing his damn mind. I don't know what he was thinking, but I wasn't moved by this none whatsoever.

"Look, I don't have time for this," I said, turning back to the cashier, who'd just finished ringing up my flowers. I look at the total, grabbed my card, and handed it to her. She swiped it, then handed me a receipt and a pen. I signed it, grabbed my copy and my things, and proceeded out the door. I didn't know what dude was up to, but I really wasn't in the mood for whatever it was he was trying to do. I had other things to be doing, and playing with him wasn't one of them.

"Look, can you just give me your phone number and let me take you out sometime? I promise that if you don't like me after that, I'll leave you alone and never bother you again," he said from behind me. I stopped, contemplating his offer. One date couldn't hurt me, and like he said, if I ain't like it, then I'd never have to worry about him again.

"Okay," I said, turning to him. "Give me your phone."

"Okay," he said, smiling and handing me the phone. I programmed my number in and handed it back to him, then headed to the car. "Hey, wait! You never told me what your name was."

"I know. My name is Brinay," I told him. "I saved my number under Nay."

"That's a pretty name, ma," he replied, "My name is Alonzo, but you can either call me Lonzo or Zo for short."

"All right, Lonzo. I'll see you later. I have to go," I said walking off.

"All right, see you later," he said as he backpedaled into the store.

I smiled the rest of the way to the car, thinking about what had just gone down. I couldn't believe I just picked up some random dude in a grocery store, and pregnant at that.

I'm a bad girl, I thought as I opened the door and got in the car.

"Damn, I thought you said that you was going to be a minute," Kourtney said, biting into my ass. I know she was mad, but I didn't intend to stay in the store that long.

"I wasn't gone that long," I said, trying to save face.

"The hell not. You were damn near gone a whole half an hour. You know we on daylight saving time. It's about to get dark."

"I know," I said, backing out of the parking space.

"So where are we about to go?" she asked, looking at the flowers that I had sitting next to me. "Who are the flowers for?"

"We're going back to the hotel, and the flowers are for my mother's grave. I'll just have to drop them off there tomorrow, because I won't have enough time to drop them off today."

"Yeah, you know we still have to fix our hair, and you still need to at least take a catnap. I don't want you stressing my baby out," she said, reaching over and rubbing my stomach.

"Oh, trust, a nap is the first thing that I'll be doing once I walk into that hotel room," I said, yawning. "I'll do everything else once I get up. Besides, the little party or whatever they want to call it doesn't start until seven, which means that we'll be rolling there at least about 8:30, nine o'clock."

"As always, we gotta make an entrance," she said, cracking up.

"And you know this," I said cosigning, "I can't wait to see the look on everyone's faces when I roll up in there. I know they ain't expecting me to come, so it's going to be one interesting night. I only hope that nothing too serious pops off."

"Me too."

SKY

I know Dontie was mad at me, and I was truly sorry about pissing him off, but I wasn't feeling up to it. I know he was probably wishing that he didn't have to go to meet my parents in a few hours. To be honest, I was wishing that I could cancel everything my damn self. My period had just come down, which means that I wasn't pregnant yet again, and I was pissed, mad, confused, and hurt—all at the same time. Only the Lord knows how bad I really wanted to have Dontie's child, but that doesn't look like it's going to happen anytime soon. I don't know if something is wrong with me and that I couldn't have children, but I was going to find out, and soon.

Randell's ass has been calling and texting me since I woke up this morning like he didn't remember what I told his ass last night. I don't know what I'm going to do with him. I have to figure something out.

We'd just gotten back from the mall, and the man didn't even have the decency to come in the house. I mean, damn! He could've come in and made sure that there was no one inside or anything. How you just drop your wife off at home and not make sure that everything was okay? I knew he was mad and shit, but he was straight bugging, and that's what I don't have time for. I already had a lot going on right at this minute. I didn't need to worry about my husband too, but he would always make shit complicated.

After making sure that the front door was locked behind me, I grabbed the bags off of the floor and made my way upstairs to the bedroom. I needed to make sure that we had everything together for tonight. Once I made it to the bedroom, I placed the bags on the bed, next to the clothes that Dontie and I had put out for tonight, and went straight to the bathroom to run me some bathwater. I would take a shower, but I wasn't trying to get my hair wet. I'd already spent half the morning doing it. I wasn't trying to do it over again.

Going over to the tub, I made sure that the water was warm before I plugged up the drain and began to get undressed. Once I had stripped out of everything, I went into the room to grab my phone. After getting that, I went back into the bathroom and got in the tub.

"Aww," I said as I lowered myself down into the water. That water was feeling too good to my body, and I wasn't fully in there yet. When I was all the way into the water, I lay my head back and closed my eyes. My body really needed this right now. All I was missing was a massage and a nice glass of wine. *Lord, I wish I could just stay in here all night and never get out,* I thought to myself.

My moment of peace was short-lived by the ringing of my phone. I really wished that I had turned that damn thing off, because it was always going off when I didn't need it to, like right now. I was trying to be in peace, and this bitch wants to ring. I moved to get it, which made me splash water everywhere. "Shit," I said, getting mad at whoever it was calling me before I knew who it was. By the time I did make it to the phone, there was enough water on the floor to fill a baby's pool.

"Shit, hello," I said, answering the phone with an attitude.

"Hey, baby girl, it's Daddy," I heard my father say from the other end of the phone.

"Oh, hey, Daddy, what's going on?" I asked, quickly changing my tone.

"I was just calling to see if you was ready for tonight?" he asked.

"Umm . . . Yes, I'm all ready," I replied. "Will the whole family be there?"

"Every last one of them that's alive and able to," he said with a light chuckle. "That reminds me, your sister is going to be there also."

"You said *what* now?" I asked, trying to be sure that I heard him right.

"I said that your sister is going to be there," he said, repeating himself.

"Umm . . . okay," I said, stunned; then I thought back to yesterday when I possibly might have seen her at the hotel. "When did she get in?"

"She came down two days ago."

"Oh, okay," I said; then everything got quiet.

"That's all you have to say?" he asked.

"I mean, what else do you want me to say, Daddy?" I asked him. I hope he wasn't expecting me to be all happy and jolly for nothing. Brinay wasn't nobody to me.

"You haven't seen your sister in years, and you acting as if you don't care one way or the other," he said.

That's because I don't, I thought, rolling my eyes in my head.

"Dang, Daddy, what do you want from me? Like you said, I haven't seen the girl in years, so it ain't like we have some type of sisterly bond or whatever," I said blowing out air in frustration.

"That's the point. I expect you to be happy to see your sister. I mean, the way she left and the relationship you all had wasn't perfect, but she's still your sister, Sky." I know he was serious, because he only called me Sky when he was mad or was about to get mad. "I don't know what's going on with you two. You act as if you all were two different people from two different families and not blood."

"That's because we aren't, and I don't give two shits about her ass," I said, not realizing that I had said it loud enough for him to hear me.

"What did you just say?" he asked. I know that he heard what I said. He just wanted to see if I was going to say it again.

"Oh, nothing. Daddy, I have to go. Keyon's calling me on the other line. I'll see you when I get there," I said, abruptly hanging up the phone, not giving him time to answer.

"Lord, help me," I said, placing the phone back where it was. I spoke on the phone with Keyon for a little while before I hung up. I was no longer in the mood to sit there and soak, so I grabbed my favorite Caress body wash and washcloth and began to wash myself. I did this a few more times before I turned the shower on and rinsed off, making sure that I got every bit of soap that was on me and didn't get my hair wet. When I was done, I turned off the water, grabbed a towel, and got out.

Grabbing my phone, I headed into the bedroom. Seeing that Dontie still hadn't made it home yet and it was almost five in the evening, I went downstairs to make sure that the door was locked. Once I'd done that, I headed back upstairs, placed my phone on silent, and put it on the charger. I hung up the clothes for this evening; then I removed the towel from around my body and climbed in bed. I didn't have much time left, but I needed a quick power nap before I went to deal with all of this. I just hoped that tonight wouldn't be as exciting as the day was.

DONTIE

When I left the house, I didn't have but two things on my mind. One was to smoke a nice fat blunt, and the other was to find out where Brinay was staying at so that I can talk to and see her without all of these emotions in the air. I called her phone a couple of times, but she didn't answer. I needed to see her, because I felt as if I was going to lose my mind any minute now, and she was the only one, besides my mom, who'd be able to calm me down. I even went as far as to check all of the local hotels, but I kept coming up empty-handed. When I couldn't get in touch with her, I decided to go with my first option. Knowing that I needed someone to talk to, someone who understands me, I phoned Chance.

"What's up, man?" he asked, answering the phone.

"Ain't shit, man. Where you at?" I asked him.

"Shit, I just came from the mall. What's up with ya?"

"Man meet me at my apartment in Miami Beach. I need to smoke me a much-needed blunt to get my mind right," I said to him.

"Yo, man, who giving you problems?" he said, ready for whatever.

"Ain't shit like that, man. I just got woman problems, and I need to vent before I go crazy on somebody's ass," I said, sighing.

"Let me find out you over there stressin' over pussy, nigga," he said, laughing.

"Ain't never that, man. You already know how I do it," I replied, trying to take back what I just had said.

"Uh-huh, I hear ya," he responded. "Let me go and drop my shit off at the telly, and I'll meet you."

"Nah, man, you can just bring all of that shit and get dressed over here," I told him.

"All right, man, I'll meet you in a minute, then."

"All right, nigga," I said, hanging up the phone. Before I headed in the direction of my apartment, I tried calling Brinay's phone again. Just like before, it rang a few times before going to voice mail. "Fuck," I said, throwing the phone on the passenger seat. "The minute I see her ass, I'ma check her ass for playing with me and not answering that damn phone," I spat. "I'm tired of these bitches playing with me. I'm about to change a few things, starting with her ass."

I'm going to show their ass about playing games with me, I thought as I headed to my apartment. "They're going to start treating me like the man that I am, or I'm going to hook my foot up their asses and not think twice about it. Either way, they are going to fall in line and get it right."

It took me all of twenty minutes to make it to my apartment, and by then, I was getting a little sleepy. When I pulled up, I thought I saw someone in my parking space, but I was just tripping. I parked my car, got my weed and cigar from out of the glove compartment, and headed inside.

When I walked in the lobby, I was greeted by the doorman. He'd been babysitting my apartment when I wasn't there, and in exchange, I always give him a hefty tip.

"Good evening, Mr. Edmon," he said.

"Evening Mr. Jeffery, how's everything going with ya?" I asked him.

"Everything is fine, sir. And yourself?"

"Same shit, different day," I responded.

"Okay, then, have a good night, sir."

"You too," I said, handing him two crisp one hundred-dollar bills. "My cousin Chance will be here any minute. Can you tell him that I'm already here?"

"No problem. Thank you."

"You're welcome. Be easy," I said, making my way to the elevator. Once inside, I pressed the button to take me to the second floor.

Getting off the elevator, I made my way toward my apartment down the hall. Pulling my keys out of my pocket, I unlocked the door and headed inside. Once inside, I clicked on the light and inspected everything. Even though I paid Mr. Jeffery to watch my shit, I didn't trust nobody. Once I was sure that everything was all right and where it should be, I headed to the kitchen to grab me a quick beer.

"Damn, I ain't been in this bitch in so long that I forgot to go grocery shopping," I said once I opened the refrigerator door and realized that it was damn near empty. There was nothing in there but a couple of bottles of water, butter, cheese, milk, an onion, and some bell peppers. Since I was thirsty, I grabbed a bottle of water and closed the door. Walking toward the den area, I grabbed a seat at the table and prepared to roll a few blunts. Since I was damn near a pro, it didn't take long at all for me to roll up. When I was finished, I opened the water and took swag, temporarily quenching my thirst. Seeing as Chance hadn't made it there yet, I decided to take a shower. That'd be one less thing I'd have to do when I get home later. Since I had a three-bedroom, two-bath apartment, I'd opted to take a shower in the bedroom.

Once I was inside of the bedroom, I stripped out of my clothes and tossed them in the hamper. I turned on the shower before going back into the bedroom to grab a pair of boxers and a wife beater; then I placed my phone on the charger that was plugged in the wall next to the bed and headed back to the bathroom. I was just in time, because the bathroom was beginning to get full of steam. I placed my things on the sink, then got in.

No lie, that water felt so good that, for a moment, I wished that I had taken a bath instead of a shower. Knowing that I didn't have no time to play around, I grabbed my Dove body wash and my bath sponge and began to wash away the dirt of the day, wishing that I could erase the memories and start the whole day over. Just then, an image of Brinay today popped in my head, causing me to smile. I can't lie. I was madly in love with that woman, and just the mere thought of me losing her was too much for me to bear.

Yeah, I know that I had a woman, hell, *a wife,* for that matter, but I couldn't get Brinay out of my head and my heart. She was too good of a woman, and I don't know what I was thinking for doing the things that I was doing to her. I can't lie. If I'd met Brinay before I met Sky, there wasn't no question in this world that she was going to be my wife, and I wouldn't have no problem with leaving Sky. Unfortunately, I didn't, and now things are way different and difficult, and I don't know what to do about them.

I'd been daydreaming about what life could be like when I heard a knock on the door.

"Yo, Dontie, nigga, you in there?" Chance's voice came booming through the door.

"Yeah, man, I'm about to get out," I yelled back at him.

"All right. I'm going to go put my things in the room down the hall," he responded.

"A'ight, cool," I replied. Jumping out of my mind, I lathered the bath sponge again with body wash and began to wash my body before I let the water rinse the suds off and got out. Taking my boxers, I put them on, followed by my wife beater. I then went to my dresser, where I kept my Degree deodorant, and rubbed some on my armpits. Opening the drawer, I found a pair of socks and black and gray basketball shorts before I went into the living room in search of Chance.

It didn't take me long to find him, because the smell of weed led me to where he was sitting in the living room, smoking on one of the blunts that I had rolled earlier.

"Damn, nigga, it's about time," he said, taking a tote of the blunt he had between his two fingers. "I thought you was going to be in that shower forever, man."

"Hell, you took so damn long to get here that I decided to take a shower," I told him.

"Yeah, man, I had to swing by the hotel to get the rest of my things for the night. That's why I was a li'l late," he said, handing me the blunt.

"Nigga, you always forgetting something," I said, taking one long pull from it. I let the smoke fill my lungs before I repeated the motion, taking an extralong pull the second time.

"Damn, nigga, your mind must really be gone the way you pulling on that blunt like that," he said, laughing.

"Shit, it's not all the way gone. I just been going through it lately," I said, taking another pull before I handed the blunt back to him.

"Looks like it," he said, knocking the ashes in the ashtray on the table. "Let's run it."

"A'ight man," I said, sitting back on the couch. I then placed my legs on the coffee table as I began to tell him everything that's been going on. I told him about the trip to Jamaica, how I bought a ring for Brinay and ended up marrying Sky. By the expression on his face, I can tell he was taken aback by that part. I proceeded to tell him about how I thought Sky was cheating on me, how I know something is up with Brinay, but she ain't telling me, and how everything happened today at the mall. He didn't say anything. He just sat there listening to me put everything on the table, including my daily growing feelings for Brinay. I know that it was a lot for him to hear, because it was a lot for me to say. When I was finished, we had done

smoked the second blunt and was about to light up the
third one.

For a minute, we just sat there in silence, as the
thoughts of what I just said played over in our minds. I
sat there with my head against the sofa as I waited for
him to tell me what he thought. When a minute too long
passed, I opened my eyes to find him staring at me.

"What?" I asked.

"Man man man," he repeated, "You done got yourself
into some shit here, fam," he said, lighting the blunt. It
was now his turn to take a drastic pull from it.

"Tell me about it, man," I said, shaking my head. I knew
I had gotten myself into some shit. The problem is that I
didn't know how to get myself out of it now.

"You want to know what I think, fam?" he asked, handing me the blunt. I looked back at him and nodded my
head, then took a pull from it.

"Yeah, man, go ahead and tell me what ya think about
all of this shit here," I replied.

"Man, to be honest with you, you need to cut one of
them loose, and since you done went ahead and married
ole girl, that someone has got to be Brinay, fam." He said
just what I thought he was going to say.

"I can't do that, man. I can't let go of Brinay, Chance," I
said, shaking my head.

"Fam, you have to. No, scratch that—you *need* to let her
go. You just said that you care about her, but you done up
and married some other chick. Did you even stop to think
about how she's going to feel if she finds this out? You
already said that she's down here and you don't know
why. What if she has people out here, and they tell her?
She's going to be devastated, and she's going to end up
resenting you. If you love her like you say you do, then
the best thing for you to do is let her go before things get
even crazier than they are now," he replied.

"Fam, I hear what you're saying, and I know that it may be true, but I love the girl too much to just let her go, man. I can't do that if I wanted to. My heart wouldn't even allow me to," I said, placing my head in my hand. I was even more fucked up now than I was earlier today. To even think that I had to let Brinay go is beyond me, and I knew that I couldn't tell her the truth, because, like he said, she was going to be devastated if and when she did find out. I knew that telling her was out of the question, and I decided right then and there that I was going to ride this thing out as long as I could and deal with the consequences when that time came.

"All right, man. That's on you, but I'm telling you now that you're going to regret it. If not now, then later on in life," he said, getting up from the couch. "I'm going to take a shower, my nigga."

"All right, man," I responded. Once he was gone, I grabbed the rest of the blunt and thought about all he was saying. One side of me wanted to tell Brinay and let the chips fall where they may, but I knew that if I told her, I was going to lose her forever, and I wasn't ready for that, at least not yet, which is why I'm deciding not to tell her at all. Like I said, I was going to ride this roller coaster until it came to an end.

Before I knew it, I had done finished the blunt and had fallen asleep. If it wasn't for Chance being here and waking me up, I knew for a fact that I would've been there the whole night, and Sky would've been even madder than she was today.

"Yo, man, get up. It's ten minutes to seven, and you got to go all the way home to get dressed," he said, shaking me and trying to wake me up. "Yo, Dontie, man, get up. You're already going to be late."

"What?" I asked confused.

"Man, it's almost seven o'clock, and you have to go," he said again. This time, I heard him loud and clear.

"Fuck!" I yelled, getting up from the sofa. "How the hell did I even fall asleep that fast?"

"I don't know, man. Must been that weed. All I know is that you need to be getting out of here before ole girl starts calling," he said, heading back to where he'd come from. I hurried into the bedroom, trying to finding a pair of jeans and my shoes. Once I found them, I threw them on, found my keys, grabbed my phone, and left the room. I checked my phone to see that I had about twenty missed calls from Sky, and two from Brinay, along with a couple of text messages. *I'll check that shit later,* I thought.

"All right, man, I'm out," I yelled down the hall to Chance.

"A'ight, cool. Text me the address when ya make it home. I'll see you later, man," he said from the bedroom door.

"All right, man," I said, and with that, I was out the door. I didn't even go to the elevator, because I knew that just because I was in a rush, it was going to take forever to come, so I took the stairs. Once I made it to the lobby, I ran all the way to my car. I unlocked the door, got in, and started it. I pulled out of the parking spot and drove off. I silently prayed that Sky wouldn't be mad, like I knew that she'd be, as I drove like a bat out of hell trying to get home, hoping that I didn't get stopped by the police or get into an accident on the way.

Chapter Thirteen

Sky

I jolted up out of my sleep in a hurry. I must have over-slept, because when I looked at the clock, I noticed that it was almost seven o'clock at night. I hurried around the room trying to get my act together. In the midst of everything, I noticed that Dontie still hadn't made it home, which only pissed me off more than I was already.

"He's going to make me hurt his ass," I said as I made my way to the bathroom. Grabbing a washcloth and my toothbrush, I prepared to brush my teeth and wash my face. When I was done, I went back into the bedroom and grabbed my makeup bag. I didn't really need any makeup, so I only added a little bit here and there. After doing that, I headed back into the room and grabbed my baby oil so that I could oil my body up. Right when I started to pour some on my legs, I heard the sound of the alarm going off. I got up from the bed and began walking to the door when I heard it being disarmed, which meant that Dontie had finally decided to bring his ass home. I was going to wait by the door and chew out his ass, but I didn't have the time or the patience for that at this moment. I'd wait until tomorrow to give his ass the business and find out what the hell was up with him and all of these games he was now playing.

I heard him before I saw him. I knew he was standing in the doorway looking at me naked. I hope he wasn't trying to get none, because that was a no-go, and even if I could've, I wouldn't have anyway. I wasn't about to fuck his ass, not knowing where he was coming from and what he's been doing.

"Why are you standing there staring at me when you need to be in the bathroom taking a shower so that we can get dressed and get out of here?" I said as I continued to oil my body.

"I don't need to take a shower," he said, now walking into the room.

"And why's that?" I asked, now looking up at him. His eyes were red, and I could already smell the weed coming from his clothes, and he hadn't made it all the way over to me yet.

"Because I already took one," he said.

"Oh yeah, and where the fuck you took a shower at if you ain't took one here?" I asked, getting up from the bed.

"I got a room at a hotel in Miami Beach," he replied.

I know his ass was lying, but I didn't have any proof to back that up. "Yeah, I fucking bet. Let me find out you got some bitch you fucking with . . . I promise you ain't gon' like what's going to happen, Dontie," I said, staring him in his eyes. For a moment, we stood there mugging each other as if we were about to start throwing punches. I know that's what I wanted to do to his ass right now. He was the first to walk away, laughing as he headed to the bathroom.

"What's so fucking funny?" I asked, walking behind him.

"You. You be having all of this mouth on you, but I never seen you back none of that shit up," he said, grabbing his toothbrush and squirting toothpaste on it. "I told your ass once before, that if you ain't gon' walk the walk, don't talk the talk."

"You don't know what I'm going to do," I said, defending myself.

"No, I just know what you *ain't* going to do," he said, then began brushing his teeth.

"Yeah, all you got to do is try me and see," I said, walking off. I didn't have time to play with him. I already let almost twenty minutes pass, entertaining his ass. Grabbing the oil, I finished oiling my body before I went to grab our clothes out of the closet and placed them on the bed. I then went over to the dresser and grabbed the purple bra and pantie set that I had gotten from Victoria's Secret earlier in the day. I grabbed my shoes from the rack in my closet and began getting dressed just as Dontie came out of the bathroom.

"Where are my things?" he asked, standing in front of me.

"They're over there on the bed. Hurry up and get dressed so we can get out of here," I said.

"Yeah, a'ight," he said smartly. I looked at him and rolled my eyes before I began putting on my dress. When I was done, I made my way to the mirror. Taking the cap off of my head, I let my curls flow freely. Thank God that none of them had gotten wet. Grabbing a comb and some bobby pins, I began pinning my hair up to the side. When I was satisfied with how everything looked, I grabbed my jewelry box, along with Dontie's box, and placed them on the dresser. I sprayed on a few pumps of my Mariah Carey perfume before I began to apply my jewelry. Once I was done, I did a quick once-over in the mirror before I went to put on my shoes. After applying everything that I needed, I went over to the full-length mirror to see how I looked. I was straight killing it, as usual.

"Are you ready to go?" Dontie asked, stepping behind me. I looked at him through the mirror, and I had to say that I was very pleased with the way he looked. Looking at him now and seeing how good he looked made me forgot about what happened earlier.

"You look good, ma."

"Thanks, baby," I said, kissing his lips. "You don't look bad yourself. Now, let's go because we're already late as it is."

"All right, ma. Come on," he said, leading the way. Grabbing my purse, phone, and keys, I made my way down the stairs. I then made sure that everything was off, the alarm was on, and the doors were all locked before I followed Dontie outside. Getting in the car, it smelled just like weed, so I made him put all of the windows down and sprayed a little perfume inside the car before we got on the road and made our way to my father's house, which was only about fifteen to twenty minutes away. I was nervous and excited that this night had finally come, and all the people who I loved were going to come together as a family . . . well, almost all of them.

BRINAY

As I sat there in the mirror admiring myself, I couldn't help but to feel nervous about this evening. I hadn't seen my family in years, and I knew that it was going to feel funny, because when I left here, me and my family wasn't on the best of terms. Hell, my sister and I hadn't been on good terms since we were first introduced, so I knew tonight was going to be weird, and eventful.

"Come on, Nay," Kourtney said from behind me. "It's already almost eight o'clock. If you stand in front of that mirror any longer, we're going to be here all night."

"Okay. I'm coming," I said, applying a little more lip gloss to my lips. "How do I look?"

"You look like you always do," she replied, causing me to frown. "Beautiful!"

"Thanks," I said, letting out a nervous chuckle. "You don't look so bad yourself."

"Thanks, baby mama," she said, smiling. "I be trying."

"All right, now that we know that we're some showstoppers, let's go find the show to stop," I said to her. I walked over to the bed and grabbed my keys, the key card, and my yellow clutch.

"Today, Kourtney, today."

"Girl, I'm coming," she said, picking up her purse. "Come on. Let's be out, Big Momma."

"You're going to stop with all of these nicknames that you're giving me," I said, laughing, as we walked out the door.

"You know I can't help it. I'm just excited to meet the baby, that's all," she said, laughing with me.

Me too, I said in my head, instead of saying it to her. *Me too.*

"Oh my God, Nay, your daddy got bank, girl," Kourtney said, her eyes beaming like she was a kid in a candy store. "What did you say he do again?"

"I didn't," I replied. My father stayed in an upscale neighborhood out in Key Biscayne. He had a six-bedroom, five-and-a-half bathroom house with all that extra shit added to it. I mean, dude had a six-car garage, a big-ass driveway, a gym, and a pool in the backyard. I can't lie, the house was nice, but I don't know why she was getting so bucked up behind it. After all, it was only a house. Ain't like he was going to be able to take any of that with him when he dies.

"Girl, you're one crazy sister. If my daddy had lived in something like this, I'd be in that bih every day," she said, getting a little too excited for me.

"That's easy for you to say. You didn't live the life that I was living. I could care less about any of this, because material shit doesn't make me. Not one bit," I replied. I guess she got the hint that I was beginning to get in a sour mood, so she ended up dropping the subject altogether.

"Damn, the entire family must be here, because I can't find a parking spot no-damn-where," I said, getting frustrated. I'd been driving around for a good five minutes, and I hadn't found a parking spot yet.

"There goes one right there," Kourtney said as a car pulled out of a spot. Just as fast as that car pulled off, I pulled in. I wasn't trying to let no one else get that spot before me. I cut the car off and just sat there, staring at the house. For a minute, I was lost in my thoughts, thinking about everything that I've been through in there.

"What's wrong? Are you okay?" Kourtney asked, grabbing my arm.

"Nothing. I'm fine, boo," I said, "You ready?"

"I'm ready when you are," she said, looking at me.

"All right, then, let's go," I said. I took a deep breath before I removed my keys from the ignition and got out.

I waited for Kourtney to walk over to my side before I began walking toward the house. I was happy that we didn't park too far from the house, because my feet were beginning to hurt and we'd just gotten there. It was cool, though, because I had some flats in the car.

With each step that I took, my heart rate sped up. My heart was beating so fast that I thought it was going to pop out of my chest any minute now. I was so nervous that my hands were beginning to shake.

"Are you sure that you want to go inside?" Kourtney asked, stopping me in front of the door.

"Umm, yeah, I'm sure," I replied, not so sure my damn self.

"I mean, if you want to leave here and go back to the hotel, we can leave right now," she said.

"No, ma'am. I'm here now, so I might as well just get this over with."

"Okay, then, let's go," she said, ringing the doorbell. As I stood there waiting, I thought I was going to piss on myself. I don't know if I was afraid or anxious, but what I *do* know is that it was too late to turn back now. I was about to say something to Kourtney when the door opened, causing my words to get caught up in my throat.

"Brinay?" she asked with a look of shock written on her face.

"Hello, Veronica," I said to my dad's wife. She stood there, staring at me as if she were waiting for me to disappear or something. As I stood there face-to-face with her, I couldn't help but to remember all of the things that she did to me as a child. I had a mind to spit in her face, but the view of my father walking up behind her stopped me.

"Who is it, dear?" he asked behind her. She didn't answer him, so he looked out the door for himself. The minute he saw me standing there, he practically threw her ass out of the way and came straight for me, giving me a hug. "You made it!"

"Yeah, I did," I replied, barely able to breathe. He was hugging on me so tight that I thought he was going to suffocate me. "I can't breathe."

"Oh, I'm sorry, baby. I'm just happy to see you. I haven't seen you in years," he said, letting me go.

"This here is my friend, Kourtney. Kourtney this here is my father, Brian Williams." I said, introducing the two of them and trying to act as if I didn't hear what he had just said.

"It's nice to meet you, sir," she said, extending her hand for him to shake.

"Same here," he said, bypassing her hand and giving her a hug instead.

"Ahem," we heard from behind us. We turned to see Veronica standing there with her arms folded and her leg shaking with a look on her face that said she wasn't pleased. I caught my dad rolling his eyes before he turned back to me.

"Come on, let's go inside," he said, grabbing my arm as Kourtney followed behind me. On the way inside, I locked eyes with Veronica. She rolled her eyes, causing me to smirk. I don't know what was her problem, but I can guarantee that she don't want none of this here. This ain't like them old days when she used to rule me. I'm not a kid anymore, and I don't give a fuck about her old ass, so I wouldn't have a problem with chewing her ass out in front of all these damn people.

"Chill," Kourtney said once she noticed the look on my face.

"I am," I whispered.

"Uh-huh."

As I followed behind my father into the dining room, I silently said a prayer, asking him to give me the patience to be able to deal with these folks tonight, because I wasn't trying to go to jail for murder, and that's what was just going to happen if anybody tried me.

SKY

Just like I had thought, once we had arrived at my father's house, I knew he was going to be asking me twenty-one questions about why I was late. I told him that I had forgotten something important back at the house and had to turn all the way around to go and get it. Just like that, he bought my story but turned his attention to Dontie and his cousin, Chance. Like any normal man and father, he wanted to know any and everything about them. Where they were from? How old they were? What did they do for a living? How much did they make? Did they have any kids? Who were their parents? Were they criminals? If so, how many times had they been arrested and for what? I mean, the man asked so many questions I thought that we were on a job interview or in an inter-rogation room or something. Hell, he had me scared, and he was *my* daddy. I thought he was going to ask both Dontie and Chance for their Social Security numbers so that he could run a background check on them.

"Daddy, please, be still," I whispered in his ear, spotting the looks on both Dontie's and Chance's faces.

"I'm just trying to get to know these men, Skylar," he replied. "How long did you say that you've been dating Dontie?"

I didn't, I thought in my head.

"We've been dating for almost two years now, Daddy," I said in a sweet voice, because I knew he was going to be mad about me keeping Dontie a secret this whole time.

"And *why* are we just *now* meeting him?" he asked with an attitude.

"Because I wanted to make sure that this was going to last before I introduced you all to each other," I said sadly.

"Are you sure that's the *only* reason?" he asked, looking me in the eyes as if he was searching through my soul to see if I was lying or something.

"I'm positive," I quickly said.

"Okay."

"Let's go in the dining room, then, shall we? Everyone's been here waiting on you to arrive," he said just as the doorbell rang. "Excuse me."

"No, honey, I'll get it. Why don't you show them to their seats," my mother said, heading for the door before he said anything else. I guess she was trying to get away from him, just like I was.

Once we made it to the dining room, I spotted my whole family sitting at the table. I mean, *everybody* was there, from my uncle to my aunts, my little cousins, and all of their children. Well, everyone besides Brinay. I'm not surprised, though. I knew she wasn't going to show up. She always chickened and bailed on things we had at home.

"Hello, everybody," I said, waving as my father directed both me and Dontie to our seats. Once Dontie, Chance, and I were seated, I began to introduce them to a few people in the family. I noticed that on one side of us there were two empty seats. I'm guessing they saved them for Brinay and whoever she was bringing, *if* she had someone to bring. I'm just glad that they were next to Dontie and not me, because I didn't want her sitting nowhere near me.

"I'll be right back," my daddy said. "I'm going to see what's taking your mother so long at the door."

"Okay," I replied. As I looked around at all of the people who I loved and I knew loved me, it felt good to know that I'd be adding Dontie to my family.

"I think your father's a cool dude," Dontie whispered in my ear.

"He is," I said, grabbing his hand. "Baby, my daddy didn't mean any harm. He was only trying to get to know you. He means good, I promise."

"Yeah. Uh-huh. I thought I was applying for a job instead of meeting my girl's family, with all of the question that he was asking," he said, looking uncomfortable.

"I thought the same thing myself," I said, trying to crack a joke to lighten the mood.

"Hell, yeah," he said, joining me in laughter. He then bent over and said something to Chance that caused both of them to laugh.

"You know I lo—" I started to say, but stopped when I spotted my father walking into the den with my sister and some high yellow chick behind him. *Fuck,* I thought as our eyes connected with each other from across the table. For a minute, I sat there just staring at my little sister. I turned to find both Dontie and Chance looking at her as if they'd seen a celebrity or something. Their mouths were so wide open that I thought something was going to fly in.

"Close your mouth," I said, kicking Dontie under the table.

"That's your *sister?*" he asked, looking confused.

"Yes, why?" I answered, wanting to know.

"No reason. I just thought y'all kind of looked alike," he said, turning his head to Chance, who was looking as if he was about to start drooling any minute. I was glad that I didn't have to worry about my husband and my sister, because I'm more than sure that Chance was going to try to talk to her, being the player that he was.

Turning my attention back to Brinay as she stood talking to our grandmother, I felt some type of way. I can't lie. Even though I haven't seen my sister in years, she still looks as beautiful as the day she first came into this world. Just like me, everyone around the room stopped and stared at her. Even in a casual outfit, she still was a showstopper, which was one of the reasons why I hated her in the first place. It's been like that since we were kids. Even thought I was the big sister, people would always stop and stare at Brinay, commenting on how beautiful she was and how long her jet-black hair was. She even had a pair of green eyes that drove every boy in school and around the neighborhood crazy. At first, my mother tried to convince my father that she wasn't his, because of her eyes, but once both of them took a DNA test and the results came back and said that she was indeed his, she couldn't say any more about it, which only made her madder and had her hating both my father and Brinay. She hated my father for cheatin', and she hated Brinay for being a reminder of the woman my father cheated on her with. To this day, my mother and father still fought about that, and the woman was now dead and gone.

My eyes followed her the whole way over to where she was sitting, which happened to be next to me and my husband. I was sitting there stuck. I didn't come out of my thoughts until my mother nudged me in my back. I looked back her, and she gave me a reassuring smile before moving to take her seat next to my father.

"Okay," my father said, trying to get everyone's attention. "Good evening, everyone. I've called the family here today because Skylar has an announcement, and she wanted the whole family here so we can hear it together. When she's done, we're going to give each person a chance to speak, announce, or say anything that they want to, and after that, we're going to eat and spend some time together as a family."

"You now have the floor, Skylar," my mother added once he was done and seated. I got up from my seat and took a look around at all of the people. Once my eyes landed on my little sister, I decided to introduce Dontie as my husband, just to mess with her.

"Everyone, I'd like y'all to meet my *husband*. Dontie, this is my sister Brinay. Brinay, this is my *husband*, Dontie."

Just like I wanted, I watched her mouth fall open. She tried to hurry and close it before anyone saw her, but it was too late, because *everyone* around the table saw it. I'm sure she was a bit surprised by that, but I didn't care. I just wanted her to know that this was one man that I had that she couldn't get or take away from me, even if she tried to. I skipped over all of the noise that I heard in the background when I introduced Dontie as my husband.

"Nice to meet you," she said, extending her hand for him to shake.

"Likewise," he said returning the gesture. She looked at me, and I smirked before turning back to everyone else.

"I called everyone here to introduce the man in my life, who also happens to be my husband. We got married two weeks ago in Jamaica," I said dangling my left hand so that everyone could get a good look at that big-ass rock on my finger. No one said anything. Everyone turned to my father, waiting for him to speak first. I watched as he looked at me, then back at the glass of wine in his hand, before he got up and walked over to the bar that stood on the left side of the table. He then poured two glasses of scotch, grabbed them, and walked toward us.

Once he made it over to us, he handed Dontie a glass before he raised the other one he had in his hand, smiled, and said, "Congratulations and welcome to the family." He then threw his drink back, taking it to the head, before he encouraged Dontie to do the same. I'm sure everyone was waiting to see if he would blow up, but surprisingly, he played it cool. Once all that was out of the way, we started hearing a bunch of *congratulations* and *welcome to the family* from everyone. I sat there, happy that everything went well and not the total opposite. I took a look at my sister, who was now sitting there confused, just as I thought she would. *Yeah, bitch, I got married first, and my nigga looks good. You can't have him, though,* I thought. As if she heard me, she looked at me, and I could've sworn that I saw a smirk sitting on her face. She then reached past her friend and talked to our cousin Keys. I knew them bitches had to be talking about me, because they never liked me, but right now, I didn't care, because I was on cloud nine and ain't nothing was going to knock me off of it . . . and I do mean *nothing.*

Chapter Fourteen

Brinay

Before I made into the dining room, something told me that some shit was about to go down and that I should just bail right then and there, but I didn't. I knew that most of the people sitting at that table wouldn't have expected me to show up to their "family get-together," so I wanted to show them different. I wanted to show them that I wasn't that same little girl anymore, that I'm not afraid of them, that they don't intimidate me not one bit, and that they can't do the things they used to do to me anymore. I wanted to show them the New Brinay. She's confident, smart, and classy . . . with a mean side if someone pushed her too far. I wanted to show them that, even though they did everything to break me as a child for being the product of my father cheating on his wife, I didn't break—that I'm still standing, and *nothing* was going to break me down. I was prepared for whatever the night had to bring.

"Are you okay?" my father whispered to me as we neared the room.

"Yes, I'm fine," I said with a smile.

"Okay, then," he responded. I was only a few seconds away from being face-to-face with everybody, and I have to admit that I was taking the shit like a G. I had my game face on, and my million-dollar smile on full display that always won people over.

Before we stepped foot in the room, there was a lot of talking going on, but the moment I came into view, all of that stopped. Just like I knew it, I was a showstopper. I made each and every last one of them stop whatever they were doing to stare at me. *Got 'em*, I thought. I mean, it was so quiet in there that you could hear a pin drop on the floor.

My eyes roamed over the table at all of the familiar faces, when they landed on my sister. From the way she was looking at me, I could tell that she was surprised to see me there. On the inside, I was smiling, knowing that I was fucking up her whole day, and it felt great. For a moment, we stood there, staring at each other as if we were the only two in the world. We kept eye contact until my father showed Kourtney and me to our seats.

"Umm, Nay," Kourtney said kicking my feet under the table, trying to get my attention.

"What, Kourt?" I asked, turning to her. She opened her mouth to speak when my father's voice boomed through the room. He started saying some shit about Sky and why she wanted us here, which instantly made me bored and caused me to turn my attention elsewhere. Just when I thought I was done hearing her name, she began speaking. She then turned my way, saying that she had someone to introduce. That's when I first noticed Chance sitting there at the table. I gave him a look as if to ask what the fuck he was doing here when she said something about a *husband*. I immediately turned back around.

Words couldn't explain how I was feeling right now. I looked at Dontie as he looked at me, and his expression was blank, as if he were wishing that he could be somewhere else and not here at this moment. Hearing my sister, the bitch that made my life a living hell, introduce the man who held my heart and who was the father of my child, saying that he was *her* husband was crazy. I felt like

I was in a movie or as if I was on the TV show *Pranked*. I thought for sure that Ashton Kutcher was about to jump out any minute now, but he didn't.

"This is one small fucking world," Kourtney whispered loud enough for me to hear.

I turned and looked and her like "Ya think?" and turned back to my sister's *husband*.

I had a mind to call him out on his shit, but I had another thought, so instead, I played the game cool and acted as if I didn't even know him.

"Nice to meet you," I said, reaching my hand for him to shake.

"Likewise," he said, returning the gesture. When our hands, touched I felt a jolt of static go through my body, so I hurried and pulled away. I looked around the table to see if anyone had caught that, but they were so tuned in to what my sister was saying that they didn't. Soon after, everyone started getting happy, congratulating her and asking when the wedding was going to be. I didn't get a chance to hear whatever it was she had to say or what anyone else in the family had to say, because I was so lost in my own thoughts. I felt so distant that I didn't know if I was coming or going.

As I sat there, I started thinking about everything that Dontie and I had, all of the things we've been through, the many times that he said that he loved me. All of that was a lie, and it sickened me to know that. I knew the man had another woman, but for that woman to be my fucking sister is crazy. Like, where in the world do you see a man messing with two sisters? *Two fucking sisters*. I mean, ain't no medal for this. This right here takes the cake, baby. I'm 'bouta have a baby by the man who's married to my sister, so that mean my child would be my sister's nephew or niece. *Ain't that some shit,* I thought, shaking my head. I had to laugh at that. It was either do that or break down crying, and if I broke down crying, everyone would want to know why was I crying, and I was nowhere ready to deal with that. At least not right now, I wasn't.

"Brinay, Brinay," I heard my name being called. I turned and noticed my father standing there looking at me.

"Hu-Huh?" I asked, turning my focus to him.

"Do you have anything that you would like to say, anything that you want to share with the family?" he asked me.

"Oh no, I don't," I quickly replied, causing Kourtney to kick my feet once again. I gave her that *bitch, kick me again and we're going to fight* look before I turned back to my father. "On second thought, I do."

"Okay, well, it's your turn. The floor is all yours," he said, taking his seat.

"Okay," I said. For a few moments I sat there quiet, but then I turned and got a glimpse of my sister and her new husband holding hands next to me, and that gave me the boost to say what I had to say, so I stood up from my seat and looked at everyone.

"Well, a few days ago, I found out that I was going to be a mother."

"You're pregnant?" my father asked me like I just didn't say that a few seconds ago. By the look on his face, he appeared to be shocked, maybe.

"Yes, Daddy, I'm pregnant. I'm going to be a mother," I said rubbing on my stomach for emphasis.

"Jesus, help me, because you girls are trying to kill me," he said, clutching his chest as if he was about to have a heart attack. "I just found out that one of my daughters has been hiding a man and is now married. Now, I find out that my baby girl is pregnant. Is there anything else that the two of you aren't telling me?" he asked looking to me, then to Skylar.

"Nah, I told you everything, Daddy," she said first.

"No, that's all," I responded after her.

"Okay, good," he said getting up from his chair. I thought he was going to pour himself another drink, but instead, he came walking over to me. "Congratulations," he said, kissing me on my forehead. "I'm going to be a grandpa," he proudly said to everyone around the table. Again, they began saying congratulations. When everyone was done, he motioned to the servant to bring in the food. Once everyone had their plates, we bowed our head to say grace. As always, my father led the prayer.

We were only a few minutes into it when somewhere around the table, I felt someone watching me. I looked up to see who it was, and I saw Dontie watching me. He mouthed the words "I'm sorry," with the saddest pair of eyes that I'd ever seen. Normally, when he does this, I'd forgive him, but not this time. This right here was unforgivable, and for that, I never *ever* wanted to see his ass again. Rolling my eyes, I placed my head back down, just in time for my father to say amen.

Not a minute later, everyone began digging into their food. I wasn't hungry, so I pushed my plate away from in front of me. Even though I tried to play hard, I felt the tears welling up in my eyes. My heart was aching right now.

"Are you okay?" Kourtney asked, looking at me in sympathy.

"Ask me that when we leave here," I said, getting up from my seat. She looked at me and tried to get up, but I stopped her. "I'm only going to the bathroom. I'll be right back."

"Do you need me to come with you?" she asked.

"Nah, I'm okay. Eat your food. I'm sure it's great."

"Nay, where are you going?" my father asked, causing everyone to stop eating and look at me. "Are you leaving?"

"I'm going to the bathroom. My stomach is a little upset. I'll be right back," I said to him.

"Okay," he said digging back into his food as everyone followed suit. I took one last look at Dontie, who was watching me like a hawk, before I hurried out of the room. I didn't need anyone else saying something. My eyes were already getting teary. Lord, I wasn't prepared to answer anything if these tears began falling down my face.

I made it to the bathroom, just as the dam broke and the tears started rolling down my cheeks. Who was I trying to kid? I felt mortified. I felt as if I was about to die any minute, that's how bad my heart ached. The one man who I broke all the rules for ended up doing exactly what I was trying to prevent. He hurt me, and this wasn't just something that I could get over with time. This was going to leave a permanent scar. This right here was probably going to make me hate men. I might even turn to the other team. Men are so selfish. They think only about themselves. I bet Dontie didn't stop to think how this was going to affect me, how I'd feel when I found this out. He was just like any other dog-ass nigga in this world. He wanted to have his cake and eat it too, no matter what was going on or who it had affected. He did just what he wanted to.

A few minutes had gone by, and I was still sitting on the floor crying my eyes out. I felt bad, and on top of that, my head, stomach, and back started hurting me again, plus, I was beginning to get a little light-headed. I decided that it was probably best if I left and went back to the hotel room. Getting up from the floor, I walked over to the sink, turned the water on, and splashed some on my face. Once I was done, I grabbed a towel and padded the water off of my face. After making sure that I looked presentable, I opened the door and was about to leave . . . when I saw the last person that I was expecting to see.

"What do you want, Dontie?" I asked. I really didn't feel like talking to him, nor did I want to be bothered.

"I need to talk to you," he said, trying to enter the bathroom.

"Nah, you don't need to do nothing but leave me alone and go attend to your wife," I said, putting a hand up to stop him.

"Brinay, I swear I didn't have no idea that the two of you even knew each other, let alone were sisters," he began to explain himself, because he knew damn well what he did was fucked up.

"Dontie, honestly, I don't care. Whether you knew if Sky and I were sisters doesn't matter to me. Well, it does, but that's not the point. Just knowing that you had another woman was fucked up. You played me like I wasn't shit, like I didn't mean a damn thing to you. You actually stood in my face and lied about the shit, and now you come with this bullshit," I said as unwanted tears began rolling down my face again.

"Baby, I'm sorry. I really am sorry," he said, trying to touch me.

"Don't touch me, Dontie, I mean it, or I will go out there and fuck everything up," I said, which caused him to back up. "From now on, Dontie, if you see me, please don't speak to me, don't call or text my phone, or stop by my apartment, and don't send Chance over there to check on me, either. I'm through with both of you. Now move."

"Ma, it doesn't have to be like that," he said, blocking my way.

"It does, and it will. Just leave me the fuck alone, Tae," I said, pushing past him.

"What about the baby then, Nay?" he asked, grabbing my arm. "What's going to happen?"

"What about it?"

"Are you going to let me see my child? I need to be there for my child," he said sadly.

"Hell, no, you don't have to worry about that. I got that covered. I don't want or need you anywhere near my baby, Dontie," I replied.

"Ma, you can't do that. I get that you're mad with me, and you don't want me around you, but please don't keep my child away from me," he begged.

"*Your* child? How do you know that it's even *your* child?" I asked, taunting him.

"Be real. You know I was the only one you was messing with, so I know that baby is mine. You can go 'head with all that dumb shit you spitting right now," he said, looking hurt.

"Yeah, keep believing that if you want to. Like I said, stay away from me. You don't have to worry about *my* child. I'll do anything to make sure that he/she is straight," I said. I stood there looking at him before I shook my head and walked off. I didn't have time for Dontie. I already saw his true colors, and even though I loved him, I know who he really is, and I didn't want no part of his ass.

When I made it back to the table, everyone was just about done with their food, and they were now serving dessert. Even though that triple chocolate cake looked great, it was time for me get up out of here. I'd already been here too long, and I was beginning to feel some type of way.

"Come on, I'm ready," I whispered to Kourtney. I grabbed my purse and keys before making my way over to where my father was seated. "Dad, it was great to see you and everyone else, but I have to go."

"Why?" he asked. "Is something wrong?"

"No, I'm feeling worse, and I'm getting sleepy," I replied.

"Okay. Well, let me walk you to the door then," he said, getting up from his seat, just as Kourtney made it over to us.

"Okay," I replied. I made sure to say good-bye to my grandmother before I followed him to the door. On our way out, I spotted Dontie and Chance talking by the stairs, I hadn't even seen when he got up and left the room. When they noticed us, their conversation halted. I'm guessing they were talking about everything that went on tonight. Whatever it was, I didn't care. I rolled my eyes before I looked away.

"It was great seeing you, baby girl," my father said once we made it to the door. "I really missed you. You have to come by more often."

"It's was great seeing you also, Daddy," I said, hugging him. "I'll come by when I'm done with school and everything."

"No, you're going to come by when my grandchild makes an appearance, in a few months," he said, pulling back. "Don't make me have to take a trip up there for you, now."

"Okay," I said, laughing.

"It was nice meeting you, young lady," he said, hugging Kourtney.

"It was nice meeting you too," she replied.

"All right now, y'all be careful and call me when you make it to your hotel room," he told us.

"Okay," we both said as we began walking toward the car. Since we were parked close to the house, it took no time at all to make it there. Turning back, I noticed that my father was still standing in the doorway. Unlocking the door, we got in the car. I then started the car and moved it out of its parking spot before beeping my horn and driving off. I know what I said to my father, but truth be told, this was going to be my last time at his house. I wasn't coming back to Miami. I was kissing this place good-bye once and for all.

Two weeks later

As I sat there watching all of the couples talk and interact with each other, I couldn't help but to feel sad. I'd finally made an appointment to see the doctor, and I was very scared about what I might find. All I wanted is for my baby's father to be here, but that can't happen, and I was okay with that. But I wasn't prepared for this at all. What if the doctor said that something was wrong with my child? Since I didn't come to the doctor sooner, I don't know if something is wrong with my baby or not. I was hoping that nothing was, because I'd be devastated if it was. I didn't sleep a wink the night before, because I was anxious and nervous about this day.

"Brinay Williams," the nurse holding the clipboard said, looking around the room. I got up from my seat and walked over to her.

"That's me," I said softly. I couldn't believe that I was actually this scared.

"Follow me this way, please," she said, leading me to the back of the office. Grabbing my chart from the nurse's station, she placed it in the little box outside of room 3 before opening the door and allowing me to go in. She walked over to the table, grabbed a paper gown, and handed it to me. "You can take off everything from the waist down. The doctor will be with you shortly."

"Okay," I said, taking the gown out of her hand. I waited until she was gone before I started undressing. Once the gown was on, I got on the bed and waited for the doctor to come in the room. Not even two minutes later, the doctor entered.

"Good morning, Ms. Williams, I'm Doctor Candice," she said, greeting me.

"Good morning, as you already know I'm Brinay," I replied nervously.

"I see that this is your first pregnancy," she said, looking over my chart.

"Yeah, it is, and I'm extremely nervous."

"That's to be expected. All of our first-time moms are nervous," she said, grabbing a pair of gloves and putting them on. "Everything is going to be fine. I'm going to check your stomach and the baby's heartbeat before I get some information. I'll be examining your lower area also; then we're going to go down and get you your first ultrasound today."

"Okay."

"Lie back for me, please," she said, walking over to me. Raising the gown, she began doing everything that she had to do. In between everything, she began asking me about how it was going so far. I started telling her about all of my problems and everything that I had experienced. The whole process must have taken about an hour, and by then, I was tired. When it was time for me to hear my baby's heartbeat, I cried, knowing that I was carrying another life inside of me. When I was done, she took me down to the ultrasound room.

"When did you say you experienced your last period?" she asked.

"In May, I think," I replied. "Is something wrong?"

She didn't say anything. She kept rolling the thing around my stomach, taking pictures along the way.

"I need you to meet me back in the room," she said, taking the pictures out of the machine. She waited a few minutes for me to get dressed; then we left the room. Going back into the room, I began worrying. I even started crying. I couldn't help but to think that something was wrong with my baby.

"Okay," she said moments later, entering the room. "I looked over your pictures, and everything seems fine, but from the looks of things, it seems that you're about six months pregnant."

"What?" I asked confused.

"You said that your last period was in May, but from the measurements of your baby, it looks like you are about five or six months pregnant, and you're having a baby boy," she said again.

"But how?" I asked. "I was still bleeding."

"It's normal for a woman to still have a cycle while she's pregnant."

"So I'm five months?" I asked again.

"Yes, you are, and your estimated due date is December tenth," she replied.

"Okay," was all I said. I was shocked to know that I was five months pregnant. I thought for sure that I was only a few weeks.

"Well, do you have any questions?" she asked.

"No, ma'am."

"All right, I'm going to prescribe some prenatal vitamins and iron pills since your iron level is low," she said, writing a few things down. "You can pick that up, along with your next appointment date, at the front office," she said, getting up from her seat.

"Okay."

"Take it easy and congratulations, Ms. Williams," she said before she left the room. I sat there for a minute, going over everything that she had said. I was five months pregnant and having a little boy. *A boy?* I thought for sure that I was going to have a girl, but I guess not. I thought about Dontie for a second, and again, I wanted to call him, but I decided against it. *No matter what, it's better off this way,* I thought as I got up and left the room. I stopped by the office to pick up my prescriptions and my next appointment date before I went back to the waiting room.

I spotted Kourtney sitting in the corner where I had left her, reading a magazine.

"Are you ready?" I asked her.

"Is everything okay?" she asked, getting up from her seat. "What did the doctor say?"

"Everything is fine," I said as I began telling her what went down. Just like me, she was surprised to know that I was already five months pregnant.

"So did you pick out a name?" she asked as we made it to the car.

"Yes. I decided to name him after his father," I told her. Even though I said that I didn't want Dontie nowhere in my child's life, I decided to name him Dontae. Only thing is I was spelling it a different way.

"That's good then," she said. "I can't wait to meet my little man."

"I can't wait to meet him either," I said, beaming with pride. After all of the things that I've been through, I decided that I was going to give my child a life that I never had. Even though his father wasn't going to be in his life, that wasn't going to stop me from loving him enough for both us.

DONTIE

Three months later

The Wedding Day

The minute the limo pulled up to the hospital, I jumped out. I didn't even give the driver enough time to stop. I was on a mission. Once I made it inside, I damn near ran to the front desk.

"Umm . . . My baby mama was brought here. Her name is Brinay Williams. She was involved in a car accident," I said to the lady sitting behind the desk.

"Can you give me one moment, please," she said as she began typing away on her computer. "Yes, she's in surgery now. If you have a seat in the waiting room to your left, I'll notify the doctor of your arrival."

"Okay, thank you," I said before I made my way over to the waiting room area. I spotted Brinay's father sitting in a seat in the corner, so I went over to him. "What's going on?"

"Dontie? Why are you here, son? Why aren't you at the wedding?" he asked, surprised to see me.

"I heard about what was going on. I couldn't be at a wedding knowing someone in the family was hurt," I said telling a lie. What I really wanted to say, but I decided not to, was that Brinay was my baby's momma and that I came to check on her and my son.

"You should be at your wedding, son. I got this," he replied.

"Mr. Williams, I have to tell you something," I said, preparing to tell him the truth.

"What is it?" he asked.

"Well, sir—" I began but was interrupted by the doctor.

"Family of Brinay Williams," he said, coming into the waiting room. Both Mr. Williams and I got up and walked over to him.

"I'm her father. What's going on with my daughter?" he asked nervously.

"Well, sir, as you all probably know, Ms. Williams was involved in a terrible car accident. She suffered a number of injuries and is in stable condition for now," he replied, causing my heart to drop. "She has a few more surgeries to go through."

"What about the baby?" I asked him.

"Luckily, the baby is fine. We had to deliver him by C- section a few minutes ago. He's being cleaned and will be transferred to the nursery," he said, which made me happy. "As for Ms. Williams, I came out here to let you all know what her condition is. I need to know if you'd like us to continue to operate on her or not."

"You do whatever you have to do to save my daughter," her father said as tears began to roll down his face.

"Okay, sir. I'll have a nurse come in and take you all to the nursery. In the meantime, let me get back to work," he said before he disappeared behind the two double doors.

I stood there, going over everything that the doctor had just said. I hoped like hell that Brinay would pull through this in one piece. I don't know what I'd do if I lost her. I knew that we hadn't talked in a minute, but that still didn't stop me from loving her and wanting to be with her. I wanted a chance to make things right between us. I needed to for the sake of our son. Speaking of my son, I was more than happy that he was fine, and I couldn't wait to meet him. No sooner did that thought come to mind than the nurse came out to take us to the nursery.

I was nervous the whole walk there. I never thought in a million years that I was going to be a father, and now that I was, I didn't know how to feel. I looked at all of the babies in the nursery, and each and every one of them were beautiful. There were babies of all colors, and I was proud to be a father of one of them.

"He's right here," the nurse said, stopping in front of the glass where a baby boy lay there wrapped in a blue blanket. I stood there staring at him. He looked just like me when I was a baby. He had my nose, my lips, my hair, and all.

"Can we hold him?" Brian asked the nurse.

"Sure," she said as she went to get him. She returned moments later with him cradled in her arm. She gave him to Brian, who, in turn, held him, before he broke down crying and had to leave. She then handed him to me.

As I stood there with my son in my arms, I felt like one of the luckiest men on earth. I had created a life. I had a minime, and all I could think about was his future. I already made a list of all of the things that I was going to do when he gets home.

"Is this your first?" the nurse asked.

"Yes, it is," I replied, beaming with pride.

"I can tell, that glow on your face says it all," she said smiling. "Do you want to know his name?"

"She named him already?" I asked, shocked.

"Yes, seems like she was awake long enough to name him Dontae," she said, catching me off guard.

"What did you say his name was?" I asked, not believing that I heard her right.

"His name is Dontae," she said, just as the baby began to cry. "I guess it's time for his first feeding. Would you like to do it?"

"Yes, I'd love to," I said as I followed her into the nursery. She handed me a bottle and showed me how to hold him properly before she left the room, leaving me and my son alone.

"Hey, little man, it's Daddy. I'm sorry that I wasn't there when you was born or for any of your doctor's appointments, but from here on out, I'm going to always be there for you. I promise you that," I said as I continued to feed him his bottle.

November 29th will always be a day that I'll remember. It was supposed to be my wedding day, but instead, it became the day that I welcomed my first seed, my son, my child, into the world. I made a vow that from this day forward, I was going to make things right. Even if Brinay never wanted to be with me again, I was going to make it right between us. I just wished that she pulled through so I can do so. Either way, I was going to be in my son's life. Sky was just going to have to accept that or leave. Whichever her choice would be, it didn't matter. I wasn't going to leave my son or his mother's side until they were both out of here and healthy enough to be on their own.

Sky

I've been standing in the same spot where Dontie left me for almost an hour or so now. I was in a trance. One minute, I was listening to my cousin, Keyon, sing at my wedding, and the next minute, I was watching my husband leave. I can't believe that he actually walked out on me. I don't know if I should be embarrassed, shocked, mad, or all three. All I knew was I felt as if I was about to explode any minute now, and if Dontie was in front of me, I'd let him have it. Today was supposed to be *our* wedding day, the day when we were supposed to celebrate becoming a union. I mean, even though we were already married, I didn't get to have my dream wedding at the time. Now that day has come, and it looks like I still won't be having it. To make matters worse, it was all because of my bitch-ass little sister.

To be honest, I don't even know why the hell she came. Like before, I didn't invite her ass. I know it wasn't anyone but my dumb-ass father who invited her ass her in the first place. However, you'd better believe that I'm going to get his ass also. I can't believe she actually showed up. I mean, who travels from state to state, knowing that they were damn near nine months pregnant anyway? Shouldn't she be at home with her baby's daddy, getting ready for their little monkey to come into this world or something? Why'd she have to come and fuck up my day? Hell, she should've stayed her ass gone in the first place. Our lives were much better when she was gone. Now she's back and causing problems like she usually does. In fact, I should be blaming my dumb-ass father for cheating on my mother and having her anyway. To be honest, I never really liked my little sister. From the moment I found out that I had a little sister, I was pissed . . .

I was sitting in the living room, playing with my dollhouse, when my father walked in from work. I was about seven years old, and I was a daddy's girl. Like any other little girl, I was happy to see my father, and since it was Friday and he was home early, I was extremely happy that he was going to be spending the evening with us. He came in carrying a bag from my favorite toy store.

"Daddy!" I said, running over to him.

"Hey, Daddy's little princess," he said, kissing me on my cheek. "How was your day at school?"

"It was great. I made a new friend, and I got a gold star," I said, extremely excited.

"That's great, baby girl. Where's your mother?" he asked. For some reason, my dad wasn't being his normal self.

"She's in the room," I told him.

"Okay, let me go talk to her. I'll be right back," he said, giving me the bag he had placed on the table.

"Okay," I said, grabbing the doll he had bought for me. I went into my room and got a comb and my hair bucket so that I could do my baby's hair. On the way back to the living room, I heard my mother and father arguing. I know I shouldn't have been eavesdropping, but I did anyway.

"So you're telling me that she's outside, Brian?" she asked, sounding as if she was crying. "What's she doing here?"

"I went to get her. I was tired of hiding her. It's time for her and Skylar to meet," my father replied. I was confused about what they were talking about.

"If you think for one minute that you're bringing her in this house, you got another think coming, Brian," my mother screamed.

"She's my daughter, Veronica, and regardless of whether you like it, she's going to be here. So you might as well get used to it," he said.

"No, the only daughter you have is Skylar. She's no daughter of yours."

"I'm not about to do this with you again. I've already taken a test three damn times. She's my daughter, and whether or not you like it, she's going to be a part of our lives," my father told her again, sounding as if he was highly upset. Everything went silent, so I assumed that he was done talking. I ran as fast as I could down the hall to the living room. A few minutes later, he came walking out of the back room and over to me.

"Sweetheart, I have someone I want you to meet," he said, sitting down on the sofa where I was playing with my baby doll.

"Who, Daddy?" I asked, wanting to know. I was tired of everything being a secret. I wanted to know what was going on.

"I'll be right back," he said, getting up from the sofa. He walked out the door. I wanted to get up, but somehow, my feet wouldn't let me. Instead, I stayed there and continued to play with my doll as I waited for whoever it was to come inside.

A few minutes later, my father walked through the door with a little girl at his side. She was so cute! She was light brown-skinned, had long, pretty ponytails, and she was skinny. She looked like a life-sized little baby doll.

"Skylar, I want you to meet someone," my father said, walking over to me. "This is your little sister, Brinay."

"My what?" I asked, because I knew for sure that my mother didn't have any more children. She couldn't from what I'd overhead her tell my father. So where did this little girl come from, and why am I just now meeting her?

"She's your little sister, sweetheart," he said again. "She's my daughter, just like you."

"But Mommy doesn't have any more kids, Daddy," I said innocently. I was trying my best to understand the situation at hand.

"Well, umm . . . Sky, baby, umm . . . She has a different mother. You both have me as y'all father, but y'all have two different mothers," he said, scratching the back of his neck. I could tell that he was uncomfortable. I still didn't understand what he was saying. All I knew was that I had a little sister, who wasn't my mother's child.

I heard a door open, and seconds later, my mother came walking down the hallway. The minute she spotted the little girl, she got mad and stomped off down the hallway, back to her room. My father immediately went after her, and that's when they started arguing again.

"Hi, I'm Skylar," I said, extending my hand for her to shake. She looked up at me, and that's when I noticed that she had a pair of green eyes. "Your eyes are so pretty."

"Thank you. I'm Brinay," she replied. I can't lie. At first, I was thrilled to have a little sister. I was happy as ever that I was a big sister. That meant I had someone to share my toys with and play with. That was . . . until we got older and Brinay started getting all of the attention. It was as if when she was around, it was Sky who? Everyone loved her and her stupid-ass eyes. She had my father wrapped so far around her finger. He would do anything for her. That was, until work picked up, and he started working all those long hours. He would leave Brinay home with my mother and me.

It wasn't me that really hated my sister, it was my mother. She said that Brinay looked so much like her mother that she couldn't even stand to look at her. That's when she started treating her badly. At first, I felt sorry for her, but then my mother encouraged me to do the same mean things. She would make me slap her, kick her, spit on her, and just beat her for no reason. So every time she'd come over to our house, we'd try to make her stay as uncomfortable as possible. Making sure that either she wasn't eating, or had less food to eat, giving her cold baths. Sometimes she wouldn't take a bath at all. Her clothes would be dirty, and her shoes would be too small. My mother would never comb her hair, which meant she never got to go anywhere. She was always forced to stay inside or stay home alone when we went out.

Through all of these things, no matter what my sister went through or how we treated her, she still managed to keep faith. She'd go to school hungry sometimes and still manage to get all As, while I was barely passing. Brinay made the Principal's List and kept winning the Science and Social Studies fair. My mother tried to strip her of everything, from her dignity to her pride, but she couldn't strip her of her brains and beauty. My little sister was always being recognized for something, while I had to fight my way to the top. Even when her mother died, she held it all together.

I remember one year her mother had beat my mother so bad, that she had to go to the hospital. They tried to get her to press charges, but my father convinced her otherwise. He'd found out the things that Brinay was going through at our hands, so he threatened to kick my mother out if she dared to press charges. Besides, Brinay's mother had threatened to call CPS on my parents.

After that happened, it would be years until I saw Brinay again, and by that time, she was already seventeen, which was the same year her mother died. Since my father was her only living relative and her brother *was in jail, she had to come stay with us. My mother tried to do the things that she used to do to her when she was young, but she wasn't having that. She put her foot down and kept to herself. The minute she graduated, she applied to a school out of state and was gone. We hadn't heard from her since. My father would try to get in contact with her and send her money, but she would never answer the phone, and she would always send the money back. He was desperately trying to make up for lost time, but it was too late. The deed was done, and his daughter really didn't care for him. She proved that when she stayed away and refused to answer him.*

The next time I saw her was when she showed up at my announcement. You'd think I would be happy, but I wasn't. My little sister should've stayed her ass gone with the wind, because I most definitely wasn't missing her.

As I stood there watching all the people who'd come to be a part of our special day leave the church, I wanted to break down and cry. Dontie had made me look like a total fool, leaving me to go be with my sister as if *she* was his wife. A lone tear fell from my eye as I quickly wiped it. I wasn't about to cry. I wasn't about to let anyone see me vulnerable like that, so I played it cool, for now. I was going to hash everything out, but at the right time and on the right people.

"Are you okay?" my mother asked, walking over to me. I ignored her question. I really didn't feel like being bothered right now, and knowing her, I knew she was going to say something that I didn't like. "Skylar!"

"What, Mom?" I snapped at her. She should've gotten the hint that I didn't want to be bothered when I didn't answer her. "What do you want?"

"I'm just trying to see if you're okay," she said, rubbing my shoulder. "Baby, I know you must be upset, but everything is going to be okay."

"I'm fine, Mother," I replied, moving out of her reach. I didn't need her touching me either, because I was liable to snap at any moment.

"No, you're not, Skylar," she said. Her voice was getting on my nerves.

"Look . . . I said that I was fine. Now, won't you please just leave me the hell alone!" I snapped at her unintentionally. My mother could be an annoying bitch sometimes. She never knew when to let shit be, and that was one thing I hated the most about her.

"Little girl, you have me confused. I am *not* your equal. I'm your *mother,* and you will *not* play with or talk to me like that."

"I have to go," I said, heading toward the exit.

"Where are you going, Skylar?" she asked as she followed behind me. "You have to call and cancel the venue, and then determine what you're going to do with the food and everything else. You need to be here."

"What do I have you for?" I abruptly turned around and asked her. "Ain't that what you're for? To handle things like this?" She didn't answer. She just stood there, staring at me. I knew she wanted to say something, but she must have remembered that I wasn't my little sister, Brinay. I wasn't about to let anyone get over on me, mother or not. She wasn't going to play with me like that. She knew better. "I'll see you back at the house." With that being said, I left the church, hopped into my father's car, and made my way to the hospital. Dontie was going to feel my wrath. No way was I going to let him leave me hanging like that.

***

When I got to the hospital, I went straight to the nurse's desk and asked for Brinay's room number. I had to act hysterical, because I don't believe they would let me see her otherwise. They told me that she was actually in surgery, but her son was in the nursery. I asked them if it was okay to see him, and they told me that I could. They gave me a visitor's pass, before instructing me where to go. On my way to the nursery, I bumped into my dad.

"Daddy," I said, walking over to him. I noticed that his eyes were red. I couldn't believe that he had the nerve to be crying over this bitch. He wasn't acting like a father for all those years, but *now* he wants to start acting like father of the year.

"Baby girl," he said, once he noticed me. He looked surprised. I guess he didn't expect me to be here. "What are you doing here? What happened to the wedding?"

"The wedding ended early, and I came here to check on you and my sister," I replied, lying through my teeth. There was only one reason I came here, and it wasn't for my damn sister or her bastard-ass baby. I noticed he gave me a funny look before he looked away. "How's she doing?"

He began telling me everything that the doctor had told him. From the sound of things, she was in bad shape. Still, I didn't care. She wasn't my responsibility, she was his. "Your husband is here. As a matter of fact, I left him in the nursery holding the baby."

"You left him *where?* Doing *what?*" I asked, thinking that I heard him wrong. Did he just say *my* husband was in a nursery holding the next bitch's baby?

"He's in the nursery with your nephew," he repeated. I could feel myself beginning to lose it.

"Okay, Daddy, I'm going to check on the baby. I'll see you in a minute," I told him. Too many things were beginning to look suspicious to me. Why would he be holding her baby? Shit . . . that was *her* damn child. It wasn't as if he was that little bastard's daddy. They should've been trying to notify his daddy or something.

"Okay, I'll be in the waiting room when you all come out," he said, walking off.

So many questions entered my mind as I made my way to the nursery. I needed to know what was going on with my sister and my husband. Did they already know each other? Why was he so quick to leave our wedding to be with her? I know for sure it wasn't because he was that concerned about her. Why would he be holding her baby? Was there something going on between the two of them? I needed answers, and I needed them fast. However, the only two people who could give them to me were my sister and my husband. When I made it to the nursery, I didn't see him right away, but I did see this little blond, blue-eyed nurse.

"Umm . . . Excuse me, I'm looking for my husband. He was supposed to be in here feeding my nephew. His name is Dontie, and he's wearing a white tuxedo," I said to her.

"Oh, he's in the room feeding his son," she replied. I looked at her as if she had lost her damn mind. Why did she automatically think that *my* husband was the father of *that* kid? Just because he was black?

"No, ma'am, that's not his son," I said, correcting her.

"Well, that's not what I was told," she said smartly.

"You may have heard wrong, because my husband doesn't have any kids." I rolled my eyes at her. "Now, can you show me to wherever he's at?"

She paused a bit before she spoke. "Yes, they're right this way."

I followed her as she led me to where he was. I couldn't get over the fact that she said someone told her that my husband was the father of my sister's child.

When we made it to the room where Dontie was feeding the baby, I had to stop and catch myself. My stomach twisted into knots as I watched him sit in a rocking chair holding Brinay's baby, with a bottle to his mouth. I placed my finger by my lips to tell the nurse to be quiet. She looked at me and rolled her eyes before she left the room. If I wasn't too busy with my husband and all, I would've showed this Barbie-looking ho how to play with somebody. Yeah, that's right. I was from the suburbs, but I also knew how to get hood too. I promise you that her little white ass would be black and blue in less than five minutes, especially with all the anger that I had in me right now.

I stood off by the door, watching Dontie interact with the baby. I see why they thought he was the baby's father. Hell, if I didn't know better, I'd think so too, the way he was sitting there, rocking and holding the child.

"Yo, little man, I'm about to go check on your mother right quick. I'll be right back," he said to the baby, as if he could understand him. He placed the bottle on the table next to them and got up. He got the surprise of his life when he noticed me standing there. "Sky! What are you doing here?"

"I should be asking you the same damn thing," I yelled at him. "The fuck you doing playing father with the next nigga's child?"

"Sky, right now is not the time for all of this. Can you please wait until we get home to do this? If you haven't noticed, we're in a hospital nursery."

"I don't give a fuck where we are. What I want to know is how you can leave me at our wedding ceremony to come and play daddy to this little monkey!" I yelled at him, which caused the baby to cry.

"Look what the fuck you done did," he yelled, as he began rocking him. "You should've stayed your ass where the fuck you was."

"I can't believe you tripping on me behind a bastard that ain't even yours," I told him. Damn, if looks could kill, I'd be one dead bitch right now. I opened my mouth to say something but immediately closed it back. I didn't want to say something else to piss him off. I stood there watching him as he desperately tried to calm the little baby down, but nothing he did was working. Finally, I left the room to get the nurse. It just so happened to be the same little bitch I interacted with earlier. "Umm, it won't stop crying. Can you come and do something about it?"

"*It?*" she asked with her hands on her hips.

Fuck, I thought, realizing what I had said. "I mean the baby," I said, trying to correct myself. Again, she looked at me and rolled her eyes before she walked off to tend to the little monkey. I followed behind her. When we first walked in there, Dontie's back was turned, and he had managed to calm him down.

"Dontie," I said, trying to get his attention. Again, the little baby started crying. It seems that whenever I come in the room, the little bastard cries.

"Sky, just go out in the waiting room and wait there for me," he said, handing the baby to the nurse. "I'll meet you there when I'm done."

"Look . . . I ain't going nowhere until you come with me. What you got to stay in here for anyway? Like I said, that child ain't for you. So why you gotta act like his daddy?"

"I'm getting real tired of you and that smart-ass mouth of yours," he spoke through gritted teeth. "Can you please just go out in the waiting room, like I asked you to?"

"I already said that I wasn't going nowhere. So you might as well stop asking me to," I yelled. The little monkey started crying even louder.

"Ma'am, if you don't leave, I'm going to have to call security on you," blue-eyed Barbie said.

"Look, bitch—" I was rudely interrupted when Dontie walked over to me, picked me up and began carrying me out of the nursery. I know I probably looked insane, because I still had my wedding gown on.

"Dontie, if you don't put me down . . ." I said harshly. He ignored me and continued carrying me. "I'm not playing with you, Tae. You better stop and put me down, or I'm going to cut up."

"I wish the fuck you would, and I'm going to bat the fuck outta you, right in your mouth," he hissed.

"Who you think you talking to like that, Dontie?" I asked shocked. "You must have gotten shit confused. I'm your wife, not your muthafucking child."

"You ain't my child, but you're sure as hell acting like it," he said, just as he reached the double doors that led to the waiting room. He stopped right in front of them but didn't open them. "I don't know what point you're trying to prove and to who, but I asked you to wait outside in the waiting room while I do what you're too stubborn to do. That is, check on your sister and her child."

"I'm not trying to prove anything to anyone. I just don't understand why you're so worried about shit that doesn't concern you. Brinay is *my* sister, *not* yours. You're *my* husband, which means that you should be on *my* side, backing me up on anything that I do," I said folding my arms. "If I don't want to see them, then that's on me."

"You're right. She's your sister, and I am your husband, but the way that you're acting is crazy. You call her child all kinds of little bastards, monkeys, and shit. Tell me what that child ever did to you? He didn't do a damn thing, because he just got here. This feud that you have going on with your sister is retarded. How could you hate her that much? Your sister could be dying in that room, and you don't look like you're concerned one bit."

"That's because I'm *not* concerned, and don't try to sit here and tell me anything. You don't have any siblings, so you won't understand."

"Correction, bitch, I have a brother and two sisters," he replied.

"And when the fuck was you're going to tell me this shit?" I asked him.

"You think I wanna bring you around my family, the way you've been acting?" he asked, ignoring my question.

"I can't believe this shit," I said, folding my arms across my chest. "The fuck is that supposed to mean, nigga? I'm your *wife*. You have no choice but to bring me around your family. I'm already in it. I carry your last name, nigga. The fuck you mean?"

"We haven't been married long. I'm sure if I wanted to, I could get a divorce with the quick—" he began to say but was cut off when my hand connected with his face. I tried to knock all last year's snot out of that nigga's nose.

"Now you trying to divorce me?" I said, feeling hurt. I couldn't believe he had the nerve to say that he was going to divorce me behind this shit. He walked closer to me before he grabbed both of my wrists and began squeezing.

"If you put your muthafucking hands on me one more time, I'm going to make you regret the day you said I do. As a matter of fact, I'm going to make you regret the day you met me. Now get the fuck in the waiting room. I'll meet you there when I'm done," he said angrily. He gave me a light push before he walked away. Before he was gone, he turned around. "I'm not playing. If you cause any more trouble, you're going to be in trouble your damn self."

I stood there as my husband chastised me as if I was his child and not his wife. I wanted to blast on his ass, but I was stuck on the fact that he was tripping on me over my sister and her child. I was beginning to think that they had something going on. Hell, why else would he be acting a fool on me? There wasn't any other explanation. I watched as he disappeared down the hall. My heart was telling me to go after him, but my mind was saying something different.

Going with the latter, I went ahead and made my way to the waiting room, where my father was still waiting.

"What's wrong, baby girl?" he asked. I guess he noticed my facial expression, but I didn't feel like talking about it.

"Nothing, Daddy. Did the doctor come out and tell you anything about Brinay?" I asked, changing the subject, I wasn't about to let him know that something was going on with my marriage. It's too early to be having problems.

"No, baby, I'm still waiting," he replied, just as a tall white man in a white coat and some blue scrubs came walking our way.

"Mr. Williams?" he asked.

"Yeah, that's me," my father said, standing up. "How's my daughter doing?"

"Well, sir, she just got out of surgery, and I'm happy to report that everything is fine. We were able to stop the bleeding and everything. She's in recovery right now. She'll be moved to a room in the morning."

"Thank God," my father said, breathing a sigh of relief. "Is there something I can do?"

"Well, not right now. I'll let you see her for five minutes, but that's all until she's moved in the morning."

"Okay, Doc, and thank you."

"You're welcome, Mr. Williams. I'll let the nurse at the front desk know that you're going to see your daughter. In the meantime, have a good night," he said, and with that, he was gone.

"Are you coming?" my father asked, once he noticed that I wasn't trailing behind him.

"Umm . . . no. I'm waiting for Dontie. I'll just see her tomorrow when she's moved," I lied. I wasn't going to see her now, and I damn sure wasn't going to see her then. He looked like he was disappointed, but I really didn't care. I was too busy worrying about my husband to be concerned with a sister who I barely got along with. As I always said, she was *his* problem, not mine.

"All right," he said before he left to go check on his daughter. I sat back down and waited for Dontie. I meant what I said, and I wasn't leaving the hospital without my husband. Even if I had to act a damn fool, he was coming home with me.

Chapter Fifteen

Dontie

I couldn't believe that Sky actually had the nerve to show up and show out the way she did. I don't know what made her come here, but I can guarantee it wasn't to check on the well-being of her sister and nephew. How one can be so evil toward her own sister is beyond me. I'm still stuck on the fact that she tried to continue a wedding and her sister was in the hospital hurt. Hell, if Brinay wasn't pregnant by me, I would've still left the wedding, because as I said, that was her family. I honestly don't know about the bad blood between the two of them, because neither of them ever told me what was going on, but I know they can't hate each other that much. Sooner or later, someone was going to have to tell me what all this beef shit was about.

If I know Sky, as I thought I knew her, I know for sure that she was going to be sitting out in the waiting room, waiting for me. Which is why I decided to let her ass wait. She needed her ass whipped for all of the things her ass was saying earlier. I wanted badly to wrap my hands around that bitch's throat for playing with my son, but I didn't want her to get suspicious, so I didn't. She'd better be careful with all that slick shit that's coming out of her mouth, because I wouldn't be saving her or her feelings too much. What she needs to know is that if I had to choose between her and my son, her ass would be gone in a heartbeat.

I stood in the nursery longer than I'd expected to. I was both excited and nervous. I was glad that my son had entered the world healthy, but I was concerned about his mother. Since I couldn't see her right now, I decided to stay and bond with my son. Since his mother couldn't be here with him right now, I wanted to fill that void. I know the nursery is going to be closing soon, so I know that my time today was going to be limited. I know I should stay with him, but I didn't want to make things too obvious, at least not yet.

As I stood there holding my son, I imagined all the things we'd do when he gets older. I thought about how handsome he was going to be. Actually, I could tell that he was going to look like me. I thought about the many trips we'd take together. About all of the money he would make me spend. The many girls he would have. I thought about it all, and the more I thought about his future, the more I thought about his mother. I just hope that everything is going okay for her. I don't know how, but I wasn't going to leave this hospital until I got a chance to check on her.

I got up from the rocking chair and went to put my son back in his little crib. I then walked over to where one of the nurses were.

"Excuse me, miss, but can I talk to you right quick?" I asked.

"Sure," she said with a Kool-Aid smile. I know this bitch doesn't think I was trying to rap to her, because that was not the case.

"Umm . . . Do you know when my son is going to be getting out of the hospital?"

"What's his name?" she asked, looking at a chart.

"His name is Dontie Edmon, or Williams. I don't know which last name his mother gave him."

"Uh-huh," she said looking at the chart. "Here he is. Dontae Williams. I don't know. You have to find out when his doctor comes in tomorrow morning."

"Okay. Thank you," I said to her. I went to take one last look at my son before I gave him a kiss and left. I still couldn't believe that I had a son. Now I was going to try to see his mother.

I was nervous as hell as the nurse guided me to Brinay's room. I had to do every trick in the book, including give her my number, before she'd even let me past the nurse's station. It didn't matter that I told her I was going to visit my baby mama, who had gotten into a wreck and had just given birth to our son. She still asked me for it. I wanted to blow on her ass, but I knew she wasn't going to let me see Brinay otherwise. I had no choice, so I just gave it to her on the strength of that. Man, this shit is crazy. I wasn't going to take her out or nothing like that. I just did what I had to.

"She's in here," she said, stopping in front of the door.

"Okay, thank you," I said. I waited until she was gone; then I took a few minutes to get myself together before I actually went in. I was nervous about seeing her like that. When I got my head on straight, I went in.

The minute I walked in the room, my heart immediately broke at the sight of her in a hospital gown, hooked up to all those machines. She looked peaceful as she lay here. I watched her chest rise up and down to make sure that she was actually breathing. As I walked closer to the bed, I could hear my heart beat through my ears. I stood there first, just watching her. Even with all of the bruises and swelling, she was still beautiful. I took a seat on the bed beside her and grabbed her hand.

"I know I'm probably the last person you'd hope to hear right now, and I don't blame you, but I want you to know that I love you, Nay. Even though things are fucked up right now, just remember that." I got choked up, just thinking that I probably was the cause of this. "I really hope that you pull through this, and if you could find it in your heart to forgive me, I promise to make it right." I was about to get up when she squeezed my hand. A few minutes later, her eyes fluttered open, but a few seconds after, they closed. I was glad to see that she was okay and that she had heard me.

"I'll be back tomorrow. Make sure you're up then, ma," I said before I placed a kiss on her forehead and left.

I honestly felt bad that my favorite girl was laid up in the hospital and I couldn't do anything to help her. I felt even worse that I had to go home with her bitch of a sister. Lord knows I made the worst mistake when I married her ass. Even when I didn't know that they were sisters, I knew I'd made the worst mistake of my life. Shit, I was catching a headache even thinking about it.

When I made it to the waiting room, I spotted her sleeping in one of the chairs. I can't lie. She was beautiful in her wedding gown. If I wasn't already in love with her sister, I would've been glad to be her husband, but my heart was already somewhere else. I take that back—if she didn't have those nasty-ass ways and my heart wasn't with another woman—I would've been glad to be her husband. Unfortunately, that's not the case, and now everything is totally fucked up.

"Sky," I said, gently shaking her. She stirred in her sleep but didn't wake up. "Skylar."

"Huh?" She jumped up, looking all around. I'm guessing she had forgotten where she was.

"Come on, ma, let's go," I told her. She looked at her phone before she rolled her eyes and got up.

"It took your ass long enough," she said, getting up and walking off. I had to rub the back of my head. Right now was not the time for her shit. Pulling my phone out, I dialed Chance's number.

"Everything's good?" he asked, answering the phone.

"Everything's okay right now, but I need you to meet me at the house," I told him.

"What's wrong?"

"Sky's on one of her bitch fits, and I'm not in the mood to deal with that shit right now. Not with my son and his mother sitting in the hospital."

"All right, I'm on my way over there right now," he said, just as I spotted Sky walking back into the waiting room.

"All right, man," I said before I hung up and went to meet her.

"What the fuck you waiting on to come ya ass on?" she asked with a major attitude. "Fuck, it's bad enough you left me at the altar. Then I had to watch you play father to another nigga's baby, and now, you took forever and a day to come out. You expect me to wait longer? You better bring yo' ass before you be walking home."

I didn't say anything back, because I knew she was just in her feelings about me leaving her on our wedding day. I could understand why she was feeling some type of way, but she needed to chill out. I'm not about to continue to let her disrespect me just because she wants to. If she only knew half of the things that was going on in my head, she'd really be on fire.

When I walked out the door to the emergency entrance, she was there waiting for me. I went to open the passenger door when I realized that she was already sitting there. I know she only wanted me to drive home so that she could be able to fuss, but this time I was cocked and ready for her. She was going to get a rude awakening.

When I hopped in the car, I didn't say shit. I threw on the radio at a decent volume and drove off. From my peripheral vision, I saw her fold her arms across her chest. *Oh Lord*, I thought, picking up speed. I was doing way above the speed limit, trying my best to get us home quickly. I silently prayed to God that I'd make it home in no time so that I wouldn't have to hear nothing from her ass. I guess the Lord didn't hear my prayers, because she reached over to lower the volume and turned to me.

"Are you going to tell me what's going on between you and my sister?" I felt my heart skip a beat or two before I shifted in my seat. I know damn well she didn't know anything. I decided just to play it cool.

"What are you talking about, Sky?" I calmly asked her. I wasn't trying to go off on her or anything like that, because that shit would've been a dead giveaway.

"Dontie, don't play dumb. Is there something going on between you and Brinay?" she asked again.

"I barely even know your sister. How could there be something going on between us?" I asked, trying to pretend as if I was hurt.

"I don't know—you tell me. You was quick to leave our muthafucking wedding to come to the hospital to see about her and her little bastard without any regard for me or my muthafucking feelings. So something must be going on between y'all, because that shit ain't normal. Like you said, you two barely know each other," she yelled. I was getting so tired of hearing her sing the same tune.

"I left because that was the right fucking thing to do. She's your sister, and she was pregnant with your nephew. I don't know how you could try to continue to have a fucking wedding, knowing that she was hurt and in the hospital. Not to mention the fact that she was pregnant," I said, trying to stress the shit to her. "You walk around here on your imaginary high horse, acting as if the sun sets and rises on your ass, but it doesn't. Ain't that much hate in the world that you can honestly say you don't give a fuck about what happens to your sister or her child."

"That's because I don't. I don't give a fuck about her, nor do I give a fuck about her muthafucking child. So you can stop with all these bullshit-ass speeches you trying to give, because I most definitely don't want to hear them," she replied, folding her arms across her chest again, sitting back in the seat. I couldn't even respond to that. I didn't know how to. My wife is basically saying that she doesn't give a fuck about my son. "And from this moment on, you don't have to go to the hospital to check on neither one of them. You can leave that up to my father. That's *his* responsibility, *not* yours or mine."

I just sat there, not even saying anything. To be honest, words wouldn't be able to describe how I was feeling right now. I'd only be able to express myself through actions. Lord knows I don't want to put my hands on her, but if she continued to piss me off, popping all that stupid shit from her lips, I was going to have to go back on that.

For the rest of the ride home, it was silent. We didn't even have the radio on. She was lost in her thoughts, and I was lost in mine. I'm sure her mind was still stuck on the fact that I walked out on her, while I was trying to figure out who was going to get my son when he comes home in two days. I knew for a fact that he couldn't go home with Brinay's father and her stepmother. I'm sure if Skylar hates her sister, her mother hates her even more, and there was no way I was going to allow them to fuck with my son. Behind him, I was ready to body both of their asses, not caring if Sky was my wife or not. I knew DJ couldn't come home with me, because his mother wouldn't allow it. That's when I thought of Brinay's friend, Kourtney. I'm not even sure if someone had called to inform her of Brinay's accident. On second thought, I'm pretty sure that they didn't, because if they did, she would've been down here right now. She and Brinay acted more like sisters than Brinay and Skylar did. I was going to have to call her the minute I get a chance. It was a good thing that I had her number, because I would've hated to have to leave my son alone and go pick her up.

"What the hell is he doing here?" Skylar asked, once we pulled up to the house and spotted Chance sitting on his car smoking.

"I told him to meet me over here, that's what he's doing here," I said to her as I threw the car in park and got out. I didn't bother to wait for the smart remark I know was coming from her nagging lips.

"Give me a few minutes, man. Let me run upstairs and get a few things," I walked over to the car and told him.

"All right," he said, hopping back into the car. I'm guessing he wasn't trying to hear her mouth either. I already had the door opened and the alarm disarmed before she came inside.

Ignoring her presence, I began walking up the stairs to our bedroom. Grabbing a duffle bag from the closet, I walked over to the dresser, opened a few drawers, and began filling it with a few items.

"Where the fuck are you going?" she asked from behind me. I looked at her through the mirror. I was really beginning to see her for who she really was. Deciding not to reply, I shook my head before I continued doing what I was doing. I didn't have the time or energy to be entertaining her ass right now. "Tae, I know you hear me talking to you. Where are you going?"

"To mind my muthafucking business," I finally said, turning around.

"Oh, so you're cursing me now?" she asked, looking a bit hurt. I cursed around her all the time, but I'd never cursed directly at her.

"Sky, please go 'head with your shit, because I'm seriously not in the mood right now," I said, turning around to close the drawers. I turned back around to see her just standing there.

"Who is she?" she asked me.

"Who is who?" I asked, confused.

"The bitch that you're cheating on me with. Who is she?" she asked, beginning to sound like a mad woman.

"I don't have time for this shit," I said, walking past her and out of the room.

"Is it my sister? Is that why you left me to be with her?" she asked, chasing after me.

"Do you actually hear yourself right now, Skylar?" I asked, turning around without warning, causing her to bump into me. "How the fuck you come up with that shit?"

"Just answer my question, Dontie," she yelled, totally ignoring me. "Do you and my sister have something going on between the two of you?"

"Look, ma, I don't have time for this stupid shit. You're trying to find any and every reason to hate your sister, but you won't be using me," I said, walking away from her. I thought she was going to follow behind me, but she didn't, and I was glad. I didn't know how much more of this shit I could take. This shit was beginning to get out of hand. I know the truth was going to come out one way or another, I just wasn't ready for it to come out this soon. I had too many things to do before I could really come clean.

Chance

Shit like this you don't normally see in real life. I mean, I'm used to seeing shit like this in a movie or reading about it in an urban fiction book. I would never have thought that my cousin would've gotten himself into some deep shit like this.

When I first learned that Brinay and Sky were sisters, I was shocked. Hell, I was speechless. Here we were, celebrating Dontie and Skylar's union when his other chick up and walks in. At first, I thought the shit was a plot that Brinay and Sky were playing, but they actually had no idea that they were fucking the same man. Well, Sky didn't. After the dinner, Brinay didn't want to have anything to do with Dontie, and I can't say that I blamed her. When she found out that he was married to Sky, the look of pain on her face was unlike one I'd ever seen. She was really hurt by that. Shit, he's lucky that she didn't put his ass out. I would feel the same way if I was in her situation. What fucked him up the most is when he found out that she was pregnant. Shit, knowing that he was married to one sister, while the other one was pregnant by him had to be stressful.

He spent months trying to get back on Brinay's good side, but nothing he did seemed to work. He tried showering her with gifts, giving her money. Hell, he even offered to divorce her sister, but nothing he proposed moved her. She really wanted nothing to do with him. She didn't even want him to be a part of her child's life, which I thought was fucked up. She always talked about her father barely being there for her, so I couldn't understand why she didn't want him to be in his child's life.

I know her coming to the wedding was her father's doing, because she and her sister couldn't get along if they wanted to. Shit, someone could offer to pay them top dollars and they still wouldn't budge or attempt to act like normal sisters. I don't know what it was, but they couldn't stand each other. They barely were able to stay in the same room together for a long period of time.

Everything is like a competition with them. That whole day, I watched her as she walked around the church. I can't lie, she was beautiful and being pregnant gave her an extra glow. I've seen some females that wore their pregnancies bad, but she, she wore it like an angel. The baby really had her hair growing beautifully. *Gosh, I wish she was my woman,* I thought.

"What you over there thinking about?" Dontie asked, pulling me from my thoughts. We were on our way to my apartment.

"Just thinking about life, man," I lied. I can't tell him that I was really thinking about his baby mama, because I knew things would probably get hectic between us.

"Shit, I don't want to even think about my life right now," he replied. I couldn't imagine how I'd feel if I was in his situation. Hell, he makes me want to do a background check on every female I come in contact with. Shit, I definitely wasn't trying to mess with females that came from the same family. I saw the way he was going through it, and I knew for sure that I couldn't go through the same thing.

"So what are you going to do?" I asked, even though he said he didn't want to think about it. His problems weren't going to go away, no matter how hard he tried to ignore them. He was going to have to face this eventually. Might as well do it now.

"Honestly, man, I don't even know. It's like I keep hoping and praying that all of this is a joke, but I know that it isn't," he said, shaking his head. I didn't know what he was going through, and I didn't want to know. "My life is spiraling out of control right now. It's like I have the woman who I really want, but I can't be with her, because I'm stuck in a committed relationship with her sister. Fucked up part about it is, I really wasn't supposed to marry Skylar. When I bought that ring, I had one person in mind, and it damn sure wasn't her."

"So you saying that you actually bought the ring for Brinay?" I asked, to confirm my theory.

"That's exactly what I'm saying," he replied, rubbing his hands up and down his face repeatedly.

"So how the fuck you end up marrying Sky then?" I asked, because the shit wasn't adding up. He went on to tell me how and why he married her in Jamaica. He told me that somehow, getting caught and temptations would pressure you into doing things you don't want to do.

"Wow!" I said when he was through telling me everything.

"Yeah . . . Shit is crazy, huh?" he asked sarcastically.

"I mean, man, this ain't something you hear on a daily basis," I replied. "So what are you going to do about the baby?"

"What do you mean? That's my son."

"I know that, but you know Nay's probably going to be in the hospital a little longer. Are you going to take him home with you and Skylar?" I asked.

"Man, you know I can't do that," he replied.

"So what are you going to do then?"

"I'm going to call her friend down here to come and get him while I work on the shit that I have to do."

"I already called Kourtney, if that's who you're referring to. She'll be here first thing in the morning," I told him, just as we pulled up into my apartment complex.

"Thanks, man. With everything that's been going on, I had totally forgotten about calling her."

"I know," I said, just as I parked the car.

He grabbed his bag out of the backseat, and we got out.

"I'm going to get through this, though. I know it may seem like I should give up, but I'm not. There's no way I'm giving up on my girl or my son. Brinay may not want anything to do with me now, but in due time, all of that will change."

I didn't say anything. Well, I couldn't say what I wanted to, because we would've probably been out here squaring up. Instead, I kept my ears open and my mouth shut. If he and Brinay were meant to be together, they would be, but if not, then they wouldn't. Even though I've had a crush on her since before they got together, I concluded that I was going to leave well enough alone. Our family had enough problems as it is. It didn't make sense trying to add fuel to already lit flames. Come to think about it, the nigga could have her. I know I was crushing on her, but after all, he was still family, and I wasn't about to go against the grain.

Chapter Sixteen

Kourtney

I've been running like a chicken with my head cut off all afternoon, ever since Chance called and told me what happened to my best friend. No wonder she wasn't answering my phone calls and text messages. I couldn't even begin to understand the things she was going through right now. To get in an accident while being pregnant and not having anyone there for you is crazy. I mean, with everything that's been going on, finding out that her sister was married to her baby daddy and stuff . . . Things have been crazy. Now, on top of that shit, she has to add this to it. My poor friend can't seem to get a break, but just like any other time, I'm going to be there for her. Always.

I know I told Chance that I was going to catch a flight the first thing in the morning, but I couldn't sit around, knowing that my friend was hurt in the hospital and I wasn't there for her. Instead, I decided to drive. Before doing anything, I went to my school and transferred all of my classes online. I then went back to my apartment and began to pack for my trip. I made sure that I brought quite a bit of clothes with me, because I knew that I'd probably be down there for a while. When I was done packing my things, I double-checked that everything in my apartment was unplugged and turned off. After doing an inspection of my apartment to make sure that I wasn't leaving anything on or that I needed, I grabbed my things and headed down to the car. Before getting on the road to head to Miami, I stopped by Brinay's house to get a few things for her and the baby.

I knew she most likely didn't have anything down there for the baby, since she wasn't scheduled to deliver for about another week or so. I tried to get everything that I thought he was going to need. Bottles, diapers, baby wipes, clothes, nipples, bibs, socks, onesies, etc. I got everything. I had to make almost ten trips to the car before I had finally hauled everything off. When I had gotten everything into the car, I did the same thing in her apartment that I had done to mine. I unplugged everything, including the stove.

Once I was through, I made sure to lock every window and both doors before I left. On my way out of town, I stopped at the gas station to fill up my tank. I wasn't trying to make any unnecessary stops. All I wanted to do was hurry and make it to my friend. I knew that she was probably looking for me. I was supposed to be there when she had my god baby, but unfortunately, God had other plans. That was fine, though, because I was on my way. I just hoped that nothing was going to happen when I made it down there. I had a weird feeling that things were about to pop off. I hoped like hell that my friend wasn't about to get into some shit behind Dontie's ass. Truth be told, I thought that they made an awesome couple, but after I found out that he was married to her sister, I quickly changed my mind. Who sleeps with one sister while married to the other one?

"God, just be with and watch over my friend and her son. I know things aren't right with them right now. Which is why she needs you now more than ever," I said, praying for Brinay and her baby. It suddenly dawned on me that I have a god baby, whose name I didn't know yet.

I couldn't wait to get there and see him. Hopefully, he looked like his mother and not his father.

After pumping my gas, I hopped in the car, threw on my Monica's *New Life* CD, and hit the road. I was going to be there for my best friend, no matter what the situation was.

I made it to Miami faster than I anticipated. I was going to go straight to the hospital, but the way my eyes were set up, I needed a quick nap. My body was drained, and I was beginning to catch a migraine from worrying too much. Besides, I really needed to take a bath. Instead of going straight to the hospital, I went to the address Chance had texted to my phone last night. I knew it was early, but I was hoping and praying they were up, because I didn't have any strength in me to look for a hotel right now. Pulling my phone out, I decided to call him first.

"Hello," he answered the phone groggily.

"Umm . . . Good morning, Chance, it's me, Kourtney," I replied. "I'm here in Miami."

"I thought your flight wasn't scheduled to arrive for a few more hours," he said.

"It was, but I didn't take a flight. I decided that I was going to drive. I couldn't sit at home waiting on tomorrow to come," I told him. "If you're still asleep, I can go check into a hotel."

"No, it's fine. I was about to get up anyways. Dontie isn't here right now. He's probably at the hospital with the baby."

"Oh my God, I can't wait to see him," I said, beaming with pride. I was finally an aunt and godmother.

"I can take you there when you get here, if that's what you want," he suggested.

"I'd like to, but right now, I really need a hot bath and a bed. I'm tired and worn out," I said, blowing out air in frustration and exhaustion.

"Okay, well, you can come over and take a nap or whatever here."

"Are you sure?"

"Positive. Besides, Dontie really needs to talk to you. So the faster you do whatever it is that you have to do, the faster y'all can come up with a solution to his problem."

"What problem?" I asked, confused.

"I don't know. You have to ask him whenever you see him, ma."

"Oh, okay, well, I'm outside," I said to him.

"Okay, I'm about to come out and help you with your things."

"All right," I said, hanging up. I got out of the car and went around to the passenger side backseat where my things were. The other side was filled with things for Brinay, and the baby's things were in the trunk. I was only able to pull two of my five bags out before Chance came down.

"How many bags do you have?" he asked, walking over to me. I pointed to the rest of my bags sitting in the backseat.

"Damn, you moving down here?" he asked jokingly.

"Hell, no, but I did bring a lot of clothes. You know a girl changes her mind like clockwork."

"Do I," he agreed just as a car pulled up behind us. I couldn't see who it was, because the windows were tinted.

"Who the hell is that?" I asked Chance, but he was already walking toward the car. A few seconds later, the window came down, and Dontie stuck his big-ass head out.

"What's up, ma?" He waved with a Kool-Aid smile. "It's nice to see you. It's been a minute, huh?"

"Nice to see you too, and yeah, it's been awhile," I said, grabbing my bags out of the car.

"Wait, hold on," Dontie yelled, causing me to stop.

"What?" I asked, stepping a few feet back.

"You can leave your bags in the car. I already got a spot set up for you to go to," he told me. "Chance, why don't you help her put her things back? Then you hop in the car with her and y'all follow me."

"All right, cool," Chance said, walking over to me. He placed my things back into the car faster than he helped removed them. I then walked around and got in as I waited for him. About a minute or so later, he climbed in.

"He's going to be waiting for us by the front gate," he said, as he leaned his seat back and got comfortable.

"Okay," I replied, starting the car. I backed out of my spot and went to meet Dontie by the gate. When he saw that we were behind him, he pulled off. I had no idea where we were going. I just hoped that we would get there soon, before I fell asleep at this wheel.

Dontie

I was up early the next morning. I had a lot of things to do and not much time. Since my son would be coming home soon and his mother would be most likely staying in the hospital, I decided to head to the store to get him some things. Before I did that, however, I drove out to my house in South Beach. I needed to check on something.

When I pulled up to my brownstone five-bedroom, three-and-a-half bathroom, three-car garage, I felt a sense of peace. However, I also felt a sense of sadness. This was the house that I was supposed to move in after I married Brinay. Marrying Sky had obviously put a dent into my future plans. The good thing about it is that Sky doesn't know anything about this house. She was too busy trying to fuck and suck these old duck-ass niggas to climb to the top of the corporate ladder. She didn't think I knew about her and that old-ass nigga she been fucking throughout our relationship, but I wasn't worried about that. If she wanted to fuck him, then that was her problem, especially since I had the woman I really wanted to be with in my life. Whatever she did didn't matter to me one way or another.

Hell, she was so busy working that she didn't pay my ass any attention anyway. Not that I cared. It just gave me the opportunity to fall more in love with Brinay. Brinay and Skylar are like day and night, which is why I could never love Sky the same way I loved her sister. Even though I was now her husband, Sky still believes that I'm somewhat beneath her. I don't know how, because the same things she can get, I can get. She's not the only one with money in this marriage.

Getting out of the car, I pulled my keys from my pocket and walked up to the house. I wanted to make sure my sister was keeping my shit in shape. When I opened the door, the scent of Pine Sol immediately invaded my nostrils. I haven't been here in a few months, since before the wedding actually, but I see that my sister has been doing her job. I wandered around the house, inspecting everything. It wasn't that I didn't trust her. I just wanted to see how everything looked. Since the guest room and a bathroom were on the first floor, I checked them first.

Once I was pleased with the way things looked, I made my way upstairs. The first place I decided to go was my son's room, which was across from the master bedroom. Slowly, I made my way over to the blue door that had the letters *DJ* written in cursive on it. I turned the knob, opened it, and made my way in. I can't lie. My sister really outdid herself on this one. The whole room was blue, with footballs, basketballs, baseballs, and soccer balls all around the room. He had a wooden crib that could transfer into two different-sized beds when he got older. On the bed was one of the softest mattresses that I'd ever felt. Shit, it made me want to hop in and take a nap. There was also a rocking chair in one of the corners.

Right across from the crib was his changing station and his dresser. I knew he didn't have much of anything in there, which is why I decided to go shopping for him. I finished looking at the room before I inspected the rest of the house and was out. By the time I was done, it was almost nine that morning. I wanted to call and wake Chance's ass up, but I knew he was tired from last night, so I made the trip alone.

When I pulled up into Walmart, I grabbed two carts and headed straight for the baby section. I started throwing any and everything into the carts. I didn't check age range or size. Everything from lotion, soaps, six boxes of diapers, wipes, baby powder, milk, two different types of bottles, onesies, socks, bibs, T-shirts, a car seat and stroller, a swinger, high chair and bouncer . . . You name it, I had it. I had so much shit, I had to get a third cart and some assistance. When I was done, I made my way to the register and checked out. I spent almost two grand in Walmart, and I wasn't finished getting everything that I needed. When I checked out, they sent two associates out to help me with my carts. Once I had everything packed and loaded in the car, I made my way back to the apartment to get Chance. I most definitely was going to need some help getting everything out of the vehicle.

I had perfect timing, because when I pulled up to the apartment to get Chance, Kourtney was also there. "Good! Now there's even more help," I said aloud. Chance was getting her luggage out of her car. I pulled my car directly behind her to stop him. She wasn't going to be sleeping there. I had already made up my mind to let her, Brinay, and my son stay in the house over in South Beach until I got everything under control.

***

When we pulled up to the house, I parked in the driveway; then I got out and instructed Kourtney to pull up beside me. After that, I went to unlock the door. I stepped inside to disarm the alarm before I went back out to the car to get my son's things to bring them inside.

"Yo, Chance, before you go inside the house, can you please come help me get these things out of the car?" I asked.

"Damn, nigga, what you did, bought the whole Walmart?" he asked, joking.

"Nah, nigga, I just had to make sure my son had everything he needed for when he comes home tomorrow," I told him.

"I feel ya, man," he said, as we began grabbing bag after bag to take in the house. It was already hot outside, and everyone knew how crucial Miami heat was. I tried like hell to get as many bags as I could, because I was trying to make as few trips to the car as possible. We still made about ten trips to the car, and by the time that we were finished, I was tired as hell.

"Don't stop. Y'all might as well go back outside and get everything out of my car," Kourtney said, as we entered the living room with the last few bags from Walmart. I sat down on the sofa, trying to catch my breath. A nigga wasn't out of shape or anything like that, but it was hot as fuck outside.

"All right, ma, give me a minute."

"Here," she said, handing us a bottle of water. I sat there, enjoying the ice-cold water, gulping it down my throat as the cold air blew on us.

"Come on, man, let's get this over with so I can go check on my babies," I said, getting up from the sofa. Chance followed me out of the house.

"All of this shit she has in here," I said, noticing every-thing on the backseat, including diapers and other baby items. I knew right away that she'd look out for my son.

"Nigga . . . that ain't even the half of it," he said, walking around the car. He then popped the trunk and headed to the back of the car.

"What the fuck! She plan on moving down here?" I asked once I saw all that she had in the trunk.

"Fuck, I don't know, but this here is some bullshit," Chance said, as we began grabbing what we could. "I'm taking a nap after all this shit. It's bad enough that she woke me up out of my sleep. Now she got me working like a damn slave."

"Shit, I want a meal or something," I joked as we entered the living room. She was sitting on the sofa with her eyes closed. Baby girl looked tired. I walked over to her and lightly shook her.

"What's wrong?" she asked, jumping up. I knew she was tired, but I had to laugh at the sight of the slob running down the side of her mouth. She must have felt it, because she hurried up and wiped it off. "I'm sorry."

"It's cool. If you're tired, you can go rest in the guest bedroom down the hall," I said, pointing in that direction.

"Thank you, but I would like to take a bath before I get in the bed," she said, getting up. She noticed that we had started bringing in her things. She walked over to them, grabbing two suitcases, before heading down the hall. "Where's your bathroom?"

"There's one right next to the room on your right," I told her.

"Okay, thank you," she replied before she disappeared into the room.

"Yo, nigga, I hope you come and help me with the rest of these bags," Chance said, walking into the room with more bags. "I hope your ass don't expect me to help bring this shit upstairs, nigga."

"Nah, I'ma call my sister and let her handle that for me. Come on, let's get the rest of these bags, so I can get back to the hospital."

When I made it to the hospital, it was way past noon. I was worn out and tired, but I needed to get there. Since I knew my son was probably sleeping, I decided to go and check on Brinay. I missed my baby more than anything else, and I was becoming frustrated. I wanted her to hurry up and wake up. Things were getting crazy, and I needed her.

When I made it to the floor she was on, I spotted her father talking to the doctor. *I wonder what the hell's going on,* I thought as I walked over to them.

"Okay," he said, just as I had reached them.

"What's going on, Mr. Williams? Did something happen to Brinay?" I asked, hoping that he would say no. I don't know if I would be able to take it if something happened to her.

"No, son, she's fine. I just had a few questions, that was all," he replied. I let out the breath I didn't even know I was holding. He looked at me as if he wanted to say something, but he didn't.

"Okay," he said, just as we entered the room. She was still lying in the same spot she was in the other day, but the only difference was, she didn't have as many machines hooked up to her as before. I walked over to the bed and just looked at her.

"The doctor said that she was doing a little bit better than she was before. I just wish that she would hurry up and wake up," Mr. Williams said from behind me. I nodded my head, agreeing to what he just said. We all wanted her to wake up. I hated to see her in this state. Every time I saw her like that, my heart ached. "I'm about to head down to the cafeteria to get something to eat. You want anything?"

"Nah, I'm good," I said, turning to him. "I'll sit with her until you come back."

"Okay," he replied, and with that, he was gone.

For the longest, I stood there staring at Brinay, wishing that she would just wake up. I wished I could hear her voice or feel her arms around me. I was truly missing her, and besides, her son needed her more than I did. He needed his mother with him. He was waiting for her.

"Hey, baby," I said, finally speaking. Every time I came here, I'd sit down and talk to her. I wanted to make sure that she was able to hear my voice, even though she couldn't see me. "I know you can't see me, but it's me, Tae."

I walked over to her and did what I normally did before I sat down next to her. Taking her left hand into mine, I sat there, gently rubbing it. "Brinay, you need to cut the bullshit and wake up. I miss your crazy ass. Our son is here, and he needs his mother. It's time for you to wake up so you can be with him."

I knew that she probably couldn't hear me, but that didn't stop me from talking to her. For the life of me, I couldn't understand why the Lord was punishing me like this. As I sat there thinking, I couldn't help but to remember when I first met Brinay . . .

It was a Friday morning, and Chance and I had just come from upstate, visiting a few of my niggas. I was supposed to just be dropping Chance off and heading back to Miami, but the nigga insisted I stay there for a damn party that night. I mean, he damn near begged my ass to stay. I know if I would've told him no, he probably would've found a reason to make me stay. Since he was my favorite cousin, and I really didn't have shit to do back home, I gave in.

"I'm telling you, nigga, this party better be as alive as you say it will," I told him as we sat there, smoking a blunt.

"Man, I'm telling you, that nigga, Blacky, be giving the hottest parties in South Carolina. Nigga be having everybody and they momma up in that bitch. Ya feel me?" he said, taking a hit from the blunt. He closed his eyes and inhaled it before blowing the smoke out and puffing again. He then passed it to me.

"Yeah, nigga, that's what ya mouth say, but let me find out otherwise," I replied, taking the blunt from his hand.

"Man, I told you that it's going to be popping, but you don't trust me, fam?"

"I'm not saying I don't trust you, but you just be overex-aggerating too much, nigga. Them hoes better be in that bitch too."

"They will, they will," he repeated himself.

"A'ight, well, let's go and hit up the mall, but first, I need to get a room to put this little shit up in," I said to him.

"A'ight, cool, but why don't you just leave that at my mom's house?" he asked.

"Because, nigga, I don't know what could go down. If the police turned up to Aunt Jackie's shit, she's going to jail, no doubt," I told his dumb ass. I wasn't one to shit where I sleep, nor was I going to let anything come to my family. Even though I didn't stay there, that was my family. I wouldn't be able to sleep if some shit popped off, and they ended in jail . . . or dead.

"Yeah, I feel ya, man," he said. "Hurry up, so we can get to the mall before it gets too crowded. I'm not trying to be in that bitch all fucking day."

"All right, man."

"As a matter of fact, I know just the place where you can get a room for the low, and it's a nice hotel too," he replied.

"Okay, well, you drive then."

"Man, I'm already loaded. I really don't feel like driving."

"Nigga, just shut the fuck up and drive," I said, getting out of the car and heading over to the passenger side. I opened the door to find him still sitting in the seat. "Nigga, go 'head on before I change my mind and decide to head my ass down to Florida tonight."

"Nigga, you lucky I don't feel like going to this party by myself," he said, getting up and going to the driver's seat.

"Yeah, whatever, nigga," I said, throwing the keys on his lap.

"And watch the way ya driving before you fuck around and have us both in jail," I told him as he cranked the car up.

"Yeah, nigga, I know," he said, pulling off.

"See why I wanted to get to this bitch early?" Chance complained as we scanned the mall parking lot for a place to park. Everyone in South Carolina must have taken off from work or something, because the place was packed, even though it was still early.

"Yeah, man," I replied, just as I spotted a parking spot. His ass was too busy fussing and almost missed it. "Hey, look, pull in right here."

He pulled into the parking spot, and then shut the car off. I removed my gun from my waistband before opening the secret compartment and placing it in there. I then opened my glove compartment to get my money and cards. When I had everything, I got out of the car.

"I hope you don't be long, nigga. I already know what I want, so I'm just going in and out," he said, as we made our way into the mall.

"Man, please. You know ya yellow ass gon' act like a female and take a few hours," I said joking, but I was still serious. Chance was most definitely a pretty nigga, and he acted like one. Don't get me wrong, I'm not gay, and I'm no ugly nigga. Take my word, nigga, Chance is just a pretty boy.

"Nigga, whatever. Don't get mad, because I like to look good, nigga," he said, stopping to flash his million-dollar smile. "I'm a have-all-the-hoes, while you be by ya lonesome."

"You don't believe that shit yourself, playboy," I replied, pushing him. I then turned in the direction of the entrance and almost lost myself. "Who is that?"

"Who is who?" he asked, trying to see who I was talking about.

"Shorty in the pink shirt and blue jeans, standing next to the bright girl with the braids in her head," I said, hoping that he would catch on without making me point toward her.

"Oh, that's Brinay," he said, just as they made it a few feet away from us. "Hey, Nay."

"Hey, Chance," she replied. "Why you wasn't in class today?"

"I had some business to take care of," he told her. I stood on the side, admiring her beauty. Shorty was bad. She was beautiful. She was short and had a banging-ass body. She wasn't a skinny chick, and she was thick with long, black hair.

"Yeah, let me find out yo' ass around here up to no good instead of being in school," she said smartly. She then turned to me, and that's when I noticed that she had a set of exotic green eyes. "Oh, hey, I'm Brinay, and that's my friend, Kourtney."

"What's up, ma? My name is Dontie," I replied, shaking her hand.

"I just told you my name, and I know I didn't say anything about it being ma."

"I'm sorry, beautiful. Brinay, is it?" I asked.

"Yeah, that's it," she said, flashing her beautiful smile, which showed off a set of perfectly white teeth.

"Come on, Nay, we have to get going. You know I hate to be in the mall when it's packed," her friend said from behind her.

"All right. Damn," she said, rolling her eyes.

"Seriously, Nay?"

"It was nice meeting you," she said to me. "Chance, ya ass better be in class next week. Come on, Kourtney."

"All right, ma," I said. I waited until they were out of earshot before I turned to Chance. "Where you know shorty from?"

"Nigga, damn. Slow your ass down. I know the chick from school, and before you try it, shorty don't even do your kind," he replied.

"What you mean she doesn't do my kind?" I asked.

"I already see that look in your eyes, and like I said, she doesn't do your kind. So you might as well leave her alone. She will not date you," he said, walking off. "As a matter of fact, I never seen her date any man before."

"Well, she going to have to make an exception for me. I ain't leaving here until baby girl is mine," I said, walking off, but he stopped me.

"On the real, man. Shorty is a good girl. She barely gets out, and like I said, I never seen or heard of her with any man."

"And you're saying all of this because . . .?" I asked his ass. He was acting as if he were her brother or something, as if he had a crush on her or something. "You acting like you're her daddy or something, nigga."

"I'm not her daddy, nor her brother, nigga. I was just telling you, nigga," he said, looking offended. Fuck it. I didn't care that nigga was throwing shade in my game.

"Know what, nigga? Don't even worry about it," he said, walking off mad. Shit, I wasn't worrying about it. The nigga wanted me to stay down here, but now when I come across a honey that I like, he starts acting a bitch.

"Is there something that you want to tell me? Do you have a crush on her or something?" I asked, trying to catch up with him.

"Nah, my nigga, you good," he said, cutting me off.

Fuck it, I thought. If he wanted to act like that, then that was fine with me. I wasn't about to kiss the nigga's ass, if that's what he thought. I don't care if he was my blood or not. Hell, the nigga could've been my own damn daddy, and I would've treated him the same muthafucking way.

Deciding not to let him spoil my mood, I went about my business and started shopping. I wanted to get some new shoes, so I decided to head there first. Since he wanted me to stay, now I had a good reason to. I hope by the time this nigga get done shopping, he won't be feeling like a little bitch.

Chapter Seventeen

Brinay

"Girl . . . Nay, I know you seen dude checking you out when you was talking to Chance just now," Kourtney said as I flipped through the many clothes. We were currently in Love Culture, looking for an outfit to wear to Blacky's party tonight. Normally, I don't go out, but since the last call I'd gotten from my brother, I needed a good drink and a nice fucking time.

"Girl, what you talking about?" I asked, trying to play dumb.

"You know what I'm talking about. Chance's cousin, Dontie, was checking you out and you was giving him nothing but attitude, heffa," she laughed, nudging me in my back. I stopped and gave her that *bitch, if you poke me in my back again, I'm going to smack the fuck out of you* look before I went back to find something to put on.

"I seen him, but I ain't paid his ass no mind. You know damn well I'm not trying to date or fuck with nobody right now. Especially since I've got my plate full of problems. The only thing I'm focused on is school. All that other shit is irrelevant to me," I said, just as I spotted a dress that I liked. I removed it from the rack and held it up. "You like?"

"Girl, get out of my face with that ugly-ass shit. I'm going to have to teach you a thing or two about fashion," Kourtney said, taking the dress out of my hand and putting it back on the rack. "Your ass has a body out of this world, and yet, you dress as if your grandmother be buying your clothes. Give that body some room to breathe. Shit, show it off for a change."

"I don't need to be showing off all of my goodies. Besides, that draws too much attention," I told her hot ass.

"Attention, my ass. You just want to be an old grandma. For all that, you could stay home, since you wanna dress like you in ya eighties."

"Bitch, whatever," I said, rolling my eyes at her. She had a real funny way of being dramatic and sarcastic. "Let me see what you find, and it better not be anything sleazy, neither."

"See, now you talking," she said, smiling. I didn't respond. I just shook my damn head at her. To say she was a geek in school, she surely did have a bad side to her. I don't know what I've just gotten myself into. I silently hoped that she wasn't trying to make me look like a slut. "Let's get out of here. I don't see shit in here I like no way."

Several hours later . . .

When we pulled up to the party, it was packed. All of South Carolina must have attended, because I saw damn near everybody I knew, and a whole lot of people I didn't know.

"Girl, Blacky's party gets better and better every year," Kourtney said, as we made our way through the crowd.

"Shit, you ain't never lying. If he keeps that up, he won't be able to throw it in a club no more. He's going to have to rent out the damn concert center or something."

"Who you telling?" she responded. "I need to go to the bathroom."

"Damn, bitch, we just got here. You gotta pee already?" I asked, rolling my eyes.

"Bitch, yeah," she said, as she led the way to the bathroom. I knew she really didn't have to use the bathroom. She was just going in there to check how she looked for the umpteenth time. I don't know why, because I kept telling her that she looked great. Shit, I should be the one trying to haul ass to the nearest mirror, not her.

Thankfully, when we made it to the bathroom, there wasn't a line. We were able to get in there with the quickness. Just as I thought, Kourtney's ass went straight to the mirror.

"I knew your stupid ass ain't had to use the bathroom. I don't know why I even followed ya lying ass in here," I told her as she began applying lip gloss to her already glossy lips.

"Bitch, whatever. I needed to make sure that I look good. Besides, I do have to use the bathroom," she said, handing me her purse. "Hold this for me."

"I hope you hurry up, because I'm not trying to be in the bathroom all night," I replied, taking the purse from her hand. "I already need me a drink."

"Girl, be quiet. I'll only be a minute," she said before she disappeared into the stall. Since I was already in the bathroom, I decided to make sure that I was looking okay. Placing both our purses on the couch, I went over to the full-length mirror.

For a minute, I stood there staring at myself. I couldn't lie. I knew letting Kourtney pick out an outfit for me was a bad idea. Even though I had clothes on, I was feeling somewhat naked. I had on a purple, crop top shirt, a black skirt that stopped a little above my knees that kept rising up every time I walked, with some multicolored wedge heels on. I had on light makeup, and my hair was bone straight with Chinese bangs. I was pleased with the way I looked . . . but I still felt naked.

"Bitch, would you just get over it already?" Kourtney commented, walking out of the stall. She walked over to the sink and washed her hands before she turned and looked at me.

"What I do?" I asked, confused. I had no idea what she was talking about.

"I'm talking about you standing in that mirror. You look fine, I don't know why you think otherwise."

"It's just that I felt awkward. You know I don't normally dress like this," I said, trying to plead my case.

"I know, but you look wonderful like that. Maybe you should start dressing more like this," she joked.

"Ain't gon' happen."

"Uh-huh. Come on, let's get out of here. It's time to party," she said, leading the way.

Dontie

When we pulled up to the club, that bitch was packed. I mean, they had a line wrapped all the way around the building. I doubted if half of the people standing outside would be able to get in. Shit, I don't know if *we* were going to be able to get in. We were barely able to find a parking spot. I damn near had to circle the block three times before we found it.

"Yo, Chance, man, you see this line?" I asked as we parked the car and got out. We ended up parking two blocks away from the club, which meant that we were going to have to walk. "I don't think we're going to be able to get in there."

"Chill, man, we getting in that thing the minute we walk up to the door," he said, pulling his phone out and texting someone. "Ain't no way we not going to get up in here, with all these people in line."

When we arrived at the club, we walked straight up to the door, but not before hearing a few niggas bitch and a couple of hoes trying to get our attention. I'm guessing they were wondering why we wasn't in line with them.

"What's up, Titus, nigga?" Chance said to the bouncer standing by the door.

"What's up, nigga? Where you been at? I was looking for you earlier. I thought you wasn't coming," the bouncer replied, dapping him off.

"Man, I had to get fresh first. You know damn well I wasn't missing this party for anything," Chance responded.

"Oh, that I do know," dude said, looking to me.

"This is my cousin, Dontie. Dontie, this my nigga, Titus," Chance said, introducing us.

"'Sup man?" I said, dapping him off.

"What up?"

"All right, man, I'm about to head in. I'll see you when you get in here," Chance said, as dude removed the velvet rope to let us through.

"Bet."

Just like the outside, the inside of the club was packed. There were niggas and bitches all over. I now know why I see security all over in this bitch.

"Let's head over to the bar," Chance said to me over the music.

"Okay," I said, following behind him. When we made it to the bar, it was crowded as well. We had to wait a minute before we were served.

"What you drinking?" Chance asked once it was our turn.

"Give me a Hennessy," I replied, pulling out a twenty-dollar bill to give to him.

"Nah, I got this round. You just get the next," he said, placing our orders.

Two minutes later, we had our drinks in our hand, scanning the floor. I wasn't too much of a dancer, so the dance floor wasn't my scene. I knew it was only going to be a matter of time before I retired to the nearest seat.

"You wanna walk over by the stage?" Chance whispered in my ear. I shrugged my shoulders, indicating that it didn't matter as I followed his lead. I thought for sure that I was tripping when I noticed the chick I met in the mall earlier making her way through the crowd. Coincidentally, she and her friend were walking to the same place we were going to.

"You remember me?" I asked, whispering in her ear. She jumped before she turned around and looked at me.

"Chance's cousin, right?"

"The name is Dontie, but, yeah. I'm Chance's cousin," I said, getting close to her. "You got a man, ma?"

"Nah, I'm single. You got an old lady?" she asked, taking a sip from the drink she was nursing.

"Nah, ma, I'm single," I told her. "What you drinking on?"

"Alizé. Why?"

"Damn, why every time I ask you something, you answer and ask me why?"

"Because I want to know why you asking me all these questions."

"Maybe because I wanted to buy you a drink."

"Okay, well, go buy my drink then," she said, looking at me with those gorgeous green eyes of hers. The way she was sucking on that straw made my dick jump.

"Don't go nowhere. I'll be right back," I said before I disappeared to the bar.

Chapter Eighteen

Brinay

I was surprised to see Dontie at the club. Okay, I wasn't *that* surprised, but I hadn't banked on seeing him a second time in one day. I was even surprised when he came at me. I knew he wanted me, but he was bold. What he didn't know was that I don't date. It was very hard for me to trust a man. Shit, especially after the shit I went through with my sister and her fucked-up mother. When I told my father about it, he didn't believe me. I haven't fucked with a man since. Shit, in a sense, my father gave me my first actual heartbreak. Lord knows I didn't want to experience that pain again, which is why I've never allowed a nigga into my fold.

It didn't take long for Dontie to return with a few drinks on a tray for everyone. He handed Kourtney and me a drink before he passed the tray to Chance, who took his drink and set it on the table next to him.

"Let me find out you trying to get me drunk," I said, taking a huge gulp of my drink.

"Nah, it ain't like that. I'm just trying to make sure you have a good time. That's all," he said, smiling. I noticed he had a set of perfectly white teeth and a dimple on his cheek. Every time this man said one word, my heart skipped a beat.

"So where are you from?" I asked as we continued to sip and talk.

"I was born and raised in Miami," he said catching me by surprise.

"Well, what are you doing in South Carolina then?"

"I'm here taking care of business," he simply replied. "Besides, my family stays down here also."

"Oh, okay," I said, deciding not to pry any further. Whatever he did was his business, not mine.

"What about you?" he then asked. "Where are you from?"

"South Carolina," I lied. I didn't want to tell him where I was really from.

"Okay. So are you single?"

"Yes. What about you? I know you got a woman or a few baby mamas down in Miami somewhere."

"Nah, I'm single, and I don't have any kids."

"Oh," I replied, paying more attention to my drink. I don't know what it was, but this man had me wanting to give him a try.

I was sipping on my drink and laughing with my newfound friend, when Usher's "Love in This Club" remix, featuring Beyoncé and Lil Wayne came on. I don't know if it was the drink, the outfit, or the fact that basically everywhere I went, a nigga was grabbing on me, but before I realized what I was doing, I grabbed Dontie and headed straight to the dance floor. I turned around with my back toward his front, and we both began slow dancing to the music.

When Beyoncé's part got ready to come on, I turned back around and looked him straight in his eyes. I didn't know how to sing that well, but I was great at lip-synching. I was feeling good, so I really wasn't caring about anything but having a good time right now.

"I know you want it
But I'm hesitating
You must be crazy

I got a man, you got a lady."

I was both surprised and shocked when he grabbed my hips and started lip-synching back to me.

"I know, we here together
So this must be something special
'Cause, you could be anywhere you wanted
But you decided to be here with me."

The way I was moving my hips all over Dontie would've made you think that he was my man. Some people were looking at us like *really?* while others had a look that said *get a room. Fuck them*, I thought. I was having fun, and if I wanted to fuck this nigga on this club dance floor, then I would. I knew them hoes were only hating, because they were two of the hottest-looking dudes in this club, and I had one of them. To make them even madder, I wrapped my arms around his neck, looked him in his eyes, and continued to sing to him.

"This right here is only for your eyes to see . . ."

Dontie

I know y'all probably thought a nigga was being corny, but baby girl was something special. She had a nigga lip-synching to her all in the club, in the middle of the dance floor, with all these people around us. I was acting as if I was the fucking man or something. Shit, I didn't care. All I wanted was to be able to get next to her. If I had to lip-synch, then I was going to. I played as if I didn't notice the many stares from a few niggas and a couple of bitches. I knew they were mad, because they weren't us right now.

The way she moved her hips to the beat of the song had a nigga wanting to take her home and fuck her like there was no tomorrow. I had to adjust my hard-on several times. One time she brushed up against it, and I knew she felt it, because she jumped. I know y'all probably thinking that I was ya typical nigga, but sex wasn't the only thing that I wanted from her. She was special, and I really wanted to get to know her. Besides, she kind of had an attitude that I wanted desperately to tame. I could also tell that she was going to be a challenge, and I loved a good challenge.

We danced through a few more songs before we both got tired and retreated to where Chance and Kourtney were. It was hot, and my undershirt was starting to stick to my chest, and my throat was a bit dry.

"It's about time you two came and sat down. I thought y'all were going to be out there all night."

"Girl, please. I'm so tired and thirsty. I need a damn water for sure," she said, fanning herself.

"Well, let's head to the bar and get you one," Kourtney said to her.

"All right, come on," she said, getting up. "You fellas want anything?"

"Nah, I'm straight," I replied.

"Nah, I'm good," Chance chimed in.

"Okay, cool," she said before they made their way to the bar.

"So you feeling shorty, huh?" Chance asked.

"Man, I like her for sure," I told him.

"Well, if you go at her and she lets you in, please be careful with her feelings. She's a real delicate chick, fam."

"I hear ya, man."

I was brought out of my thoughts by the sound of foot-steps behind me. I turned to see Brinay's father standing there looking at me.

"I don't know what's going on, but I find it real funny, you know. You're always here more than my daughter, and this is *her* sister, not yours," he said, causing my heart to skip a beat. I wanted so badly to tell him what was going on, but I wasn't quite ready yet. "Is there something you need to tell me, son?"

"No, sir, I just think that since my wife can't be here, then I should step up for her."

"Are you sure that's all that's going on, son? I've never seen anything like this in my life," he said, walking toward me. It was in that moment I decided to tell him, but the sight of his wife walking up behind him made me opt not to.

"Hey, honey," she said, kissing him. She then turned to me. She looked as if she was surprised to see me.

"Oh, hello, Dontie. Where's Skylar?" she asked, looking around to see if she was somewhere in the room.

"She's at home, Mrs. Williams."

"Well, what are you doing here if she's at home?" she then asked, turning up her nose at me.

"He came here to check on his sister-in-law, Veronica," her husband said before I could say anything.

"Oh," she replied before everything got quiet.

"Well, I'm going to get going," I said, heading to the door. "I'll see you all later."

"See ya later, son," her father replied.

"Yeah, and can you tell Skylar that I'll be around to check on her later," her mother called after me. I didn't even answer her. Something about that old broad just rubbed me the wrong way.

On my way to the nursery, my phone began ringing. Looking at it, I saw it was my lawyer calling me. I was praying like hell that he had some good news for me, because right now, I truly needed some.

"What's up, Chris?" I asked, answering the phone.

"Nothing much, where you at?"

"I'm over at the hospital. What you got for me?"

"I need you to meet with me. There's some things I need to discuss with you, and I need to discuss them in person," he replied.

"All right, I'll come and see you when I leave here," I said, just as I arrived at the nursery. My son wasn't in his normal spot, which worried me.

"All right. Make sure you come and see me later."

"I will, man," I said before I hung up the phone.

When I walked into the nursery, I didn't see anyone. I was about to turn around when I spotted one of the nurses that was here when I first came in to see my son.

"Excuse me, miss," I said, trying to get her attention.

"Yes, sir."

"I'm looking for my son, Dontie Williams. Can you tell me where he is? I went to look for him, but he's not in his normal spot."

"Oh, he's in the room. His aunt came to feed him today."

"Okay. Thank you!" I replied. *I guess Kourtney finally came here after all,* I thought as I made my way to them. My phone started ringing the minute I made it to the door entrance. Seeing that it was Skylar calling, I placed the phone back in my pocket and proceeded to go see my son.

When I made it in the room, I thought for sure I saw a ghost. Sitting there, holding my son, while feeding him a bottle, was none other than his aunt. His aunt—my wife—Skylar. I damn near passed out.

"I should've known when you didn't answer the phone earlier that you were here," she said, looking up at me.

"What are you doing here and why are you holding your sister's son?" I asked, babbling off at the mouth. I was trying hard to hold back what I really wanted to say.

"So now I can't come see my only nephew now?" she said, as she continued to rock back and forth in the chair.

"I mean, you can, but with the way you've been acting, I don't think you should," I said, being honest.

"What the fuck is that supposed to mean?" She bucked now, getting up. I was about to answer her, but a nurse came in, preventing me from doing so.

"Hello, Mr. Edmon. There's a few things that I'd like to talk to you about," she said, walking over to me.

"Okay," I responded, waiting for her to continue. She looked from me to Sky, then back at me.

"In private, please."

"No, thank you. Whatever you have to say to him, you can say in front of me. In case you didn't know, he's my husband," Sky said, flashing her ring finger.

"Okay, well, as you know, the baby is doing fine and most likely—" was all she got out before Chance and Kourtney walked through the door.

"Hey, Dontie," Kourtney said, speaking to me. Her eyes then traveled to where Sky and baby Dontie were sitting in the rocking chair. She had a *what the fuck?* look on her face, before she looked back at me.

Most people really didn't know Kourtney that much. Hell, I'm just learning about her. She was normally quiet, but when pushed or not in the mood, she could be a hothead. If anyone was to walk in the room and look at her now, they'd think she was being as calm as possible, but Chance and I knew better. From the minute she began tapping her hand on her leg, we knew she was about to have one of those moments if we didn't hurry up and change her mood quickly. Since seeing Sky holding Brinay's baby is what had her like this, that meant we had to get Brinay's baby from Skylar's arms, with a quickness. Chance and I exchanged looks with pleading eyes before he walked over to Skylar.

"Can I see the baby?" he asked her. She was about to put up a fuss, but he took him anyway. My eyes immediately shot to Kourtney. The minute she stopped tapping on her leg, I knew she was good, and we didn't have to put up with her ranting and raving today.

"Is everything okay?" the nurse asked. She must have sensed that something was going to pop off too.

"Yeah, ma, everything is straight," I told her. "Now what was it that you were trying to tell me?"

"Oh, yeah," she suddenly remembered. "Like I was saying, as you all know, the baby is doing fine, but his mother isn't. He's going to be able to go home tomorrow, but what we want to know is who's going to be taking him? We can't release the baby to just anybody."

"That's fine, because he'll be going home with me until his mother gets out of the hospital," Sky said from behind me. My neck twisted in her direction so fast, I was afraid that I was going to get whiplash. "Well, with me and my husband."

"Like hell he is. You and Brinay don't even get along. What makes you think you can take her baby home with you?" Kourtney asked, outraged. I knew she was heated by the tone of her voice.

"Bitch, who are you even?" Sky answered smartly.

"I'm her fucking sister."

"But you could never be. Her mother only has one daughter, and her father has two. I'm one of them, and she's the other one, and I know you ain't no kin to me."

"We may not be blood related, but trust when I say that *I'm* her sister," Kourtney said matter-of-factly.

"Like *I* said, you *ain't* no kin. Therefore, my nephew goes nowhere with you, bitch."

"You must have me confused with some bird, bitch," Kourtney said, taking a step closer to her.

"Nah, I don't have you confused with anyone. I got you just right. You acting like you big and bad, all behind a baby that ain't for you," Sky challenged her.

"Y'all need to stop all of this," Chance said, trying to defuse the situation.

"I don't have to stop anything. Like I said, *my* sister's son ain't going nowhere with this hoodlum," Sky threw in there.

"Bitch, you can say that a million times, but you think your sister gon' choose you over me?" Kourtney challenged her. When she didn't say anything, Kourtney continued. "You making noise for this baby like you really care. You don't even care about your own sister. How many times have you talked to your sister in the last few years? Where were you when your sister needed her family? Now you want to pull this? Bitch, get yaself a life, please. Nay don't even care about you like that."

"You can say whatever you want to. How do you know that I don't care for my sister? How do you know anything? You're a fucking *friend*. I'm sure my sister don't tell you everything."

"Look, we can go back and forth all you want. Truth of the matter is, I don't give a fuck. You still ain't leaving this hospital with Nay's baby," Kourtney yelled.

"Look, right now is not the time for all of this," I finally said. I was getting tired of everything.

"Well, what about the child's father?" the nurse asked me. My eyes went to Kourtney, whose eyes immediately traveled to mine. I was happy that Sky was standing behind me, because the look on my face would've been a dead giveaway.

"Umm . . . He's not here at the moment," Kourtney answered.

"Well, we're going to have to think of something, because this baby goes home tomorrow," the nurse said before she walked out of the room. I stood there stuck.

I needed to come up with a solution, and quick. There was no way I was going to let my child go home with Skylar, and I damn sure wasn't about to let my child go home with just anybody. I was going to make something happen in those twenty-four hours. I just don't know what it is yet.

Chapter Nineteen

Kourtney

I don't know what this looney bitch, Sky, was smoking, or who the fuck she thinks she is, but she had things all fucked up. She had to be out of her rabbit-ass mind if she thought she was taking baby Dontae anywhere. I don't know what they've been telling this ditsy broad, but she needs a wake-up call and fast. I know damn well her and Brinay weren't on any speaking terms, so her talking that bullshit about her nephew and all that was nothing but a front. I don't know what she had up her sleeve, but I'd be damned if I let her pull anything with *my* sister's baby.

I stood there as she popped her gum, hollering about "her sister and her nephew this," and "her sister and her nephew that." She hollered about how she had more rights than any of us in this room. All I could remember, however, were the many stories Brinay told me about how she and her bitch of a mother would treat her. How they wouldn't feed her, and did all kinds of fucked-up shit to her, and yet, this bitch was trying to take her son home. I immediately got teary-eyed just thinking about it. Who's to say that she wouldn't do the same thing to him? Who's to say that she wouldn't treat him bad, especially when she finds out who his daddy is? No way in hell. This bitch would really have to kill me before I let baby Dontae go home with her.

I knew how I could get when a bitch pushed me, so I had to get out of that hospital nursery. I wasn't leaving at all. I just had to get away from the Wicked Bitch of the West. To be honest, I had a feeling that the hospital was going to release Nay's baby to Sky and them. I mean, they were, in fact, sisters, and I didn't have any weight. That's why I wished that Dontie would come clean already. It was time for him to tell his bitch about him and Brinay. Shit, after all, he didn't know they were sisters. Besides, he was messing with Nay before he started fucking with ol' girl, from what I knew. What I don't know is why he fucked around and married her ass. Then he had the nerve to spit that bullshit about buying Brinay the ring first. It didn't matter who he bought the fucking ring for, what mattered was who was wearing it and who got the last name. Him saying that he bought that ring for Nay was a waste of time, since he had another bitch wearing it, along with his last name.

"You all right?" Chance asked the minute he reached me. I was outside the hospital, sitting on the bench by the emergency entrance.

"Hell, no, I ain't all right," I replied. "You didn't hear that bullshit Dontie's wife was spitting just now in that hospital? Ain't no way I'm letting her take my sister's baby home with her tomorrow. Fuck that shit. I'll kidnap him out of here before I let that shit happen."

"Man, you know Tae will not let Sky take his son home. So you don't have to worry about none of that shit there," Chance said, trying to cover for his boy, but fuck all that.

"I don't know shit. Fuck, I don't even know Dontie like I thought I knew him. For all I know, he could be behind that bitch, making her say she's going to take him home," I said, meaning everything that came out of my mouth. Brinay and I obviously didn't know Tae as well as we thought we knew him, so that meant I didn't trust his ass as far as I could've thrown him.

"Ma, chill out. All that there ain't even called for. If it's one thing I do know about Dontie is that he do love Brinay and his son."

"Yeah yeah yeah . . ." I said, tuning him out. I didn't have time to put up with none of that bullshit. I pulled my phone out and was about to make a call when it started ringing. The number was unfamiliar, but I still answered it anyway.

"Hello," I said, answering it on the third ring.

"Hello, Nay, is that you?" a male voice asked.

"Who is this?" I asked, because I didn't recognize the voice, nor did I recognize the number.

"This me, Brandon," he answered. I ran the name through my memory bank but didn't come up with anything. Then I remembered I had all of Brinay's calls forwarded to my cell phone.

"Brinay's brother, Brandon?" I asked, because I remembered her brother was in jail, and he wasn't supposed to get out for another two years.

"Yeah, that's me," he answered. "Who this and where is Brinay?"

"Umm . . . I'm Kourtney, Brinay's best friend," I answered, trying my best not to answer his other question. I didn't know how to tell this man who was in jail that his sister was laid up in the hospital.

"Nice to meet you, Kourtney. I've heard so many things about you," he said.

"All good things, I hope."

"Yeah. Where's my little sister? I've been calling her for the past few days, and she has yet to answer me. Is something wrong?" he asked again. I was about to answer when I realized that he wasn't calling me from the jailhouse phone.

"Where are you, Brandon?"

"Umm . . . I'm in Miami."

"I thought you was in jail," I said.

"I was, but I got out this morning. That's why I've been trying to call Nay these last few days to let her know that I was getting out earlier," he said, sounding a bit excited. I know that excitement was only going to last a few minutes until I told him about his sister.

"That's good to hear, but about Brinay. Umm . . . She's in the hospital," I said slowly.

"What?" he asked. "What's going on with her?"

"Well . . ." I replied, just as Dontie and his wife walked out of the hospital door. They looked at me, and I rolled my eyes at them. I didn't have time to be playing with them. I then proceeded to tell Brinay's brother about her accident. He wanted to know more about her situation, but it wasn't my business nor was it my place. If she wanted to, that was her place to tell him whenever she got ready.

"Damn . . . man . . ." he said after I finished telling him about everything that was going on. "What hospital she in? I got to get to South Carolina to come see my BriBri."

"Actually, we're in Miami as well," I told him. "I thought I told you that."

"What hospital is she in?" he asked. I quickly told him the hospital name.

"Okay, thank you. The minute I find a ride, I'll be there."

"Wait. Tell me where you are and I'll come get you," I told him. This might be good for my girl. She might wake up for him. I waited for him to tell me where he was before I hung up, promising him that I'd be on my way in the next ten minutes.

Right when I hung up the phone, I spotted Tae walking back to the hospital. I didn't see his wife with him, so I'm guessing he sent that ho home. Good, because I don't know how much more of that ho's mouth I could take.

"What's up, Kourtney?" he asked when he made it to where Chance and I were.

"Ain't shit up," I dryly answered his ass. I wasn't trying to be friends with this nigga when he was playing both sides.

"Oh, so you got an attitude now?" he asked, once he heard the way that I had answered him.

"Fucking right, I got an attitude. You need to put yo' ho in her place," I said, matter-of-factly. "You out of all people should know how I am behind Brinay and her baby. Ain't no way I'm letting that sadity ho take my friend's baby home with her. I don't care how much she claim to be Brinay's sister. She know my girl doesn't fuck with her like that. That ho was just talking to hear herself talk. You lucky I didn't punch that bitch in her face for the way she was popping off at the mouth. Only because we were in a hospital and my nephew was in the room did I not fuck her ass clean up. Next time, she won't be so lucky."

"Man, I already know that's why you were mad, but you can chill on all that. Sky ain't taking my son no-damn-where," he spoke, getting angry. I didn't give a fuck about anything right now. I was prepared to go to jail if Dontie's dog ass didn't come up with a solution, and the hospital ended up giving her baby to her sister.

"You better look like you feeling the same way when it's time for him to be released tomorrow," I told him as I began walking off, heading to my car. I stood a few feet away from where Dontie and Chance were standing and turned around. "Just be prepared to be outed if the hospital doesn't want to give me Brinay's baby. I don't care how you're going to feel, but I'm bringing the daddy into that situation. I don't care if your wife is there or not."

I stood there for a few more seconds as his jaws clenched. I knew he was mad, but I wasn't playing. I was prepared to let them know who Brinay's baby daddy was if the hospital refused to let her son come home with me tomorrow. Dontie had better be ready for whatever it was that his wife was going to do tomorrow. Brinay's baby wasn't going anywhere with her ass, and that was a bet.

Throwing my shades over my eyes, I walked off. I was going to pick up Brinay's brother, and we were going to come straight back to the hospital. I didn't even get a chance to see my friend. Hell, with all of the things going on with the baby, she'd understand why I hadn't. I hope like hell she hurries and wakes that ass up.

Chapter Twenty

Brandon

I've been waiting on this day to this to come for years now. I would've done geophysics to be a free man. I don't know how much longer I could've taken being locked up. I hated that I had to be locked in a cage as if I were an animal or something, but all of that is in the past now. I'm a free man, and I couldn't wait to see all of the things that I've been missing. Besides, I haven't seen my little sister since she was sixteen. She was now twenty-five, and I missed her little ass like crazy.

Yeah, we kept in contact, and she sent me a few pictures here and there, but I made sure that she never came up here. I didn't want her to see me like this, because I knew it wasn't going to do anything but depress her, which is why when she got accepted into a college out of state, I made it my business to make sure that she went there. The farther she went away to school, the better she was. I didn't want her to get caught up in this Miami life. That shit took eight years of my life. There was no way in hell I was going to let it get my little sister too.

I had all hopes of my little sister being there for me when I got out, but they were shot down. I kept wondering why she wasn't answering her cell or house phones. I had been calling her for the past week, and now I know why. It hurt me to my soul to know that my one and only sister was laid up in a hospital, and I couldn't be there for her. It was a good thing the people released me two years ahead of time, because now, I could take care of her.

I stood outside the gas station, waiting on my little sister's friend to come get me. I was glad that she had offered to come, because I knew it would've taken me a minute to get there if she hadn't. I didn't have any friends. All of them, including my girlfriend, turned their backs on me the minute I got locked up. If it wasn't for my sister, I don't know how I'd have been able to survive up in jail.

"What's up, young blood?" an old dude asked as he walked out of the store. "You waiting for someone?"

"Yes, I'm actually waiting for my little sister."

"Oh, okay," he said, walking off.

"Hey." A bright yellow girl yelled from a window of a car. "You Brandon?"

"Yeah, that's me. You're Kourtney, right?" I asked as she got out.

"Yeah, that's me," she said, walking over to me.

"Nice to meet you," I said, reaching out my hand for a handshake. Instead, she wrapped her arms around me, giving me a warm hug. At first, I was caught off guard but quickly realized that shorty was just trying to show me love.

"Nice to meet you too," she said, pulling back. "You can put your things in the trunk."

"Okay," I replied, doing as I was told. We both then hopped in the car and were on our way to the hospital.

For the first part of the ride, it was silent. Shit, we really didn't know each other. The only thing we had in common was my little sister. As I sat there, I decided to check shorty out. She was light-skinned, which wasn't my thing, but she was cute with it. She had a cute face and a nice body. Her eyes were odd-shaped but cute, and she had a nice pair of lips that I wouldn't mind sucking on.

Oh my God, I thought. Here it is, I barely knew this chick, and I was already thinking about having sex. I blamed that on all of the years I spent locked up. My hormones were raging, and I needed relief bad. *Get it together, Brandon,* I said to myself. Since she was in my sister's life, that meant she was now going to be a part of my life too, so I might as well get the formalities out of the way.

"So you're my sister's friend, right?" I asked, turning to her.

"Yes," she said, never taking her eyes off the road.

"Where did you all meet?"

"We met in school back in South Carolina," she answered. "We both started school together, and we've been friends ever since."

"Oh, cool," I said, nodding my head. "Y'all keeping y'all grades together?"

"Most definitely. Your sister wouldn't have it any other way," she said, flashing her beautiful smile. That was the first time I noticed she had a set of dimples. "She's a school freak."

"Good. She don't need to be out in the streets. I've always preached to her how important school is, and she should keep her head in her books and finish it."

"Oh, so that's where she gets it from," she joked, finally taking her eyes from off of the road, but only for a quick second.

"Hey . . . hey . . . I just want my little sister to be better than I was. I don't have a high school education or anything. There were many days when I wanted to stop everything I was doing to go back to school, but I couldn't. I had to make sure that my mother and sister were able to eat and sleep well at night. I'm not saying that I regret being the man of the house. I just wish I would've went about being it another way. I should've stayed in school and gotten myself a good job that paid good money. Then

I wouldn't have had to lose out on eight years of my life, you know," I told her. "Being locked up made me realize all of the mistakes that I made. I was young and dumb. If I knew then what I know now, I would've been smart about the choices I've made through my thirty-one years of life."

"I feel where you're coming from," she replied. "But your sister is going to be fine. She already knows what she should and shouldn't be doing. Again, you've taught her well. It's time that you trust in what you've instilled in her and see how things go."

"I hear what you're saying, shorty, but me and my sister don't have anyone. It's just us two in this world."

"Nah, that's not true," she quickly interjected. I was about to ask her how, but she answered before I could. "Y'all have me."

"Is that right?" I asked, with a raised eyebrow.

"Hell, yeah, it is. So not only do you have one sister to look after, you now have *two*." She poked her tongue out.

"Well, in case you didn't know, everything I just said for Brinay applies to you too," I said, playfully mushing her head.

"My head is not big, but I can't say the same for you," she teased. "You got a water jug head."

"My head ain't big, li'l sis."

"Aww. You called me li'l sis."

"That's what you are now," I said genuinely. Shorty was giving off a good vibe. I spent so many years worrying about my little sister, wondering how her life had been since I wasn't there. I never stopped to think that every-thing I taught her about responsibility and people, she understood properly.

"That I am," she giggled. I knew she said that she was my little sis, and I agreed with her. On the inside, though, I really wanted to get to know her and possibly bang her out. "It's going to be fun having a big brother now."

"You don't have no brothers?"

"Nah, unfortunately, I was adopted when I was a baby. So, honestly, I don't know," she said sadly.

"Shorty, I'm sorry, I didn't know," I said, feeling bad now.

"It's cool. You had no idea of knowing that. I'm good. I've gotten past the idea of not being wanted when I met your sister. She's shown me so much love, that all of that doesn't matter to me anymore," she responded softly, but I could tell by the sound of her voice that she was still feeling some type of way.

"That's good, shorty," was all I said. I didn't know how to address her. I'd never been in a situation like this before.

For the remainder of the ride, the car was silent. I felt bad for shorty, but really, we were in the same situation. She'd never met her family and was placed up for adoption, while Brinay and I only knew our mother. Well, Brinay knew her father too. She just acted as if he wasn't around. I only met my father while I was in prison, and our mother died when we were teenagers. We were all missing love from somewhere in life.

Before I knew it, we were pulling up to the hospital. Shorty found a parking spot right in the front, pulled in, and killed the engine. She sat there for a minute looking into space, not even moving.

"Look, shorty," I said turning to her, "I'm truly sorry. I had no idea that you were adopted."

"I told you that it's cool. I'm fine," she smiled weakly.

"No, you're not, and it's okay to still feel bad about the situation. People never really get over that, but you don't have to worry about not being loved. You have Brinay and me. That all the love you're going to need," I told her. She nodded her head as I spotted a lone tear falling down her cheek. I reached over and wiped it with my finger. "It's okay, li'l sis. Big brother is here, and I promise not to disappoint any of you gals again."

"Look at me. I barely even know you. Hell, I just met you all of twenty minutes ago, and here I am, crying like a big-ass baby."

"It's cool, li'l mama," I told her.

"Thank you, Brandon, I really needed that." She reached over and hugged me, placing a kiss on my cheek before pulling back. Her lips felt so soft against my cheek, I felt my dick jump.

"Come on, let's get out here. I know you can't wait to see your sister, and I need some fresh air," she said, getting out of the car. She waited for me, and together, we walked into the hospital, where we headed straight for the elevators.

"Oh shit," she suddenly said. "Do you want to go see your nephew first or do you want to go and see your sister? I forgot to ask you."

"It's cool, shorty, it don't matter. As long as I get to see both of them, then I'm fine."

"Okay," she said, pushing the elevator for the second floor. The elevator bell rang a few seconds later, and we were heading to my sister's room. With each step we took, my heart skipped two beats. I didn't know what to expect when I walked in that room.

"Now, I have to warn you. She's hooked up to a few machines, so she won't look like her normal beautiful self," she said as we stopped by the door.

"I'm cool. I can handle it," I told her.

"Okay, well, in that case, let's go," she said, pushing the door to the room open. I got the shock of my life when I spotted my sister sitting up in the bed. There were two other dudes sitting in the room with her.

"Oh my God, Nay," Shorty screamed, running to the bed. "I can't believe it. You're up!"

"She got up right when you left," a light-skinned dude said to her.

"Why didn't you call me then, Chance?" she asked, with her hands on her hips.

"We did, but you didn't answer."

"Uh-huh, I bet," she said, turning to Brinay, whose eyes were fixed on me. "I'm so happy to see you up, sister."

"Say it ain't so," she spoke, just above a whisper. "Tell me that my one and only sibling is standing by the door, and I'm not tripping."

"You're not, Nay Nay," I said, calling her by the name I gave her when she was just a baby. "It's really me."

"Come here, big bro," she said, reaching her arms out to me. The minute I reached her and pulled her into my arms, she began sobbing uncontrollably. "When did you get out, and why you ain't call to tell me?"

"I did try, but you wasn't answering the phone, Nay Nay."

"I was tied up, as you can see," she said, with her eyes traveling to the dark-skinned dude. She rolled her eyes and turned back to me. Obviously, there was something going on between the two of them, and I was surely going to find out what.

"I'm Brandon, Brinay's brother," I said to the two of them.

"Oh, my bad, B. B, this here is Chance, and that one is Dontie," she said, introducing the three of us. I noticed the way she introduced the dark-skinned dude as if she hated to say his name. I made a mental note to ask her about that later.

"What's up, man?" I said, shaking their hands. "Where's the baby?"

"He's downstairs in the nursery. I just called for them to bring him up before you got here," she said, just as the nurse came in with him. She rolled him over to Brinay's bedside; then she took him out of the bed and handed him to her.

I sat there watching my sister interact with her son. I was somewhat disappointed, but I was proud of her for standing up and being a woman about hers. Most females would've had an abortion, knowing that they were in school, but she didn't. I wanted to know more about her baby daddy, and where that nigga was, but that was a topic for later. I was free, my sister was up, and my nephew was healthy. Right now was a joyous moment, and I wanted to enjoy it.

Brinay

When I woke up this evening, I didn't know where I was. My vision was blurry, my head was hurting, and I couldn't speak due to something in my throat. After a few minutes of blinking, my vision cleared up, and I found that I was lying in a hospital. I couldn't remember how I got there. I used the hand that wasn't filled with IVs to call the nurse. A minute or two later, the door flew open, and the nurse came in. When she noticed that I was the one who pushed the call button, she walked right back out, only to return moments later with a doctor.

"Hello, Ms. Williams. It's nice of you to finally join us," he said to me. "I'm Doctor Martin. I've been your doctor since you were brought in. Do you remember why you're here?" I shook my head, because I honestly had no idea. Everything in my mind was just a blur right now, but hopefully, as the day goes by, I'll remember.

"Well, you were involved in an auto accident a few days ago. Luckily, you and your baby are fine," he said. The minute he said "baby," everything that I've been through these past few days came speeding back. Remembering my baby, my hands flew to my stomach. It wasn't big anymore, and I immediately began to panic. "You can calm down, ma'am. We had to deliver your baby by emergency C-section. He's fine and healthy, and he's in the nursery. You can call for him whenever you want to, and the nurse will bring him in. Now, let's get started on you. First, I'm going to check you to make sure that everything is fine, and then, we're going to get that nasty tube out of your throat. Okay?"

I lay there as he and his team of nurses went about poking and probing me. They checked everything, and I do mean *everything*. I was all for getting better, but when they got to my stomach and began pushing down on it, I wanted to scream. The staples had me in so much pain, I thought for sure that I was going to pass out or something. After they were done checking and making sure that I was fine, they removed the tube, gave me some ice chips, and handed me a few pills for the pain. They then left, but not before saying that they were going to be back later to run some more tests to make sure I was coming along fine and that I was healing properly. I nodded my head that I understood and lay back. I was tired, and I didn't have any energy.

I lay there as the medicine began to work. I was going to take me a good ol' nap before I called down to the nursery so I can finally meet my son. Well, that's what I *thought* I was going to do. Just when I closed my eyes, Chance and Dontie came walking into the room. They were the last two people I expected to see or want here. Figuring they'd leave knowing I was still out, I continued to lie there with my eyes closed.

They began talking about any and everything. I wanted to bust their bubbles, but the minute my name came up, along with Skylar's, I decided to continue to listen.

"So what are you going to do about your situation?" Chance asked Dontie.

"What situation?"

"*This* situation," Chance answered. "I know your wife is becoming suspicious. You've been running up here every day since she's been in here, sometimes two and three times a day. Ain't no way Sky don't know something is going on now."

"Bruh, to be honest, I don't even know. I'm still trying to work some things out. I love Brinay with every fiber in me. I love my son also, and I want to be with them so we can be a family, but I got to handle this Sky situation first. I really regret the day I said I do to that bitch, but I can't change it. I'm trying to get my boy down at the courthouse to help me out with this marriage shit, but it's taking me longer than I expected."

"So, what are you going to do in the meantime?" he asked.

Shit, *I* wanted to know also. I don't care how much he professed his love for me, he shouldn't have married that bitch in the first place. Hell, he lied and said he didn't have a woman, and that shit there still had me pissed. I can't front, though . . . I love the hell out of Tae. I just wish that things didn't happen the way they did. I'd be happy to be a family with him and my son, but now, I don't know.

"I'm going to fight for my family, *that's* what I'm going to do."

"But what about Sky?"

"Man, fuck Sky. I'm not trying to be bothered with her ass anymore. Truth be told, I don't know what made me begin fucking with her in the first place. Something is seriously wrong with her. I'm really starting to miss the woman I was being with."

"I'm thinking the same thing. It's like when I first met her, she was cool and shit, but now she's not. She's beginning to act as if she's one of those crazy, stalking-ass broads. I'm just happy she's your problem and not mine."

"She won't be my problem for long, my nigga, believe that," he said before the room grew quiet. I then felt his hand rubbing against my cheek, scaring me. My eyes immediately shot open.

"Oh fuck!" he yelled, jumping back. "Aye, man, go call the nurse or something. She's up. Her eyes are open."

I rolled my eyes at him because he was acting all concerned now, when his ass was part of the reason why I was in here. "You don't have to call anyone. They've been in here already."

"So you been up?" he asked taking a seat on the bed beside me.

"Yup," I said dryly. I really wasn't trying to have a conversation with him. I was still trying to figure how I felt about him and this whole Sky situation. I guess he got the hint, because he didn't say anything after that.

I cut the TV on, and the three of us sat in the room quietly watching it. I really wasn't watching, I was busy trying to process everything. I wanted to be with Tae. I wanted us to be one big family, but the fact of the matter is, he's married to my sister, and I still don't know how to feel. Shit, what would my father think if he knew the man his daughter was married to, was the same man that his youngest daughter was pregnant by, and now had a baby by. That's just not something you hear or see in real life. This shit was something like on *The Young and the Restless*. I've never seen anything like this before in my life, and to know I was living this life was crazy, but that was unimportant. Right now, I had to focus on getting better so that my son and I could get up out of this hospital. I needed to leave Miami and go back to South Carolina so that I could clear my head and get myself together.

As I sat there, I was thinking about what had happened. Truth be told, I was still feeling a bit shaken up about the accident. Lord knows I had enough going on in my life. I'm just glad that I wasn't seriously injured. All I can say is that I was blessed and highly favored. I thought for sure that when I had gotten into that accident, I was never going to see the light of day again, but my God had other plans. Not to mention, my guardian angel was there with me through the whole thing. I needed to talk to Kourtney. I was missing her like crazy, and I needed some advice ASAP. Sitting up, I reached for the phone to call her, when she and my brother walked through the door.

The moment I laid eyes on B, my eyes got misty. Suddenly, nothing else mattered. My one and only brother was home, and I was beyond happy. I haven't seen my brother since my mother died, and I missed him like crazy. He thinks I didn't know that he was trying to keep me away from him, but I did. Every time I'd try to go see him, he'd always make up an excuse or change the subject. One time I came, and he denied my visit. I was hurt. I understood what he was doing, but I was still hurt. He was the only person I had until I met Kourtney. Since he was shutting me out, I was alone. It was a good thing when I met Kourtney, because I was damn near about to lose all of my sanity.

I spent the next few hours catching up with my brother, Kourtney, and my son. Chance and Dontie had to leave, which I was fine with. I didn't want to be bothered with them no way. Besides, I could tell that something was bothering Dontie. I think it was the fact that I didn't want him to touch my son, or the fact that I ignored his ass the whole time. That didn't stop him from trying, though. He finally got the hint after an hour or so. That's when he decided to bounce. He said that he was going to be back later, but I told him not to even worry about it. I was going to spend the rest of the night catching up with my son. I didn't want any disturbance.

"So what's going on with you?" I asked Brandon.

"What you mean?" he asked as he sat in the chair, feeding my baby a bottle.

"Are you going to stay in Miami, or are you going to come to South Carolina to live with me?" I asked, wanting to know what plans he had now that he was out of jail. I didn't need him staying in Miami, getting into trouble, and possibly going back to jail.

"Honestly, I haven't given it any thought yet."

"Well, you know that you're always welcome to come and stay with me if you want to move. Besides, I got a hideaway out here too, if you want to stay here. Just know that if you stay, I'm coming back home," I said, letting it be known. I was always my brother's baby. We didn't have much as kids, but he would always baby me with the little things that we did have. He was more like my father than my real father was.

"Let me give it some thought first. I'll let you know when I decide."

"That's all I ask," I said, sitting up. "Now, can you give me my son? It's Mommy and son time."

"No problem. I was about to get out of here anyways," he said, standing up. He handed me my son before he attempted to walk out the door.

"Where you going?"

"I have a few things to do. I'll come back and see you tomorrow."

"Really, Brandon?" I asked. I had no idea what his ass was up to, but I knew it couldn't be anything nice.

"I'm not going to get into trouble, little sis. I just want to hit up the mall, get myself a new wardrobe, and get something to eat."

"Well, if that's all you're going to do, then take Kourtney with you. She's not busy, and I'm more than sure she doesn't want to sit around Dontie and Chance all day," I suggested. I know he was mad, but I didn't care. I heard what his mouth said, but I wanted to be sure that my brother wasn't going to get his ass in any trouble. "Besides, how are you going to get to the mall? You don't have a ride."

"Nay Nay!" he yelled. "I told you that I'm going to be fine."

"I heard what you said. Since you're going to the mall, then let Kourtney drive you there. Besides, if you're going to get a new wardrobe, you should take her. She knows all the latest fashions. She'll take you from looking like a chump to looking like a model with the quickness."

"Nay, that's a grown man. He don't need nobody following him around. Shit, he just got out of jail. What makes you think he want to be supervised?" Kourtney asked, looking at me sideways. I gave her a *shut the fuck up and go with it* look. "Leave the boy be. He'll be fine."

"I know he's going to be fine, because you're going to be there," I said, folding my arms across my chest. I knew if I pouted, he was going to give in to what I wanted.

For a minute, everyone sat there, not saying a word. Kourtney and Brandon were both looking at me as if I was getting on their nerves, while I sat there, being the spoiled little brat my brother made me into. He knew I was only trying to look out for him and make sure that he would stay out of trouble. He was all I had. I'd be damned if I let him come home and go back to doing the same shit he was doing before he got locked up. There was no way I was going to lose my brother again. He's lucky I'm up in here and unable to move, because *I'd* be the one going with him, but since I can't, I'll let Kourtney do the job for me. She's just like me when it comes to life. She'll make sure that he stays out of trouble, and I know that for a fact.

"Okay, you win this time," he said, which caused me to smile. I knew my brother like the back of my hand. I knew all along that I was going to win. "Don't be getting all happy. I'm going to start putting my foot down."

"Yeah, well, until that time comes, I'll continue being the brat you made me into," I said, laughing.

"Girl, you're a mess," Kourtney said, getting up from her seat. She walked over to the crib and gave baby Dontae a kiss before she came and gave me a hug. "I'll call you later . . . brat!"

"I'll be waiting on your call too."

"See you later, Nay Nay," Brandon said, kissing my cheek. "Come on, li'l sis, I got places to be."

"Aye, don't be getting too comfortable with my girl, now."

"Girl, please, that's gon' be bae, and y'all don't even know it," he said, shocking both Kourtney and me. Before I could say something, he pulled her by the arm, and they were gone.

"Lord, please give me strength," I said aloud. I reached over and got my baby out of the crib before I snuggled closely to him, prepared to get some rest.

The saying, *what's done in the dark will come to the light,* kept running through my mind as I drove to the hotel to meet Randall. My life was hectic already, and here his old ass was, making it worse. I know he wasn't calling me to talk business since I'd taken a vacation until further notice. I'd told everyone from the office not to bother me unless it was very important or an emergency. I especially told him not to ring my phone for anything. I had gone as far as to block his number, but he ended up calling me from a different number, saying that he had information on my husband that I should know about. So here I am, running to see what it was.

I seriously doubt that my husband was just *checking* on my sister because I failed to. There was more to this story, and I was going to find out. There was no way they could form a bond like that this fast, and they barely knew each other. Hell, I'd never seen them hold one conversation. So how could he care for her or her bastard-ass son, when he doesn't know the bitch? This situation was fishy, and there were so many unanswered questions that I needed answered right this minute. I was hopeful that Randall could help shed some light on this sticky situation.

I pulled up to the hotel just as my phone began to ring. I picked it up and checked to see that it was my father calling. Knowing that he wasn't going to do anything but talk about his precious daughter, I ignored his call. He was trying to rekindle things with her. I don't know why he was trying to include me in anything. As I'd told him and my darling husband, that was *his* responsibility to have a relationship with Brinay, *not* mine. I didn't care before, and I absolutely don't care what happens to her now. Whatever he was calling me about wasn't important, one way or another.

Pulling my car all the way to the back of the hotel, as I always do, I found a spot next to the building. Since it was daylight, I wasn't trying to risk my car being seen by anyone. Before getting out of the car, I made sure to check my makeup and add some lip gloss. It wasn't that I was trying to look good for him. I was making sure that my shit was still intact. No one has ever seen me looking torn up, and I wasn't about to let them see me looking torn up now. When I was done checking myself in the mirror, I turned off my car and got out.

Throwing my shades over my eyes, I made my way into the hotel and headed straight for the elevator without stopping at the front desk. There was no need to.

Randall and I would always get the same room every time we came here. He made sure of that. Hopping off the elevator, I took a seat in a chair by the elevator door and looked in my purse. I fished out the pills my doctor prescribed for me three months ago and took two. I didn't take my pills on the regular, but I did at times like these. Then I waited a few minutes before I got up. I knew what Randall wanted. Every time he found something out or did something for me, he'd always want sex from me. Since I didn't have a choice, I'd always give it to him.

"Is there something wrong, ma?" a man asked as he stepped off the elevator with a handful of bags. I looked up to see one of the most handsome men I've ever seen in my life. He was about six foot one, dark skinned, with a buff body as if he worked out daily. Dude was sexy with a low fade, a bunch of waves, and a pair of hazel eyes that made my pussy wet.

"No, I'm fine. Thanks for asking," I answered, looking into his eyes. *I wouldn't mind staring in them at night while making love,* I thought. "Why did you ask?"

"Oh, okay. I saw you as soon as I stepped off the elevator and thought that something was wrong."

"Oh, thanks. I was looking for my phone in my purse," I lied.

"Okay, cool. Well, have a great day then," he said, as he continued down the hall. I don't know why, but something in me was calling out to him.

"Hey!" I yelled, stopping him.

"What's up?" he asked, turning around. I got up from my chair and went to meet him.

"Are you single?" I asked out of nowhere.

"Umm . . . Yes, I am," he said, smiling.

"Can I get your number?" I asked, handing him my phone.

"Sure," he said taking the phone out of my hand. He programmed his number before he handed it back to me.

"Thanks," I said, preparing to walk back to the chair I was sitting in.

"Wait, what's your name, ma?" he asked, just as the bell rang for the elevator. I was going to sit back in the chair, but I felt kind of thirsty, and I just had to get out of there.

"Sky," I said, getting on the elevator. I pushed the button for the first floor.

"Okay, Sky. My name is—" he began to say, but the door closed before I could hear his name. Oh well, I'll get it whenever I decide to call him. I rode the elevator to the first floor and was about to get out when Randall called my phone. I had completely forgotten I was there for him.

"Where are you?" he asked, sounding impatient.

"I'm coming up on the elevator now. Be fucking patient," I said, snapping on him. It was a good thing that my pills had started kicking in because I would've cursed his ass out and left.

"Yeah, whatever. Just hurry your ass up," he said, before hanging up. I looked at the phone confused. I couldn't wait to get up there so that I can curse his ass the fuck out. I quickly got back on the elevator, pushing the button that led to the second floor multiple times. Tapping on my leg, I waited impatiently for the elevator to come to a stop on the second floor. The minute the elevator beeped and the doors came open, I stomped down the hall, straight to the room. When I arrived at the door, I raised my hand to knock, but somehow, he knew I was there and opened the door before I could begin beating on it.

"What the fuck you playing with me for?" I asked, still standing in the door. He didn't answer me. Instead, he looked at me from head to toe before walking into the room. When he noticed that I wasn't following behind him, he turned around.

"You can come in, Skylar," he replied. I don't know why, but for some reason, I liked the way that old man said my name, even though I barely could stand his ass. As I stood there looking at him while he looked at me, licking his lips, my pussy practically began begging for some attention. I stood there looking at him for a few seconds longer before I walked into the room, closing the door behind me. "I don't know why you insist on playing hard when you know you can't."

"Shut up and come eat my pussy," I said, walking over to the bed. Removing my skirt, I sat on the bed, making sure to leave my underwear on. I spread my legs open wide before I stuck two fingers inside of my already dripping wet pussy. Moving my fingers around in a circular motion, I pulled both of my fingers out. I raised them in the air, signaling for him to come near. It didn't take him any time to walk over to the bed. Taking the two fingers that I had into his mouth, he licked ever drop of come off them.

"Lie back for me," he said as he gently pushed me down flat on the bed. Opening my legs as far as they could go, he sat there admiring my honeypot. If it wasn't for the fact that I was hot and horny, I would've felt uncomfortable since it was him. Since my husband has been neglecting my needs and worrying about my sister more than me, it left me wanting. I watched as Randall took off his clothes and sat back down. He then began playing with himself, which began aggravating me, because all I wanted right now was some sweet licks. Frustrated, I began pleasing my damn self. It was as if he was reading my mind, because before I knew it, my panties were being ripped off, and his tongue was replacing my fingers.

"Ummm . . ." I moaned, feeling his tongue brush over my lips. I was so turned on, and my lips were so swollen, any light touch would make me cream right now. I spread

my legs more as he began sucking my pussy fiercely. "Oh
yes . . ."

He wrapped his arms around my waist and pulled me
closer. He was eating my pussy as if it were a five-course
meal at one of his favorite restaurants.

"Umm . . . You taste so good," he said in between licks.

I bet his old-ass wife don't taste as good as me, I
thought. My eyes damn near rolled in the back of my
head when he began tongue fucking the shit out of me.

"Oh yes . . . Right *there* . . ." I moaned out in pleasure.
"Eat that shit, eat this pussy, boy."

"Your wish is my command," he said, as he began to
feast on my wet honeypot. Moments later, I felt my toes
curling as my legs began shaking.

"I'm about to come," I yelled. I tried to move back, but
he stopped me. Seconds later, I began shaking uncontrollably as I released everything into his awaiting mouth.
Just like every other time, he lapped every drop up.

He stood up from between my legs and sat on the bed.
Normally, I'd be ready to go after I got my nut off, but
today, I was feeling different. I sat up on my elbows as I
watched him begin stroking himself. I knew he wanted
some and because I was in a good mood, I was going to
give it to him.

"Lie back," I said, grabbing him by his shoulder.

"What?" he asked confused.

"Just lie back," I told him.

He did as he was instructed. I could tell that he was
confused and worried, but I was about to give him
something special. Taking his dick into my hand, I
began stroking it. To say that he was an old man, he was
still packing. I looked into his eyes and noticed that he
was surprised. I hope he didn't think that I was about to
suck that shit. Hell, I don't even suck Dontie's dick, and
he's my husband, so I know damn well I'm not about to
suck his.

"What you're about to do?" he asked.

"Just lie back and let me please you," I told him, getting up and straddling him. I lifted my hips a bit, but only enough so that he could enter me.

"*Sssssh* . . . Shit!" he hissed as I slid down on to him. He lifted his hips, allowing me to fully slide all the way down. Throwing my head back, I began rocking my hips back and forth as I prepared to take him into another world.

I can't front . . . There was a time when I just loved having sex with Randall. This old man really knew how to please a girl, and I loved that about him. To be completely honest, I used to love him, but that was before I realized that he was never going to leave his wife, and I'd always be his mistress. Yes, I know that I had begun sleeping with him only to get where I wanted to be in life, but things happened. I met Dontie and put all of my feelings for Randall to the side. I had a man of my own now. I didn't have to share and be a mistress any longer. I'd have been a fool to continue to love somebody else's man.

Placing my hands on Randall's chest, I began bouncing up and down on his dick. I just love feeling his dick. It felt so great right now.

"Umm . . . yes . . . That's the Skylar I know . . ." he moaned, grabbing hold of my hips. He began pumping in and out of me from the bottom. I threw my head back as I enjoyed the feeling of being fucked. Before I knew it, Randall had flipped me over on the bed and entered me from behind. Any other time I'd be upset, but today, I kind of liked this.

"Yes . . . beat it up just like that . . ." I hissed, as he fucked the shit out of me. I could already feel my orgasm forming, so I began to throw it back hard. Every time he slammed into my walls, I threw it back. I tightened my walls around his dick, just as I felt it jump. Knowing that he was going to bust in a matter of minutes, I crossed my legs at the ankles and fucked the shit out of him.

"I'm about to come," he yelled out in pleasure.

"Me too . . ." I said, just as I felt him release his kids inside of me. Moments later, I released all over his dick. I fell forward on the bed as I struggled to catch my breath. "That was so intense and so much needed," I groaned.

"Thank you," Randall said, getting up from the bed.

"For what?" I asked, turning over to look at him.

"For giving me my old thing back," he said, smiling.

"Oh! No problem," I replied getting off the bed and heading into the bathroom. I didn't bother to close the door behind me. Shit, Randall and I have been through too much, and I trusted him enough to leave the bathroom door open.

Walking over to the toilet, I relieved my bladder. When I was done, I flushed the toilet and turned the shower on. I then went back into the room to get my purse. I spotted Randall by the bed smoking a cigar while nursing a drink. I shook my head, because I hated the smell of those things. I headed back into the bathroom, ready to wash him off me. Grabbing two washcloths from the towel rack, I grabbed the soap out of my purse and got in the shower.

Knowing that my makeup was all messed up, I decided to wash my face first. When I was sure that all the makeup was gone, I put the washcloth aside and grabbed the other one to begin showering. When it brushed against my now-sore kitty, I hissed. Since Dontie stayed put all those other nights, I really hoped he did the same thing tonight. Speaking of Dontie, I remembered that Randall had something he wanted to share with me. Hurrying up, I rinsed off, turned the water off, and got out. Grabbing a big towel, I wrapped it around my body and made my way into the room.

When I looked around, Randall was gone. There was a huge folder waiting for me in the middle of the bed, along with my clothes, which were folded neatly. I guess he really cared about me and not just the sex. I went back into the bathroom to get my purse before going back into the room to put on my clothes and shoes. When I was fully clothed, I took a seat on the bed and grabbed the envelope. There was a white note folded underneath it with my name on it. I decided to read it first.

My Darling Sky,

I'm sorry that I had to leave while you were still in the shower, but something came up. I promise to make it up to you. Here's the envelope with the information on your husband. There are also pictures of your husband with a pregnant female, who I now know is his baby mama. Please think rationally after reading everything in here. I've been having him followed ever since I found out about the two of you. If you need me, you know how to find me. Be easy, baby. See you later!

Love Always,

Randall

My heart raced after reading what the note said. I was anxious to see what information Randall had on Dontie. I didn't want to be *that* wife who spies on her husband, but it's obvious that Dontie was never 100 percent truthful with me from the beginning.

Picking up the envelope, I opened it. Slowly, I pulled out a piece of paper. I was confused about what was on the papers until I began reading them. The first gave a few details about Dontie. There was a copy of his birth certificate, along with a list of his siblings, his parents, and other family in the area. On another paper, it had his business listed and other miscellaneous things. It was the third paper with a picture of my sister and husband stapled to it that had me. On the paper, it said how and where Dontie and Brinay knew each other, and other information. There was also a picture of Chance, Dontie, Brinay, and her little friend Kourtney. The picture had to be taken a few months ago, because she was still pregnant.

"So those two muthafuckers really tried to play me," I said, as I continued to read the information. I lost it when I got to the fact that Brinay's baby was indeed my husband's. There was a paternity test to prove it. "Oh fuck, no. These bitches really got me fucked all the way up if they think I'm going to just sit down and take this shit!" I was not that bitch. I don't give a fuck about Brinay, Dontie, or their bullshit-ass baby. "I'm going to make these bitches pay for fucking with me."

I grabbed all of the papers that were now on the bed and shoved them back inside the envelope. I then grabbed my phone from my purse and dialed Dontie's number. The phone rang twice before going to voice mail.

"I know this nigga didn't send me to voice mail," I said hanging up. I dialed his number again, only to be sent to voice mail again. I didn't give up, though. I kept redialing, but by my fifteenth call, the phone didn't ring. Instead, it went straight to voice mail. Which could mean one of two things: Either Dontie had me on the block list or powered his phone off. I don't care. He and that bitch were going to hear my mouth about this shit.

I threw my phone in my purse, grabbed my purse and the envelope, and headed out the door. I was about to fuck shit up, and they wouldn't even see the shit coming. However, I had to stop by my parents' house first.

Chapter Twenty-one

Dontie

I was on my way home to see what Sky was up to when Brinay called me. She wanted me to come back to the hospital so that we could talk and spend time with our son together. I was surprised and yet confused. When I was at the hospital with her earlier, she acted as if it bothered her that I was there. Which is why I left. I wasn't trying to make her uncomfortable. I knew what she had been through and that she needed to rest. So if me leaving put her in a better place, then I had to leave, even if I didn't want to. Her calling and asking me to come back to the hospital was a surprise to me. Knowing that I really didn't want to be bothered with Sky, I busted a U-turn in the middle of the road and headed straight to the hospital. I was anxious yet nervous to see what it was she wanted to talk about.

As I made my way to the hospital, Sky called me. Knowing that she was probably bitching about me not coming home again, I sent her to voice mail. I really didn't have time for her mouth right now. I needed to be straight for when I had this talk with Brinay. I'm guessing she didn't get the hint, because she called back. Just like before, I sent her call to voice mail, but Skylar wasn't letting up. By the time I pulled up to the hospital, she'd called me fifteen times. Knowing that she was going to keep on calling, I powered my phone off. Even though

I didn't want to, I didn't have time for it to be constantly ringing once I was in the room with Brinay. Lord knows I wasn't trying to mess anything up. I needed to be extra careful when dealing with her. She was delicate. If my phone rang twice without me answering, she'd flip. That was my fault, though! Nay was never that type of chick. I made her like that, and I'm sorry for that.

After getting myself together, I got out of the car and went straight into the hospital, headed to the elevator, and up to Brinay's room. When I walked in the room, I didn't see her, but my son was lying there in the crib. I walked over to it, picked him up, and took a seat in the chair next to the bed. I sat there admiring him. He was so tiny and yet so handsome. I hadn't held him for the past few hours, and that killed me. Therefore, I knew me being away from him for a long period of time was going to have me feeling some type of way.

"Hey, little man," I said, placing my index finger in the palm of his hand. He closed his hand around my finger and held it as he slept. My heart beamed. I still couldn't believe that I was actually a father. I was about to get up and look for his mother when I heard the toilet flush. Moments later, the bathroom door swung open, and out she stepped.

"Damn, you scared the hell out of me." She jumped back holding her chest. "Next time, make some noise or something when you come in the room."

"My bad," I said, laughing at her dramatic ass. She stood there staring at me as I held my son in my arms. Her mind looked as if it was rolling a mile a minute. I wanted so bad to know what she was thinking about, but I didn't want to push her. I was going to wait until she was ready to say what she had to say.

"Tae," she said softly, after standing in the same spot for several minutes.

"What's up?" I asked her. She looked at me before she walked over to the bed and climbed back in.

"Do you love her?" she blurted out.

"Love who?" I asked, confused.

"Sky, Tae. Do you love her?" she asked again.

"Why are you asking me that?" I asked, getting mad. If I knew she was going to call me here just so she could question me about this shit, I wouldn't have come.

"Because, Tae, I need to know," she said, looking me in the eyes. I could tell that it was bothering her and that she really needed to know. I don't know why, because she should know that all of my love belongs to her, and her only.

"No, I don't love her."

"Well, tell me why you married her then, Tae," she said. I noticed that her eyes were teary. It hurt me to know that she was hurting because of me and something I did.

"Honestly, I bought the ring for you. I was supposed to break things off with Sky and propose to you, but—" I said, stopping myself.

"But what?"

"But she asked me to go on vacation with her to Jamaica, because her boss had given her an all-expense trip for a week. I didn't want to go, because I already knew what I was planning on doing, but she kept asking and begging me. I gave in and went. One day while we were there, she went through my suitcase and found the ring. I wanted to tell her that it wasn't for her, but the look on her face when she saw it was of pure happiness. I knew that if I told her that the ring was originally for someone else, she was going to be devastated. Instead, I proposed to her, and she suggested that we get married on the beach the following day. I didn't want to, but—" I explained. The look on Brinay's face as I went over the details on how I married Sky hurt my heart. "But I had no idea that you and her were sisters. Hell, I didn't know you was from Miami. I'm sure you knew that the day you came over to your father's house with Kourtney."

"You had to know that it killed me when I found out that you and Skylar were married. I loved you with everything in me. You were the man that I wanted to spend the rest of my life with. When I found out I was pregnant, I was beyond excited, and I couldn't wait to tell you. Then you started playing those games and not answering the phone. My gut instantly told me that you had another woman, and no matter how much I wanted to be wrong, I knew I was right," she said, her voice cracking up. "I never in my life thought that I would've experienced this amount of hurt again. I shielded my heart from love from a man because of what happened between my father and me when I was young. I never told anyone this, but when my father sided with my sister and her mother over me . . . that shit hurt me deep. From that moment on, I made a vow never to let a man break my heart again. Then you came in, and I decided to give you a chance, because I thought you weren't like the rest of them. You hurt me, Tae, and I don't know if I'm going to be able to recover from that."

"Ma, I'm sorry. I never meant to hurt you . . . never. I wanted to tell you about Sky, but I couldn't. I knew that if I would've told you about her, you was going to leave me and I couldn't have that, because I was in love with you. I decided to break things off with her and keep it all the way 100 with you. Like I told you, I bought you that ring. I wanted to settle down and make you the woman of my life, but everything went wrong," I told her honestly. I knew it wasn't what she wanted to hear, but at least I was being real.

For a minute, we both sat there staring at each other. Even when she was sick with her hair tangled all over her head, she was still beautiful. I honestly regret the day I messed shit up. If only I could go back and change the day I got married to Sky, everything would be all right.

"So what are we going to do?" she asked, surprising me.

"I'd love for you, me, and baby Dontie to be a family, but that's up to you."

"Tae, honestly, I'm still in love with you, but everything is still complicated. If we be together as a family, what will our family say? You're my sister's husband. How are we supposed to be together peacefully without all of those interruptions?"

"I'm happy to hear that you're still in love with me, but as far as that other shit goes, I really don't care. I'm not fucking the people in your family, and you're not fucking the people in my family, so what they say or think don't matter. As far as Skylar, I'll gladly get my lawyer to draw up some divorce papers and serve them to her tomorrow," I said, dead ass. I'd move a fucking mountain right now if it meant that I could be with her.

"Are you sure you want to be with me, Tae?" she asked.

"What the hell kind of question is that? You know there's only one woman I'd rather spend my life with, and that woman is you," I answered.

"Okay, well, if I said that I wanted to be with you too, then what?"

"I'd say we are going to be a family. As a matter of fact, the minute you get out of here, I'm moving you in with me and my son," I told her.

"Moving me in where?"

"In the house that I bought for us after we were supposed to get engaged."

"What about Sky, Tae? Isn't that the house you all stay in now?"

"No, Nay . . . Sky doesn't know about this house."

"And why is that?"

"I told you before . . . that was the house that I bought for me and you. I wasn't going to move her in, when I had no intentions on her being there in the first place," I said, just as baby Dontae began crying.

"Give him to me. He's probably wet and hungry," she said, ignoring what I just said. I handed him to her and sat down in the chair. I watched as she changed my son. I smiled slightly. It was a warm feeling watching the one you love, the one who had given birth to your seed, doing things like this. Most niggas made babies and got ghost, but not me. I wanted to be there, to be able to see and do things like this. I wanted to stick by my baby mama through every step of our child's life. "Are you going to at least think about what I said, Nay?"

"Think about what?" she asked, playing as if she was dumb or something.

"About us being together as a family."

"I'm fine with it, but I doubt that my sister will be," she said, turning to the TV.

"But I just told you that I really don't give a fuck about her. I shouldn't have married her. I was supposed to marry you. That was a mistake. I bought the ring for y—" I began, but she stopped me.

"For me, yeah, I get it, Tae. You don't have to keep saying it," she screamed, scaring the baby. She began rocking him until he had quieted down. "You repeating the same thing ain't making this any better now. I hear what you saying, and I know you say you love me, but your actions be confusing me."

"Ma, I love you, ain't no confusing that," I stressed. I was getting tired of saying the same thing repeatedly myself.

"Okay, Tae," she said, blowing me off. I got up from the chair and went to sit next to her on the bed.

"Look at me, ma," I said, because she had turned her head away from me. She ignored me, so I used my hand to turn her head myself. "All that shit in the past is gone. We're going to be together, ma . . . me, you, and Dontae. You don't have to question shit else about me and where my heart at, because I'll be 100 percent devoted to you and our son."

"You really mean that?" she asked. There was uncertainty written all over her face, but I know in due time, all of that was going to change. We were just going to have to take this one day at a time.

"Yes, I do," I said, giving her a long, passionate kiss that spoke volumes. "I'm going to make you my wife when all of this is over and done with."

"I love you, Tae," she said with so much passion, I knew it was nothing but the truth. She leaned in and gave me a kiss before she placed her head on my shoulder.

"I love you too, ma," I responded. Pulling out my phone, I took a quick selfie of the three of us, because this moment was worth a picture. I set the picture as my screensaver before I placed the phone back in my pocket. "This is exactly how I want it to be, just the three of us. Nobody but us . . . no distractions, no nothing, just our little family."

"It will be, just as soon as you handle your business," she said, with a little hint of an attitude.

"Get up for me," I told her.

"Where are you going, Dontie?"

"Chill out, ma, I'm not going anywhere," I said, pulling my phone out. I looked for my dude Chris's number and dialed him up.

"Yo, Chris," I said when he answered the phone.

"What's up, man?" he asked.

"You remember that thing we talking about the other day with that homie, Randall?"

"Yeah, why? What's up? Don't tell me you having second thoughts?"

"Hell, no," I replied. This nigga was crazy. There was no way I wanted to stay married to Skylar's ass any longer than I already was. "I want you to put that plan in motion and draw up them divorce papers for me today."

"All right. I'll call up old dude and start on them papers right this minute. It shouldn't take me that long," he said, just as the phone beeped. Pulling it away from my ear, I noticed that it was Skylar calling. Ignoring her, I went back to my call. "You want to go with the same angle we discussed the other day, or do you have something else in mind?"

"Yeah, let's go with what we talked about the other day. I want to see her face drop when she finds out I know," I told him. If everything goes as planned, this was going to be over faster than it began. "Thanks, man, I appreciate it."

"You know you my nigga, man. Besides, I'm only doing what you paid me to do."

"Yeah, I know. Call me when you're done so I can come through and pick that up."

"Okay. Holla at you later, man."

"All right . . . one," I said, hanging up the phone. I placed the phone back in my pocket before I walked back over to the bed.

"What was all of that about?" Brinay asked, looking at me sideways.

"I know you heard me say something about divorce papers. So what do you think?" I said, sitting back down beside her. She kissed my cheek before placing her head back on my shoulder.

"So how long do you think this is going to take?"

"With the information and connections that Chris has, I doubt that this will even take a month."

"Are you serious? I know people whose divorce lasted for a year or two."

"Well, mine won't. My boy Chris is A-1 when it comes to getting things done."

"Okay, but please don't do anything stupid," she said to me.

"I won't be doing anything stupid. We're just going to—" the door opening suddenly cut me off. I stood up immediately when I spotted Skylar walking through the door, followed by her parents. Brinay's eyes grew wide before they turned a dark color. This was my first time noticing that.

"Well . . . well . . . well . . . If it ain't the big happy family," Skylar said, walking over to the bed. "I knew I was going to find you here when you didn't answer the phone. You're spending quite a lot of time here with Miss Thang, aren't you?"

"I just dropped by to check on them. I was actually on my way out," I said, attempting to leave.

"I bet you was, huh, Tae?" Sky asked sarcastically, cocking her head to one side. "I'm going to need you to stay here. I have something to tell you."

"What do you want, Sky?" Brinay asked, rolling her eyes. She and I both knew she was about to come with her bullshit.

"Bitch, first of all, don't speak my name. I knew you were a slick bitch from the moment my father walked in with your Little Orphan Annie-looking ass, all of those years ago. I should've treated you like the skank you were." She spoke with venom in her voice. Brinay didn't say anything. She placed the baby back in the crib before she sat all the way up, as Sky continued. "Bitch, if you wanted my life, all you had to do was say it."

"Look, bitch, I have no idea what the fuck it is that you're talking about or referring to, but know that I was never a hater. That was all you. What the fuck did you have for me to hate on anyway?" Nay retorted.

"I had everything, while you had nothing. Most importantly, I had a father when you didn't, and when your mother died, I had a mother too. You've always wanted everything that I had, and I see that that jealousy shit followed you into your adulthood."

"First of all, bitch, like I told you before, I was *never* jealous of you. I mean, why would I be? I look better than you do, I'm smarter than you are, and I'm prettier than you are. So again, tell me why I'm jealous of you. If anybody was jealous, then it would be you. You've always felt the need to compete with your little sister, but you couldn't," Brinay said, letting her have it.

"You and your mother tried desperately to break me, but you couldn't. Then when I told my father about it, he ignored me. He never believed anything I said. It's because of your lying-ass mother that he and I don't have a normal father-daughter relationship."

"First of all, little girl, you can leave me out of this. This isn't about me. This is about you and your little whorish ways," Skylar's mother said to Brinay, while her father just stood back, taking it all in.

"Bitch, this has *everything* to do with you."

"You will *not* speak to my mother like that, and she's right. This has *nothing* to do with her," Skylar told Brinay. "But it has *everything* to do with you and my cheating-ass husband."

"What the fuck are you talking about, Sky?" I asked, finally speaking up. I was tired of all the riddles they were in here speaking.

"How long have you and my sister been messing around behind my back?"

"What are you talking about?" I asked her. She took a folder out of her purse and removed an envelope. She opened it, removed a few pieces of paper, and handed them to me. "Here. Explain this shit to me, because it's still a little mystery to me."

Taking the pictures from her, I noticed that they were pictures of Brinay and me. Some were new, while others were old. There was information on me and a few other things, along with information on Brinay. I wanted to ask her how the fuck she got this, but that wasn't the issue right now.

The cat was out of the bag. She now knew about Brinay and me, but I really didn't care. I handed the pictures to Brinay, and her facial expression told a different story.

"Okay, so you know about me and Dontie. So what?" Brinay said, shocking the hell out of everyone in the room.

"So this is true?" her mother asked. I pulled out my phone and sent a message to Chris, telling him to get the information he had gotten for me the other day and bring it to the hospital right now. He texted back okay, as I walked over to a now-screaming Dontae. I picked him up and gave him his pacifier. He immediately stopped crying.

"Yes, it is, and so what?"

"You don't see a problem in this?" Skylar's mother then asked. "Is he the father of that bastard baby?"

"Yes the fuck he is, and you have one more time to call my baby a bastard . . ." Brinay replied, just as Brandon, Chance, and Kourtney walked in the room.

"Hey, sis," her brother said, walking over to her. "What's going on?"

"Hey, I know you," Skylar said, looking at Brandon.

"Skylar, right?" he asked.

"Yeah, that's me. What are you doing here?"

"I'm here to see my little sister and her baby," he said, pointing to Brinay. "What are you doing here?"

"Is that right?" she asked. "So we have the *same* little sister?"

"Seems so."

"Well, I'm here to find out how long my little sister and my husband have been fucking behind my back," she told him. He had this confused look on his face before he turned to Brinay's father.

"Dad?" he asked. "Is that you?"

"Yeah, son, it's me."

"Dad? Son?" Veronica asked with a confused look on her face as she looked at them. "What the fuck is going on, Brian? Is this your son?"

"Yes, Veronica, he's my son," Brian answered. Her face went from happy to sad to mad in a matter of seconds. I looked at Brinay, who looked back at me with a look of confusion on her face. I could tell that she knew nothing about what was going on now. Her brother, on the other hand, stood there as if he already knew about everything that was going on.

I turned to see Chance and Kourtney looking like two deer caught in headlights. They had this expression on their faces as if they just knew some major shit was about to pop off. Hell, with all these secrets coming out all at once, we all knew something was about to happen.

Skylar

Initially, when I came here, the only thing on my mind was fucking up both my cheating-ass husband and my scandalous-ass sister. I had all intentions on busting them up in front of my parents, but the rest of the crew interrupted us. The moment Kourtney and Chance walked in, I started to give them a piece of my mind also, because I knew damn well that they knew about everything that was going on behind my back. Shit, they were too close not to. However, my words were trapped in my mouth when I spotted the dude I'd met at the hotel walking in behind them. I was confused at first, until he walked over to Brinay, kissed her, and called her his little sis. When I found out that he was Brinay's older brother, I was shocked. Hell, the world was really fucking small. How was it that the nigga that hollered at me earlier was also my little sister's big brother? Damn, the world is smaller than I thought and it was about to get even smaller.

Just as I was about to continue going in on Brinay and Dontie, Brinay's brother called my father *Dad*. Again, the world is much smaller than we thought. At first, I thought I was tripping, but when my father confirmed it, I knew it was true. I watched my mother's world come crashing down, right before everyone's eyes.

"So where did *this* son come from, and how do you know that he's your son?" my mother asked, turning to her husband.

"His mother is Brinay's mother. I had him tested when I first went to see him in jail. He looked so much like me that I knew that he was mine. Hell, I didn't even need a test, but I wanted to be sure," my father answered her. He didn't even look as if he regretted the shit.

"So you knew about this and didn't tell me?" Brinay asked her brother, heartbroken.

"Yes, I've known about it. How do you think he knows your phone number and where you stay? When he came to see me, I told him. I was surprised, just like you, when I found out he was my father also. He wanted to tell you, but I asked him to wait until I got out to break the news to you. I mean, I already knew the type of relationship you and him both have. I wanted to be there when he told you," he said.

"So you let him come and see you, but you didn't let me?" she asked in an angry tone.

"Chill out, Nay. I didn't want you to see me locked up like that, which is why I never allowed you to come and see me. Him coming see me was a whole different story, sis," he explained. She didn't say anything, but she rolled her eyes and folded her arms across her chest without saying a word.

"So that means you'd already fathered a child, way before this little bitch came along. How could you do this to me and not tell me?" Veronica said, pointing to Brinay, going completely off. "I can't believe you've had two kids while we were together."

"You know what—" my father began. He looked over at Brinay and her brother before he turned back to my mother. "I've had all I can take from you, Veronica. I let you run my daughter out of my life once before, but I'll be damned if I let you do it again. You've had all the say from the beginning of our marriage, but no more. I'm breaking my silence and putting my foot down. You're going to stop playing with me and my children."

"Your children?"

"Yes, I said my damn children," he said, in a no-nonsense tone. I was kind of proud of him for finally standing up to her. "You've been a bitch and a pain in my ass since the day I first met you."

"What did you just say to me?" my mother asked, getting in his face.

"You heard just what I said. You walk around like everything and everyone is beneath you, but truth be told, you wouldn't have *any* of this if it wasn't for my money and me. I'm tired of you treating my kids as if they don't matter. You're going to start treating my kids better—or else."

"Oh, Brian, please. I've spent enough years of my life with you to earn everything that I've gotten. And what do you mean *or else?*" she asked.

"Or else I'm going to do what I should've done a long time ago."

"And what's that? You're not going to do a damn thing," she replied. I stood there watching as my parents argued with each other as if there wasn't a room full of people.

"I'm going to leave you. As a matter of fact, the minute we get home, I'm calling my attorney and have him draw up the divorce papers," he said. As soon as the last word left his mouth, my mother's hand went directly across his face.

"Don't play with me, Brian. I'll take you for *everything* you have," she told him. He looked at her and laughed before he walked over to the bed by his children.

"You and I both know that your hoeing ass won't get a dime. So, as far as you taking me for everything that I have, you can kill that. You'll be lucky if I let you leave with the clothes on your back," he said, taunting her. She looked at him, rolling her eyes, before folding her arms across her chest. There was something they weren't speaking about, but that was on them. I had my own problems, with my own husband.

"Like I said, you're not going to do a damn thing. You actually think I'm going to let you leave me, all because of the two bastards you made when you cheated on me? As far as I'm concerned, they don't matter. They never have and never will. As long as Skylar is taken care of, then I'm fine. She's probably your only biological daughter anyway," my mother spoke with venom.

"It's funny you say that," my father said, with a light chuckle. "Because I know, Skylar is the only one who is *not* mine."

"What are you talking about?" she asked him.

"Dad, what are you talking about?" I asked, confused.

"Skylar, honey, I'm sorry, but when you were small, I had a blood test done on you," he said to me. "There're some things that you don't know about your mother, baby girl."

"What . . . why?" I asked, dumbfounded. *Why would my father have a blood test done on me, and why does he figure I'm not his?*

"Why don't we ask you mother why," he said, with a look of disdain. "She's been walking around here, acting as if she was the perfect wife when in all actuality, she started cheating way before I did. The only thing is, she didn't know that I knew about it."

"Brian, don't do this," my mother pleaded, with tears in her eyes.

"Mom, what is he talking about?" I asked her. "Is this true?"

"Skylar, can we talk about this when we get home?" she begged, looking around at all of the people in the room.

Fuck that! I was not going to wait. I'm tired of people keeping secrets from me. I was going to get answers from everyone, and today was going to be the day.

"No, Mom, tell me what is going in. Is what Dad's saying true? Were you cheating on him before you had me? Am I his real daughter?" I threw out question after question. She stood there with her hands on her hips, looking like a lost puppy.

"Sky . . . baby . . . Can we please talk about this when we get home?" she asked again.

"I said no. You all have kept y'all's secrets long enough. It's time to tell me what you don't want me to know," I said, just as someone began knocking on the door. In walked some dude in a suit, carrying a few envelopes. He walked over to Dontie and handed them to him before he walked back out the door.

I stood there looking at Dontie, wondering what was in those envelopes. I was about to ask him when my father's voice brought me back to reality. I needed to address this issue with my parents and find out what's been going on.

"Tell her, Veronica," my father said to my mother. "Tell her that I'm not her real father . . . that you cheated on me and got pregnant with her. Tell her!"

"Brian, just stop it already. I don't have to tell her, since you've *already* told her," my mother said, with tears falling from her eyes. I was shocked and surprised, because this was actually my first time seeing my mother ever cry.

"So, this is true?" I asked, heartbroken. "He's not my real father?"

"No, he's not," she answered, fully breaking my heart. I couldn't believe that the man that I've known as my father was actually *not* my father. "Like he already told you, I cheated on him with your real father before you were even born. Baby, I'm sorry. It was around the time your father first started working. He was putting in so many hours, and I was lonely at home. So one day, me, my friend, and Brandon and Brinay's mother went out to get a few drinks.

"We were sitting at the bar when a man came and offered to buy us a drink. I'd already had more than enough, but since my man wasn't home and I was lonely, I accepted it. We sat there and chatted for a while before he asked if I had a man. I told him no, which I shouldn't have, because I did. He told me that he was also single and that he wanted us to hook up. I knew that it was wrong, but as I said, I was lonely. So I took him up on his offer. What was supposed to be a one-night stand turned into a three-year affair.

"Then I became pregnant with you. I knew you weren't Brian's, but he didn't know that, or so I thought. I wanted to tell him about the affair, but I was afraid that if he found out, then he was going to put us out. I didn't have anywhere else to go. So I didn't tell him, but somehow he found out. That's when he began having an affair of his own. Even though they didn't think I knew about them, I did. I just never said anything. I turned a blind eye to it, because I knew what I did and was still doing to him was hurtful. I thought that as long as he was getting what he wanted, he was satisfied, even if it wasn't from me. When I found out that their mother was pregnant with Brandon, I was devastated. I knew about him, but she said that he was from another man that she was talking to.

"So I left it at that. I knew my husband was in love with her. I even overheard him on the phone saying how he was going to leave me for her. I couldn't let that happen, so I ended my affair and started playing the devoted wife. It was enough to get my man back, but it wasn't enough to keep him away from the woman his heart truly belonged to.

"Our friendship broke up after that, and we hadn't seen or spoken to each other in about ten years. That's when Brian showed up with Brinay. The moment I laid eyes on her, I knew who her mother was. Hell, she looked just like her mother, which is why I hated her so damn much. She reminded me so much of the friend that I missed daily. I didn't know what to do."

"So you mean to tell me that you and my mother were *friends?*" Brinay asked her.

"Yes, we were good friends . . . until we let a man come in between our friendship."

"Fuck all that shit. Who the fuck *is* my father?" I asked her. I could feel my palms beginning to sweat. My nerves were getting worse by the second.

"Her old slutty ass doesn't even know. The man she had an affair with isn't even your father."

"How do you know that?" she asked, shocked.

"Because once I found out that I wasn't the father, I had him tested. Come to find out, he wasn't the father either."

"So my mother was out here being a ho, and now she doesn't even know who my father is?"

"Watch your mouth, Skylar," my mother said, walking over to me. "I may be a ho, but I'm still your mother. If you keep playing with me, I'm going to whip your little ass."

"You're not going to do a muthafucking thing," I yelled at her. I had finally had enough. I pulled out the gun I had in my purse and pointed it at Brinay.

"Sky, don't do this," my father yelled from behind me. "This is *not* the way to handle things."

"Do what? This bitch has been the cause of me and my mother's problems from the minute she came here," I told him. "Not only that, but I found out that she and my husband been fucking around since before we were even married. They played it off really good, though, because at first, I didn't suspect a thing, but then she had her accident and my husband was at her side every damn day. That's when I became suspicious and knew that something was going on, but it was all just a theory. It doesn't take a rocket scientist to know that little baby is my husband's child. I wouldn't have known about it if it wasn't for Randall."

"It's funny that you even mention Randall's name," Dontie said to me. He walked over to me and handed me the envelope. "Since you over here pretending to be a saint and pointing out everyone else's sins, why don't you tell everyone about yours as well?"

"Don't try anything, or I swear I'm going to shoot your baby and his mother," I said, cocking the gun.

"I'm not doing anything. I'm just going to hand you this envelope."

"What is this?" I asked, taking the envelope from him.

"Just open it," he said, taking a step back. I looked from him to the envelope and back at him before I decided to open it. I wanted to know what this was, and obviously, he wasn't going to tell me, so I had to find out on my own.

It was a struggle holding the envelope while holding a gun, but I managed to make do. I was shocked to see information about Randall and myself. There were records of our e-mails, as well as our text messages and call logs. I was stunned when I noticed the records of all the times that we were at the hotel. There were also pictures of us.

"What . . . You can't say anything? What . . . Cat's got your tongue?" Dontie asked with a smirk on his face. "You weren't the only one doing dirty work as you can see."

"And so what?" I asked, trying to play it off. I couldn't believe that he was doing the very same thing that I was doing.

"While you was trying to make it like I was the only one doing dirt, you was doing it yourself. Check the second envelope. There's a surprise in there for you, shorty," he then said. I looked in the second envelope and almost lost it when I saw some divorce papers.

"What the fuck you think you're doing?" I asked him, dropping the papers on the chair.

"I'm doing what I should've done the day after we got married," he had the nerve to say.

"Is that right?"

"Yes, I wasn't supposed to marry you," he stated calmly. "I didn't even buy the ring for you, ma. It was for Brinay."

"Ain't this some shit," I said, laughing to myself.

"Sky, I'ma be 100 percent honest with you," Brinay began saying, "when Dontie and I first began messing with each other, I knew nothing about you. Hell, I didn't even know he was from Miami, and he most definitely didn't know that I was from there either. We fell in love in South Carolina."

"But the nigga was in my bed almost every day of the week."

"Yeah, that's true, but I wasn't worrying about where he was those five days. I was too busy with school to even notice that shit," she said, sounding like a damn fool. "When I found out I was pregnant, everything changed. Then the dinner came, and that's when I found out about you, me, and Dontie."

"You can save your little sob story, because you should've told me right when you found out. How you could continue to live your life, knowing that you and your sister were sleeping with the same man is beyond me," my mother blurted out.

"I've tried to play nice, but I see this ain't working. To say y'all some bougie bitches, it looks like I have to get ghetto with y'all," Brinay said, getting up from the bed. I could tell that she was still in pain, but she ignored that.

"Nay, sit down and rest your pretty little head. You're in no condition for any of this," our father said.

"No, Dad, I'm tired of Sky and her mother. They've picked on me enough without me saying anything, but here's where I draw the line," she replied, as she turned to my mother and began going in. "You, I don't care to know about your past or whatever it was that you and my mother had going on. All I care about now is that you leave my son and me alone. You've picked on me enough, and I allowed you to, but I'm putting my foot down now. You will *not* fuck with my son in the same manner that you fucked with me. What's killing me is that you walk around here, pretending to be perfect and Miss Goody Two-shoes. You're nothing but a bona fide ho, and a sad-ass mother and wife. You bashed my father about cheating when you were cheating all along. You've been having your daughter call another man *daddy* for her entire life. Bad thing is, you don't even *know* who her *real* father is. You bashed my mother and me when you and your daughter ain't no better than us. In fact, if you ask me, y'all were worse."

"Look, you two-bit ho," my mother began to speak, "you have no room to talk about anyone."

Shut them up now, a little voice in the back of my head said. "Shut the fuck up. Shut up now!" I yelled at them. I was tired and wasn't making any progress. "I've had it with all you bitches."

"Skylar, put the gun down before you hurt somebody," my father said.

"Daddy," I said to him. My eyes began to twitch as sweat began forming on my forehead. I was minutes away from having a meltdown, and no one knew it. "That's *if* I can still call you that."

"Even though I'm not your real father, I'll always be your daddy," he replied. I was beginning to feel overwhelmed. Everything was becoming too much for me to take in. I came here to bust my husband and ended up being busted my own damn self. Had I known that Randall would fuck over me like that, I would have never continued to sleep with him. Unfortunately, I did, and now everything has come back to bite me in the ass. I remembered a quote someone told me. It was, "One thing about them tables, they always turn." I was just realizing what it meant, and I couldn't do anything but laugh. God surely does work in mysterious ways. I screamed as loud as I could before I turned the gun on myself. I was ready to be put out of my misery, but first . . . I had to take a few people with me.

Chapter Twenty-two

Brinay

I can't believe the things that were going on in front of my eyes. To say that I was shocked was an understatement. I didn't know what to think. I couldn't believe that my brother was actually my father's son. What shocked me the most was when my father broke the news that Skylar was actually not his daughter. I couldn't believe it. I mean, no . . . She didn't look anything like my father and me, but that's because she looked like her mother. I never would've thought that she was not actually my father's child. It's funny how things happen. They used to treat me bad and bad-mouth me, all because I was actually my father's daughter—and *she* wasn't. Her mother probably knew that all along, which is why she treated me so different. Now, here we are, with all of these secrets being revealed, and I can't believe it. My mother and Sky's mother were actually friends—hell, I don't see it. I wonder how that came about.

I was brought out of my thoughts by the sound of my father's voice. When I looked up, Sky had a gun pointed to her head, but she quickly turned and shot her mother. I stood there with my mouth open. This bitch is crazier than we all thought. No sooner had we heard the shot than the alarms started blasting throughout the hospital.

"Sky, what is *wrong* with you?" my father asked. Before anyone could answer, she turned the gun on him and shot him too. I immediately began screaming. I was stuck on numb. I couldn't believe the things that were going on right before my eyes.

"You next, my dear sister," she said, pointing the gun at me. "I thought about killing you, but that would be too easy. Instead, I'm going to kill the one thing that means the absolute most to you." She looked to Dontie with love in her eyes. I knew it was killing her that she was in love with someone she couldn't have, but I was not going to let her kill him.

"Sky, your problem is with me, not with Tae. If you want to kill someone, shoot me," I told her.

"Nay, no, don't do this," Dontie said to me.

"Nay, Nay, please . . ." my brother said.

"Who said that I was going to kill Dontie?" she asked with a crazed look in her eyes. She then turned the gun toward the crib where my son lay screaming.

"Oh my God . . ." Kourtney began screaming.

"No! Not my baby!" I yelled as I began crying.

The next thing I knew, the door was being kicked open. Standing there were a dozen law enforcement officers trained with their guns on her. They told her to put the gun down, but they knew, as we all knew, that wasn't going to happen. The Skylar we all once knew was gone and replaced by a lunatic.

"Ma'am, we're going to ask you one more time to put the gun down," screamed a white officer. She looked at him with her gun still trained on my son and shook her head no. Tears began rolling down her face as her hand began shaking. Even though I couldn't stand my sister, my heart went out to her. Love would make you do some crazy-ass things in life, and this, by far, was the craziest thing I've seen someone do behind a man. I understand that everyone loves different, but love ain't that serious to shoot my parents' behind. Speaking of parents, I looked to the floor to see my father's limp body. Even though we had our issues, he was still my father. We were just getting back on good terms. I never wanted to see him dead. My sister was really on one.

"I'm sorry . . ." she said to no one in particular. I saw it coming before it even happened. I tried to move to her, but I was too slow. Next thing I knew, a gun went off before my body hit the cold-ass hospital floor. I'd failed my son as a parent, and his life had only begun.

Brinay

Three months later

After everything that went down at the hospital, I was mortified. Luckily, my son wasn't harmed. The gun that went off was the gun of one of the officers. Sky was shot in her leg. If you ask me, they should have killed the bitch and spared us all the heartache. Instead, she's still alive, but I feel safer, knowing that she was locked up in a mental institution for the rest of her life. At least, I know my son was going to be much safer, knowing that she was there and not in the free world. I would've preferred that they threw her in jail, but I didn't get my way.

It turned out that in the past years, she was diagnosed with major depression, anxiety disorder, bipolar disorder, ADHD, and schizophrenia. Yeah, that's a whole lot, huh? I thought the same thing when I heard it the day she went on trial. She was supposed to be taking her medication, but it turns out that she wasn't. That caused her to freak out the way she did in the hospital. Hell, she had to be crazy to kill her own damn mother. That shit was sickening. My father survived somehow, but he was shot in his abdominal area, which led to him having to get a colostomy bag. It hurts my heart to know that he's going to have to live with a constant reminder of the day he was shot, but he's taking it like a trooper. He and I are getting along great now. He and my brother are extremely close.

As for my brother, he stood by his promise and became a changed person. He goes to school at a community college in Miami, and my father found him a job. I was very proud of him. He and Kourtney decided to hook up and become an item. I was shocked at first and disapproved, but once I saw how well they went together, I left that alone. Besides, I feel much better knowing that Kourtney was going to be around him the majority of the time. At least, I knew for sure that she was going to keep him out of trouble, so that was something that I didn't have to worry about.

As for Dontie and me, we're still going strong. His divorce was finalized a few weeks ago. It's official. He's no longer married to Skylar's crazy ass, and I'm happy about that. I was just glad that she gave him the divorce without any trouble. He stuck to his word when he said that we are getting married. Here I was, standing in the mirror, admiring my beautiful wedding gown. I was so amped about getting married to my son's father. I never imagined my life would turn into this. To be in love and actually marry the man of my dreams was just that . . . a dream come true. Yes, I've been through my fair share of troubles, but all of the good things in my life outweighed all of the bad things. If I had to do it all over again, I would, heartbreak and all.

"You look beautiful, darling," my father said from behind me.

"Thanks, Daddy," I said, turning around to face him.

"I wish your mother was here to see you. You look just like her. She would've been so proud of the woman you've become."

"I know. I wish she was here also, but she's here in spirit," I told him.

"It's time," Kourtney yelled from the door.

"We'll be out in a minute," I told her.

"You look absolutely gorgeous, Nay," she beamed.

"Thanks, baby, you look beautiful yourself," I told her. She winked at me before she left.

"Are you ready?" my father asked, holding his arm out.

"I'm as ready as I'll ever be," I said, entwining my arm with his. I then placed a kiss on his cheek. I was more than happy to have at least one of my parents here to share my special day with. "Thanks, Daddy."

"For what?"

"For being here with me."

"There's no place I'd rather be than right here, giving my only daughter away on her wedding day. I'm just glad that we were able to move past everything that has happened," he said, kissing my forehead.

"Me too! I love you, Daddy," I said, with a smile on my face. It's been a minute since I said those words, but I'm happy I got a chance to say them again. Having my father in my life meant a lot. After everything that we've been through, we both deserve to have some happiness.

"I love you too, pumpkin. Now, let's get on with this wedding before I change my mind," he joked.

"Daddy . . ." I pouted.

"I'm just playing, princess. I'm just playing," he said with a chuckle. I laughed too before we left the room. I was excited and yet nervous I was about to become Mrs. Edmon, and I couldn't be happier.

Dontie

I stood at the altar as John Legend's "You and I" played in the background. Today was going to be one of the best days of my life. As I watched Brinay walk down the aisle in her wedding gown, I couldn't help but to feel a sense of peace. I could actually say I felt complete. I can't lie. I never imagined this ever happening. I never thought she would've given me a second chance, and to think that she's going to be my wife is unbelievable. I can't believe it took everything we've been through with Sky's crazy ass to see that we were really meant to be together. To think, we almost never got here. I couldn't even stand to say Sky's name without it leaving a bad taste in my mouth.

As I stood there watching two of my most favorite people in this world walk over to me, a lone tear fell from my eyes. Only the Lord knows how much I prayed for this day to come. How much I hoped and wished for the day when my son, his mother, and me could come together and be a family. Now that this day is here, I couldn't have thanked the man upstairs enough for hearing my prayers.

"Aww, my Pooh Bear is crying," Brinay said, the minute she reached me and noticed that my eyes were a bit misty. She removed her hand from her glove before she used her thumb to wipe the tear away. Her hand then traveled to my lips before her lips replaced them. She gave me a long, passionate kiss before she broke it. "Let me find out you're getting sensitive on me."

"I'm just happy that this day has finally come," I said, trying to kiss her again, but she stopped me.

"Patience, my darling. Let's get on with our wedding," she said with a slight giggle. She then said in the sexiest voice I've ever heard, "After we say I do and are united as one, you can do whatever you want to me."

The way she said that made my dick jump at attention. I couldn't wait to say *I do* so we could get going on our honeymoon. "Well, let's get going, shall we?" I asked, pulling her a little close to the altar, which made her laugh.

"Eager now, are we?" she whispered so that only I could hear it.

"Very much so, my dear," I said, sounding like white folks would sound.

"Well, in that case," she said to me, and then turned to the pastor, "let's get this thing going, shall we?"

Together, we stood there as the pastor began the ceremony. Since we were now living in South Carolina and most of the people we knew stayed in Miami, we decided to have a small wedding. The bridal party consisted of Brinay's cousin, Keyon, as the matron of honor, Kourtney, as the maid of honor, and the two bridesmaids, whose names were Jordan and Latoya. The junior bridesmaid was Keyon's daughter, Emoni. The best man was Keyon's husband, Kane, and the other three groomsmen were Chance, my older brother Donovan and Brinay's brother, Brandon. As I said, we weren't trying to have a big wedding. The only thing important was that we be able to say I do.

"The couple has chosen to recite their own vows," the pastor said. He looked at Brinay and nodded his head, telling her that she can proceed. She turned to me before blowing out air.

"Tae, my Tae . . ." she said, causing people to laugh. "Where do I even begin? From the moment I first met you, you made my heart skip a beat. I never met a man like you. You were both good and bad for my health. You were so bold and yet so thuggish. I tried to blow you off, but the more I tried, my heart threw a curve ball. It's true that we've been through more than a little bit. There were times when we gave up, more times than I care to share, only to realize that we belong together. I love you more than life itself. There's no man I'd rather live my life with beside you and DJ. Promise to love me forever, and I'll do the same."

"I promise to love you forever and ever and ever," I said, kissing her cheek. "Ma, I have to admit, these past three years have not been easy. We've been through hell on earth. From finding out who you were to escaping death a time or two, but like two people who're meant to be together, we've overcome every obstacle that was thrown our way. Yeah, I know I messed up and married someone else, but I promise to this day that it wasn't intentional. I'm just happy that you forgave me and gave me another chance. Well, chance number three, but who's counting? You're my sun, my star, and my moon. Without you, my world is incomplete. I promise to love you forever and a million days. Don't ever give up on me. I'm more than honored to have you as my loving wife. There's no woman I'd rather spend the rest of my life with, but you. Don't ever leave my side, because if you do, I'll be lost and broken."

"The rings, please," the pastor said. After getting the rings, we went through the process of blessing the rings and our marriage. "I now pronounce you man and wife. You may now kiss your bride."

"I love you," we both said before we shared a long, passionate kiss.

"Thank God, I give you Mr. and Mrs. Dontie Edmon," the pastor said, addressing the crowd. Brinay smiled and waved before we jumped the broom and headed down the aisle along with our wedding party.

"I can't believe that we're actually married," she said, during the whole walk to the limo.

"Well, believe it, baby, because we are. You're my wife, and I'm your husband," I said, as the driver was opening the door for us to get in. "You're stuck with me forever and ever."

"I love you, Mr. Edmon," she giggled, kissing me once more. "Oh, that sounds so good."

"I love you too, Mrs. Edmon." I laughed at her. She was acting like a little schoolgirl in love. "Now get in the limo. We have a plane to catch, and you know I don't wanna be late."

I turned to wave at the people before I got in the car and closed the door. I rolled the window down as I continued to smile at all of our friends showering us with love and congratulations. I continued to say thank you until we pulled off. I then rolled the window up so that I could enjoy my wife.

"So, how do you feel?" I asked my wife. "I can't wait until we arrive at our honeymoon spot."

I waited for Brinay to answer, but she didn't. When I turned to her, she had this scared look on her face. I followed her gaze and almost passed out my damn self. Sitting in the back of the limo with us was none other than Sky. I was tripping hard about this whole thing, because Sky had on the wedding gown she wore when we were married.

"Surprised to see me?" she asked, looking crazed. She had a gun, which was pointed at Brinay.

"What are you doing here, Skylar? What do you want?" I asked her.

"I want my husband back," she said, never taking her eyes off Brinay.

"You can't have me, Sky. I'm Brinay's husband now."

"Bullshit. I never signed any divorce papers, which means that you still belong to me," she said, cocking her head to the side.

"But you did. You signed it the day I came to see you in the hospital," I told her. I knew this bitch was crazy, but she wasn't *that* crazy. She knew just as well as I did that she signed those divorce papers.

"I didn't do any such thing, and you're not going to make me believe I did."

"Look, I really don't have time to be playing any of these games with you," Brinay said, speaking up.

"So she finally speaks," Sky smirked. "I thought you was going to hide behind what's mine, since you like taking things that don't belong to you."

"Bitch, he was *always* mine. I just let you borrow him," Brinay said, smirking back. "You're one of the thirstiest-ass broads I've seen thus far. How you come to *my* wedding, in a wedding dress, trying to kill me over *my* husband?"

"Bitch, because he was mine first. You have all this mouth, but where was it a few months ago?" Sky said as she began inching our way. "Talking 'bout he was always yours. No, bitch, he was *ours*."

"No, bitch, he was always *mine*. The nigga didn't want you. He wanted me. He spent countless days with me and our son. Your desperate, delusional ass is only stalking and trying to kill people. He was by my side every day, and guess what? He's *still* by my side. So like I said, bitch, he was, and will always be, *mine*."

"He can't be yours if you're dead, now, can he?" Sky retorted, cocking the gun.

"Look, Sky, you don't have to do this. I'll go with you, just don't hurt her," I pleaded. "Let her go and we can get on the plane and leave today."

"You're going to come with me?" she asked, getting excited.

"Yes, I'll come, but you have to let Brinay go first."

"I can't do that, Dontie," she said, as her hands began shaking.

"Can't do what?"

"I can't let her go!"

"Why can't you?" I asked as I watched her finger caress the trigger.

"Because as long as she's alive, I'll never have you to myself," she said, as tears began rolling down her face.

"Please, Sky, don't do this. Think of the baby. Think of his life . . . What would happen if you killed his mother? He's going to need his mother. Don't do this. Don't leave my son without a mother," I said, trying to get her to see things clearly. More tears began falling from her eyes as she gripped the gun in her hand.

Pointing the gun at Brinay's head, Sky uttered, "I'm the only mother he needs."

The tears continued to cascade down Sky's face, and her voice dripped venom as she spoke. "I've always envied you, little sis. You're so beautiful, you always have been. You was always the center of attention. No matter wherever you went, people love you and those damn eyes. I stood off on the sideline many days, while people gave you all of the attention. You even had Daddy wrapped around your finger, until Mommy made that call and had the office give him more hours. The more time he spent at the office, the more you spent at home, and the more time you spent at home, the deeper my hatred dug. You stole everything from me. You stole my boyfriends, you stole my attention, and you stole my father, but here's where I draw the line. I'm not about to let you steal another fucking thing from me!" she screamed.

She cocked her head sideways before looking me dead in the eyes. Her eyes went from brown to black. I knew my pleas fell on deaf ears, and the Skylar I once knew was long gone.

All of a sudden, the car jerked, which caused her to fall back. The next thing I knew, Brinay was on her feet, charging toward Sky. She punched her in her face, and then in her stomach, which caused her to drop the gun. Sky returned two powerful licks to Brinay's face. She then grabbed her hair, pulling her down. The two fought as if they were two grown men, matching each other, lick for lick. Brinay dug her nails in deep and ripped Sky's face.

"Bitch!" Sky yelled, grabbing at her bleeding face—a big mistake on her part. That gave Brinay all the time she needed to send a two-piece combo to Sky's head, dazing her, but Brinay didn't stop there. She got on top of her and continued to rain blows all over her face. Whatever Sky wasn't blocking, she was hitting. My heart fell when I noticed Sky pick up the gun again. From where I was, I watched as they both began fighting over the gun. I wanted to intervene, but the fear of Brinay getting shot behind my mistake weighed heavily on my mind. If she was to get killed behind my mistake, I don't know what I would do.

"No," I yelled, finally moving from my seat, but by then, it was too late. My heart fell the minute I heard the shot ring out.

Kourtney

I was more than happy for both Brinay and Dontie. The wedding was absolutely gorgeous. Everything was put together well, and the bridesmaids and groomsmen were on point. The flower girls were absolutely adorable. Not to mention Brinay's dress was spectacular and beautiful. It kind of had me wanting to get married. I said kind of.

As I stood there watching my best friend and her husband get into the limo, I couldn't help but to be happy for her. The Brinay who I once knew was gone, and I was glad. She wasn't shy, self-conscious, or scared to love anymore. She wasn't a little girl anymore. She was all woman, and I was proud of her. My girl has been through everything, and I was finally glad that she got some happiness.

"What are you smiling about?" Brandon asked, walking over to me. I was standing outside the church, holding baby Dontae.

"I'm just happy for Nay, that's all," I replied.

"I know. I still can't believe that my little sister is married and has a baby, for that matter," he said, reaching for the infant. I handed baby Dontae to him as we began walking over to the car.

"I'm so tired," I said, yawning. "When I get home, I'm going to bathe Dontae and me, and we're going to be in the bed early tonight."

"You sure have been extremely tired lately. I don't even get any attention no more. I'm starting to think that you're getting tired of me already," Brandon said just as we got to the car. He went around the back to strap the baby in before we got in.

"There's no such thing. You know you're my baby," I told him. I reached over and pecked his lips.

"Oh, so that's all I get," he fake pouted.

"If you be good now, I'll treat you good tonight," I replied, licking my lips. My phone began ringing, just as we backed out of the parking lot.

"Hello," I answered.

"Hello, is Ms. Williams around? It's an emergency!" a female voice asked from the other end of the phone.

"No, she's not. May I ask who's calling?" I said, sitting up, I don't know why, but something was telling me that something was very wrong.

"Umm . . . this is Annie from the institution where Ms. Skylar Williams is being housed. I'm calling to inform you all that this morning she broke out."

"She did *what?* When?" I screamed.

"She broke out of the institution this morning," she repeated as if I didn't hear her the first time.

"If she broke out this morning, tell me why the fuck you all are just now calling to tell us?" I asked, enraged.

"Because we were having trouble finding Ms. Williams's file."

"I swear to God, if that looney bitch shows up anywhere near my family, I'm calling to get y'all shut down," I said, hanging up the phone.

"What's wrong?" Brandon asked, worried.

"Sky broke out of the institution this morning, and these people are just now calling to tell us. I have to call and tell Nay and Dontie about this," I said, dialing her number. The phone rang a few times before it went to voice mail. "She's not answering!"

"I'm about to call her," he said, pulling his phone out. He dialed her number and placed the phone to his ear. "She's not answering me either."

"I've got a bad feeling about this," I said, as I tried calling her again, but the phone rolled over to voice mail once more.

"Me too," he replied before he busted a U-turn in the middle of the street.

"Where are you going?" I asked as I tried to call Dontie's phone, but it was turned off. I dialed Brinay's number again, only to find out that it too was turned off.

"We're going to the airport. I know their plane hasn't left yet, and I need to know if they're okay," he answered, picking up speed.

"Okay, but please hurry up. Both of their phones have been turned off," I said, already fearing the worst.

Dontie

I sat in the back of the limo defeated. I was afraid to move, to speak, to blink. I looked over to where Sky lay on top of Brinay. Neither one of them was moving. I just knew for sure that my worst fear had come true. Sky had killed my wife, and I didn't do anything about it.

"Tae," I heard a weak voice say.

"Brinay?" I asked.

"Help me, Tae. Get her off of me."

"Okay, hold on," I said, moving over to them. I carefully pushed Sky off my wife, allowing her to move. She had blood all over her dress and hands, and she was an emotional wreck. I began checking every inch of her body, trying to make sure that she wasn't the one that was hurt.

"I shot her, Tae," she said to me. "I can't believe that I shot her."

"Shush, it's not your fault," I said, grabbing her. "Come on, let's get out of here." The minute we stepped out of the limo, there were about six police cars pulling up.

"Where's the suspect?" one of the officers asked with his gun out.

"She's in the limo," I told them. Without saying a word, he and the rest of his fellow officers surrounded the limo. A few seconds later, they went in with their guns out. Not even two minutes later, they came right back out. The same man who asked about Sky just a few minutes earlier came walking over to us. I knew what he was going to say before he even said it.

"She's dead," he informed us.

"Oh my God," Brinay screamed, as she broke down crying. I thanked the officer for filling us in with the information before I took my wife into my arms.

"What . . . Are you crying?" I asked her, shocked. I can't believe that she was crying for someone who had brought us a great deal of pain. "She's no longer going to be a problem for us."

"I know, and for that, I'm happy. These aren't tears of sadness, but tears of joy. I can now live my life in peace, knowing that my sister will not be a problem for me and my husband anymore," she said before she wiped her eyes.

Brinay

I know that I shouldn't be, but I was happy on the inside when the cop came and told us that Sky was dead. I know it looked like I cared because I was crying. Truth be told, I was only putting on an act. I did feel sorry for my sister before, but I knew now that the only way I was going to be able to live in peace was if she was dead. The minute the cop walked over and told us she was dead, I wanted to jump for joy, but I didn't. I couldn't let them see me happy because she was dead. What was that going to make me look like?

Therefore, I played it cool that whole time while we were in the police station. I told them everything that happened. I told them how Sky ended up dead. Of course, some of it was a little suspicious, but I didn't give a fuck. After all of the shit Sky has done to me and my family, death was the only thing she deserved.

"Are you okay?" Dontie asked once we were out of the police station. We were headed to the car.

"I'm fine," I said, getting into the vehicle. He started the car up and pulled off.

"Do you think the police will come and arrest me?" I asked the minute we hit the highway.

"No. That was self-defense. Sky came after you. Why would they come and arrest you?" he asked, looking at me.

"Because I shot her on purpose. You didn't notice that the gun she was holding and the gun the police collected as evidence were two different guns?" I said to him. He looked as if he was a bit confused, so I decided to explain the whole thing to him. "I knew Sky had broken out of the institution this morning. I was going to see her when I spotted her sneaking out of the building, getting into Randall's car. I was going to call the police, but I knew she only snuck out because it was our wedding day. What made it more obvious was when I overheard her talking about it to him when I snuck around to her house to see what she was up to. She thought she was going to surprise me, but she was the one in for a surprise. I bought the gun off the street a few months ago, but I never used it until now. I knew exactly what I was doing when I did it. I played as if I was traumatized when the police showed up earlier, but I wasn't. Skylar got just what she deserved. I was tired of her fucking with me and the people I love."

I looked at him and noticed that he had this blank expression on his face. He opened his mouth but closed it back when he couldn't form the proper words to say.

"It's okay. You don't really have to say anything. I did what I had to for my family. Just know that if you try to play me with any other bitch, I'm killing you *and* her," I told him before I leaned back in my seat. I hope he knew that I was serious, because I was really going to kill him if he played with me again. I didn't go through everything just to have my husband cheating on me every time you look. I wasn't the same Brinay that I was before. The bitch that now lived inside of me was heartless, and I wasn't afraid to use her. "Now, let's head to the airport. Don't we have a honeymoon to attend?"

He sat there still looking at me as if I was crazy. Oh boy . . . If he only knew how much these last few months have made me just that—crazy.

"Make me divorce you," he said, laughing.

"No, baby, you can't divorce me. It's until *death* do us part, remember?" I said, showing him my wedding ring. He flashed a smile before he reached over and gave me a kiss. I kissed him back before I sat back in my seat.

"I love you, Mrs. Edmon," he said, squeezing my hand.

"I love you too," I replied, meaning every word.

THE END